# DICK CLARK DIED TODAY

*Mike Cleary*

ISBN: 1518658334
ISBN 13: 9781518658334

*To Mary Ann*
*Proof there is a happily ever after.*

## CHAPTER 1

# THE INBETWEENERS

They were not close. They were not buddies, chums, pals, mates or bros. Given their ages, bro was probably not in any of their vocabularies. What this unusual assortment of men did enjoy was a casual acquaintanceship built on occasionally being in the same place at the same time. The place was Bar OSA located in the heart of North Berkeley's thriving Gourmet Ghetto. More specifically, it was that portion of the bar closest to the front of the restaurant. That was where these gentlemen of an advanced age would sometimes perch on high wooden chairs with rungs to rest their feet. The nondescript, oddly named tapas bar was designed for comfort, partying and quick cleanup. The name OSA was an acronym for On Shattuck Avenue, not the Spanish word for she-bear. That distinction, however, did not stop the mostly Mexican kitchen crew from calling their place of employment Bar-She-Bear. The front of the restaurant boasted floor-to-ceiling, folding glass doors with thick dark wood frames that opened onto the wide street when the weather was agreeable. Plebeian decor aside, Bar OSA's atmosphere was welcoming and cheerful. The owner, Duffy Hart, relied on his customers for any additional color and personality. Being Berkeley, they didn't disappoint. The bar itself ran the length of the north side of the room allowing those first few stools to best catch the afternoon sunshine. A bonus was the optimal viewing of UC coeds dining on slices of the Cheeseboard's vegetarian pizza of the day on the lawn of the Shattuck Avenue median. On a warm day near a city-posted sign that read KEEP OFF MEDIAN, the students and others would huddle, chew and chat; all blithely ignoring the city's official warning. To their good fortune, so did the Berkeley police.

Duffy Hart called these men his Inbetweeners as they mostly popped in and out during the restaurant's downtime; that yawn-inducing stretch between lunch and dinner. Rare was the weekday when nary a one showed up. Even rarer was a time when all were present and accounted for. When one of these gentlemen did chance upon another, first names rolled off their tongues with ease, and they all seemed to know about the other's persistent aches, ailments, prostates and various orthopedic repairs if nothing more. Except for one who enjoyed a certain notoriety, they would be hard-pressed to fully identify each other. Even so, they were friendly enough, and on every visit each hoped he'd run into one or two of the others. That they were a congenial bunch there was no doubt. Duffy Hart's wife, a fiery, attractive, by-the-books businesswoman known to one and all as The Redhead once described their conversations as collegial banter with a dash of bullshit thrown in to flavor.

The men had no idea they were thought of as a group, much less one called the Inbetweeners. Duffy kept that close to the vest. To them, Bar OSA was just a friendly, welcoming place to drink; an ideal spot to fight off the ennui of a long afternoon. None of them saw it as a kind of clubhouse or meeting place. Nor did they ever feel those first few barstools were theirs by decree. If they were occupied when they dropped in, so be it. They would simply sit elsewhere.

On Wednesday, April 18th, 2012, the three Inbetweeners who decided to take a recess from the day's petty pace by visiting Bar

OSA had no need to worry about their favorite barstools being occupied. There was a pleasing idleness about the place on that idyllic spring afternoon. Thanks to a gentle breeze and a bright sun, the day was so warm and dreamy, Duffy opened the folding glass doors; moving the front tables closer to the waist-high wrought iron fencing that separated the bar from the sidewalk. A young woman wearing a men's short-brimmed fedora and a leave-me-alone expression sat at a table for two against the wall staring into a MacBook, sipping a Mojito while a plate of potato bravas cooled. At the bar, a bearded, tattooed young man in a black tee-shirt nursed a Lagunitas IPA. In years past, he might have been lost in his thoughts. This day he was lost in his smartphone. The two remaining customers from an unusually slow lunch were outnumbered by the Bar OSA staff. The lone server at lunch, the efficient, hard-working Elena Mendoza was treating herself to a Cappuccino. Nearby, Cary Willis, the tall, taciturn bar manager, was on a ladder mumbling to himself in his own version of Spanglish while taking inventory of expensive Spanish sherries. The Redhead was paying bills in the tiny, cramped back office just off an equally tiny but hugely efficient open kitchen where the the day crew of three huddled over an experimental plate of pollo en pepitoria. Duffy Hart was just about to wrap up a discussion of menu changes with his chef. The very popular fried hama hama oysters with jalapeño aioli were coming off the menu and a new dish, a fideo calamares a la plancha stuffed with house made chorizo and migas, was going on. The coming and going of favorite plates was inevitably cheered by some and jeered by others. Most regulars knew, however, that was the practice of a true tapas bar and their favorites would always return.

While there was movement in the restaurant, it was so passive, so static if a passerby were to peek in they might think they were looking at a still-life painting. One could imagine Renoir ordering the occupants to remain as still as they were for the rest of the afternoon so he could attempt to capture the bar's tranquil but fleeting moment. Fleeting because minutes later, Bar OSA was infused with a goofy liveliness thanks to the staggered arrivals of three Inbetweeners.

Walt Gillespie was first, barging in like a member of a SWAT team entering a suspect's house. Having just been on the receiving end of an an acid-tongued, angry woman's scathing reaction to his plumbing repair charges, the tall, heavyset man couldn't get to the barstool fast enough. Once firmly planted, he realized he was very thirsty. He didn't need to order, though, as Duffy, seeing him enter, had already gone to the two beer taps behind the bar and drew a Stella Artois from one of them.

"Duffy, how do you know I don't want... Say, a Margarita?" Walt asked, his voice still edgy over his recent encounter with an irate client.

"When have you ever had anything but a Stella? By the way, this one's on me," Duffy said, placing the beer in front of him. "You look like you need it."

Walt surveyed the quiet bar and answered back, "Are you sure you can afford to be that generous?"

"Call it a teaser beer. I'm hoping it lightens your mood and lifts your spirit so you'll order more. Maybe, just maybe, you might be tempted to try something with a higher alcoholic content and a stiffer price."

Feeling every bit the harassed plumber, Walt leaned into the bar to make his case. "I just left a woman who can now bathe thanks to me. That's because I spent most of the afternoon fixing a major pipe problem. She's got one of those old wood shingle houses in the Elmwood with ancient plumbing. Actually, ancient everything. Anyway, all she did was bitch about my bill."

Before Duffy could comment that people in his chosen profession and their seemingly unreasonable prices have been fodder for comics, cartoonists and myriad story-tellers since the days of the

Roman Aqueducts, Walt tapped the bar with the knuckles of his left hand and interjected, "Actually, I know why she complained."

"You do, huh?"

"Sure. Take a good look at me."

What Duffy observed was a large but trim man who hadn't shaved and his mottled grey crewcut was in need of alignment. He was wearing old, baggy work pants and a blue shirt with a faded Gillespie Plumbing emblem loosely sewn onto a torn pocket. His hands were as clean as he could get them but you knew he'd been in some nasty stuff.

"See, Duffy, when you look like this and you fix something that most people assume just needed a little brawn and no brain, they tend to go ballistic when they see what it costs them," he explained.

Duffy nodded, "I get that."

"Take this lady, for example. I'm sure if she decides to throw a big party, she'll hire some… I don't know, some cupcake with a singsongy voice who calls him or herself a professional party planner. You've seen the type. They're always well-dressed in a sort of froufrou way and they're always well-coiffed and bossing everyone around."

"Well-coiffed? That means they don't live in Berkeley," Duffy quipped.

Walt's face froze into an I-don't-get-it expression. "Yeah, I suppose so," he muttered. "Anyway, they'll come to her house and put a bunch of daffodils here, some mums over there and hang little paper lanterns all over the place and then they'll charge her twice what I charged and she will happily pay it and then brag about what it set her back. Of course, she'd stink to high heaven if I hadn't come to the rescue so she could bathe, but does she give a shit about that."

"Maybe it's time to hang up your plunger or whatever it is you plumbers hang up when you're through."

"At my age! What are you talking about? Do I look like I'm old enough to retire?"

The bar owner, in a playful mood, gave Walt a studious stare. "If sixty-five is the standard retirement age, I'd say you blew by it four years ago."

The plumber was aghast. "How the hell did you guess I'm sixty-nine?"

"Walt, you guys are forever talking about your age."

"That's bullshit," he snapped. Walter Samuel Gillespie did not like to do what he called old things. He tried very hard not to sound old, talk old or look old. Thus, he was embarrassed at being caught breaking one of his own commandments.

Duffy glanced up and spotted the second Inbetweener, Ambrose Dowling, shuffling toward the bar. He took his sweet time crossing the room as he was never in a hurry. He also had a strange custom of walking the length of the bar from one end to the other, occasionally straightening a stool until he inevitably took a seat near the other Inbetweener.

While he watched this little ceremony, Duffy put his bar towel down and leaned in toward Walt. "Up for some fun? I'll bet you I can get Ambrose to tell us he's eighty in less than fifteen seconds. How about five dollars?"

"Okay, but no tricks. And no asking him outright," Walt whispered back.

Rubbing his hands together, Duffy grinned. "This is like taking candy from a baby."

A slightly built man of medium height with a full head of uncontrollable white hair set atop a kindly, avuncular face, Ambrose Dowling was never seen in anything but wrinkled khakis, a poorly ironed but always clean white or blue button-down Oxford shirt and a Harris Tweed or Herringbone jacket. This day he was in Harris Tweed. Most of the time, the section of the New York Times that contained that day's crossword puzzle was rolled up and sticking out of his left jacket pocket. A retired professor of English Literature at the University of California at Berkeley, Ambrose always carried a book. That afternoon, a paperback on the essays of Montaigne was in his right hand. Walt and every other Inbetweener and the Bar OSA servers knew it was a grave mistake to ask him about whatever book he was lugging around for his answer would be, even if interesting, extremely lengthy. It was also the reason no one dared ask him about his bar stroll before sitting down.

Gingerly lifting himself onto the stool next to Walt, he nodded first to the plumber and then to Duffy. "Good afternoon, gentlemen. How are you on this exquisite April day?" For Ambrose, all days, rain or shine, were exquisite.

Walt merely shrugged; a gesture he considered an appropriate response.

More cordial, Duffy replied, "Everything's fine on this side of the bar. How about you, Ambrose?"

Tossing the book on the bar, making sure the front cover was upright and visible to all, he smiled at the congenial bar owner, rubbed the palm of his left hand over his mouth and stated rather proudly, "Actually, not bad for an eighty-year-old."

Walt groaned. Reaching into his pants' pocket, he pulled out some crumbled bills. Finding a five dollar bill, he slid it across the bar to Duffy.

Noticing the exchange, Ambrose asked, "Are you leaving already, Walt?"

"No, no," he grumbled. "Hey, what are you drinking, Ambrose? I'm buying."

"Well, thank you, kind sir. I'm going to have a Cuban Manhattan" Reaching into his pocket, he put the crossword puzzle next to his book. "You do know that in this establishment, it might take a little more than five dollars to cover it?"

Duffy nodded and went to work making two after deciding it was time to treat himself as well. "Ambrose, it seems like you've been eighty forever," he remarked while pouring the rum into a shaker.

"That's all about to change, Mr. Hart. I turn eighty-two next Wednesday."

Duffy finished making the Cuban Manhattans which were served up in Martini glasses with two dark cherries resting on the bottom. "Run that by me again, please."

Taking great pride in his moving up a notch on life's calendar, or in his case two, he repeated slowly, "I will be eighty-two a week from this very day."

Walt turned on his stool and glared at the professorial, grey-haired bundle sitting next to him. Then glancing at Duffy, he snapped, "Come on, give me my five dollars back."

Duffy handed the bill back to Walt. The action did not go unnoticed by Ambrose. "What are you two playing at?" he asked.

"I bet Walt you would tell us you were eighty as soon as you got here," Duffy confessed.

Ambrose took the five from Walt and handed it back to Duffy. "I am eighty and I did tell you. As I see it, Walter, Mr. Hart won fair and square."

"Ambrose, if you are going to be eighty-two next week, that means you are now eighty-one and you have been for the last eleven months and three weeks," the plumber said, his manner testy. "So it's my five. Give it back, Duffy."

While they were going back and forth over the wager, George Crowder who, thanks to advancing age and any number of football injuries, hobbled in to Bar OSA. He nodded hello to the other two while he slowly and painfully worked himself onto the barstool next to the professor.

"Hey, George," Duffy said, putting a cocktail napkin on the bar near him.

"How you doing, Duffy?" Not waiting for a reply, the former Oakland Raider offensive lineman continued, "You still have that albarino on the wine list?" His manner of speaking matched his physical appearance. Both appeared to be menacing. He was, though, one of the sweetest men on the continent.

"Jeez, what kind of an idiot winemaker names a wine albino? Wait, let me guess. It's a white wine." Walt laughed heartily at his own joke.

Crowder leaned forward to look past Ambrose at the plumber. "Walt, get a hearing aid. It's al-bah-RI-no," he said, sounding it out slowly.

"Get a hearing aid, Walter" the plumber mimicked in a sing-songy voice. "George, you sound just like my wife."

"Your wife has a deeper voice," Duffy said, reaching into the large rubber tub filled with that day's white wines by the glass. "George and your wife are correct, you know. You do need hearing aids."

The idea was anathema to Walt. Like giving out his age, hearing aids were just another sign of aging. He'd rather not hear what people had to say. What he didn't realize, though, was that all too often his responses in conversations were foolish or embarrassing due to his not hearing what had been said. Even so, no one, not his wife or a menacing ex-football player, was going to talk him into wearing them.

Crowder on the other hand had no problem with giving his ears a little audio boost. "Hey, Walt, you're almost at an age where eventually everything will need a little help. Hearing aids for your ears, glasses for your eyes, braces for your knees and maybe some Viagra for your dick."

"George, that's not going to happen," Walt said softly but emphatically.

The former Raider heard him as he wore two behind-the-ear devices and was thrilled with now hearing the words and sound effects of life that had eluded him for years. He, too, had resisted getting them. "So what were you guys talking about when I came in?" he asked.

"Ambrose's age," Duffy replied.

"He's eighty. Lord knows he's told us enough times."

Walt looked around Ambrose at Crowder and explained, "He's got a birthday next week and he's going to be eighty-two."

"What happened to eighty-one?" Crowder asked, clearly puzzled.

Walt shrugged and suggested he ask the professor.

"How can you suddenly be eighty-two?"

Enjoying the attention, Ambrose straightened a bit in his bar chair. Putting both hands on the bar, he said slowly, "Gentlemen, like you I accept the fact that Social Security, Medicare, the DMV and other assorted bureaucracies that play prominent roles in our lives still insist on honoring the twelve month Gregorian calendar. That means they consider me to be eighty-one years of age."

"Good. Let's just it leave it there," Walt huffed, his manner surly. Ambrose was beginning to try his patience.

"Walter, Mr. Crowder here asked for an explanation and I plan on providing him one," Ambrose said, his voice composed as he thought all of this was grand fun. "Try to imagine your world as a kingdom. Thus, you would have the Kingdom of Crowder and the Kingdom of, uh, Walter." Ambrose was unaware of his last name. "You two, of course, are the rulers." Looking at the former football player, he said, "You could call yourself King Crowder the First. Better yet, how about King Crowder the Raider. That's apt." Turning to Walt, he said with a chuckle, "And you, kind sir, can be King Walter of the Faulty Ears. Now I dwell happily in the Kingdom of Dowling and I have taken the title of King Ambrose the Ambivalent. I have, by royal decree, declared that a year be two dozen months even though it has its downside. For instance, a twenty-four month year plays havoc with determining whether it was an annus horribilus or an annus mirabilis. With that length of time, the year actually becomes a bit of both. Now having explained all that, I can proudly state that on April 25th, 2012, I will be eighty-two."

Duffy bit his tongue. Smiling, George shook his head. Walt, who was still trying to wrap his head around the annus comparisons, studied the professor. Wanting to say something, anything at all, he pulled out of his limited mental word file an old chestnut. "You are so full of shit," he said matter-of-factly.

"Of course, I am," the retired professor said, laughing. "Although, I would have found a more erudite way of telling me. But seeing it is you, Walter, one can easily accept the crudeness with which you wrapped the obvious truth. Of course, the monarchy business was all nonsense. Although, I've always felt I have some royal blood in me."

"So then what's the real reason?"

"If you must know, it is because I detest odd numbers. I abhor them. Does that satisfy?"

"When did you start this twenty-four month calendar year business?" Duffy asked.

Before Ambrose could answer, Walt, who was now fed up with the professor's nonsensical rambling, interjected. "Christ, give it a rest, Duffy. Can we move on to something else?"

"Would you like us to revisit the topic of egregious plumbing repair prices?" Duffy teased.

While not a stirring change of subject, that idea appealed to George. "Speaking of plumbing," he said, "I just wrote a fat check for a simple pipe repair. The guys opened up the wall in our powder room and after they replaced the pipe they just left the mess. Now we've got to find someone who does sheetrock and painting to put it right. So more money out the door."

"Why didn't you call me?" Walt asked.

"Why? You know a contractor?"

"No. I'm in the plumbing business."

"So if you did the repair, you'd put it all back together like it was?"

"Well, no. I mean I'm just the plumber," he said, leaning back to show him the emblem on his shirt.

Squinting, the former football player examined the sorry looking logo. "All I see is something pie Plumbing," he read aloud. "Sorry, I can't see the rest. Your pocket's torn and it's fallen over part of the name."

Self-promotion was not one of Walt's talents. Pointing proudly to his shirt signage which was partially covered by a torn pocket was not the way to win over a potential client. Still, he decided to defend the company name. "At least Gillespie Plumbing would have turned you on to someone who does work like that and doesn't charge an arm and a leg."

"Walt, I had no idea you were in the plumbing business," George replied, demonstrating how little the Inbetweeners knew about each other.

Walt's reaction was immediate and not well-thought-out. "It's right here on my fucking shirt," he huffed, forgetting the damaged pocket. He wondered, too, if it was a good idea to speak so harshly to a former NFL lineman who even at seventy-two looked like he could still play.

Walt's fear of George was yet another example of the Inbetweeners' loose relationship. Like many a man of his size, strength and years of dishing out serious amounts of hurt, George was known to one and all as someone with nothing to prove and, as a result, slow to anger. So you can imagine the plumber's surprise when he heard him reply in almost apologetic terms that the next time a leak occurred in the Crowder house, he would certainly call Gillespie Plumbing.

"You would be the first plumber I'd call as well, Mr. Gillespie," Ambrose added cheerfully. "However, I have a landlord who sees to this sort of thing. I can certainly slip your business card under his door if you wish."

Never sure if Dowling is playing with him, the plumber dismissed his offer and decided to abandon plumbing as a topic. He was also aware that sooner or later someone would inevitably bring up the idiosyncrasies of toilet flushing. Temperamental toilets were the bane of plumbers. Thus, he decided, against his better wishes, to revisit the age issue. "Okay, Ambrose, I'm sticking with you being eighty-one and a lot of months. But I'm curious. When did you start this every other year thing? More importantly, I guess, is why?"

"When I turned seventy," he replied. "You also asked why. You see, I was always attracted to even numbers, even as a kid. To me, they are gentle, soft and very kind on the ear. So when I hit seventy, I decided from then on I was going to skip the odd years. My dear Emily got such a kick out of it. She had her own thing when it came to age, you know. She and her closest girlfriend decided to just pick an age and stick with it. Emily always liked the number fifty-two so that is what she became. While remaining fifty-two suited my wife, I liked piling on the years. My friends, let me say this: How you think determines how you'll live. Over the years, I have become good friends with my thinking and I like things just the way they are." With that, Ambrose waved his Cuban Manhattan in all directions and then took a well-earned, satisfying sip.

## CHAPTER 2

# EMILY'S PEACEFUL PASSING

Bar OSA's owner had participated in enough Inbetweener conversations to know they could on occasion become delightfully weird and, thus, highly entertaining. He also knew these exchanges could turn on a dime. Sometimes, dizzyingly so. It was too soon to tell where this group was taking things but judging from the bravura performance of their leadoff chatterbox, Ambrose Dowling, with his whacky explanation of a twenty-four month calendar year, he sensed that this Wednesday's banter might rank right up there with the best of previous Inbetweener ramblings. He decided to stick around to see what further foolishness awaited. It wouldn't be long before he was rewarded for making that decision.

Deciding to stir the conversational pot, Duffy, his eyes fixed on the already spotless wine glass he was still cleaning, commented, "So, Ambrose, you have lived almost a dozen years since you decided to skip the odd years. I"m safe in assuming then that you didn't recognize seventy-five? That one, you know, is a biggie."

"Actually, Mr. Hart, Emily and I did call a time out on that particular birthday and we celebrated my three quarters of a century of quasi-fruitful existence with plenty of champagne, oysters and raucous sex." He glanced at all three men; anxious to see how they handled his purposely playful response.

The plumber leaned back in his chair and threw up his arms. "Way, way too much information there, professor."

George, on the other hand, seemed thrilled: "Hey, I'm only seventy-two. I'm glad to hear I have a few years to go in the raucous sex department. I don't know if that news is going to thrill my wife, though."

Then a distant voice added, "Sorry to butt in but I quite agree. I think it's incredibly cool and inspiring to hear a gentleman at that age was still getting his leg over." That unexpected comment came from the bearded, tattooed young man at the other end of the bar. A trace of an English accent explained his use of a colloquialism not often heard in Bar OSA.

Ambrose looked down the bar, lifted his drink and said gallantly, "I thank you, kind sir." His gratitude fell on deaf ears as the young man had immediately returned to whatever was entertaining him on his smartphone.

Walt frowned and mumbled, "I'm guessing by a leg over he means you're still..."

"Screwing, balling, canoodling, bonking, shagging and... Dare I say it, fucking," Ambrose noted with a wink. Always on the alert that only his intended targets hear such well-placed indelicacies, he had lowered his voice at the end of his mischievous statement. "Of course, that was several years ago. Now those bawdy, colorful gerunds are of no use to me at all."

"Duffy, I know I said I was buying him that drink. Any chance we can cut him off after this one?" Walt asked.

Ambrose patted the plumber's arm. "There's no need for that, Walter. I'm quite all right. You see," he said with a contented sigh, "I just feel really good and I haven't felt that way for quite awhile. All this unexpected silliness has been thoroughly enjoyable."

"You haven't been feeling well?" George asked with real concern.

"Oh, my health is fine. You see, Sunday was Emily's birthday. I suppose now I should say birth anniversary. I do so miss her," he said in a low, sad whisper.

It was well known that Ambrose was a widower and had been for a little more than a year. No Inbetweener knew much more than that. Now that the subject of his wife's death was on the table, Walt wanted more information. Actually, he needed more information, such was his obsession with one specific aspect of death. Knowing his particular interest was peculiar, he thought it best to first ask something general of the twinkly-eyed man sitting to his right. "So how long were you and Emily married?"

"Forty-two years, five months and three days," Ambrose answered soberly. "I've since forgotten the hours."

"Did, uh, Emily...," Walt stammered, not sure how to frame what he knew would be a tactless question.

"How did she die? Is that what you want to know?" Ambrose asked.

No, that wasn't what he wanted to know. Walt Gillespie was not interested in how one died; violently, accidentally, peacefully, surrounded by family, quickly, painlessly, etc.. Whenever he read the occasional obituary or was told of someone's death by natural causes, he honed in on what they died of; what specific illness did them in. Was it a cancer or possibly one of those diseases with a long name that can also bring one to death's door? His curiosity was fed by hypochondria. Once informed of what ailment felled a fellow being, he would perform a quick physical checkup which inevitably convinced him that he had one or two of the symptoms of that particular malady. It was just enough information to worry him for a bit of time. He sometimes wondered why he found such morbid information so irresistible but there it was. He wasn't likely to change nor did he think he could.

Before Walt responded, George Crowder took command. Ordering Walt to let it be, he put a massive hand on Ambrose's shoulder and said, "Time to change the subject and lighten the mood. Let's get back to that, uh... What did you call it? Silliness. I was enjoying talking about a twenty-four month year."

"Thank you, George, that's very kind of you. Actually, I don't mind answering Walter. After all, I was the one who mentioned her passing."

Duffy Hart brought another beer to Walt and poured an inch more of white wine into George's glass. "Can I top your Cuban Manhattan, Ambrose?"

"I would like that," he said, sliding his glass toward the bartender. Turning his attention to Walter, he continued, "You asked how Emily died. Quite simply, my wife died of natural causes and quite peacefully."

Yet another answer that was not going to satisfy. Walt wanted symptoms and the term natural causes generally closed the door to further inquiry. Still something more specific might present itself if he just continued to seem interested. After all, the retired professor loved to talk. Walt glanced at his barstool neighbor whose pale face resembled an untended garden with light grey hairs growing wildly from his eyebrows, ears and nose. He didn't always sport such a look as Emily saw to it that he was properly groomed. Skilled with a scissors and comb, she enjoyed trimming her husband's full head of hair, paying close attention to all those other places where hairs love to grow on older men. Since her death, Duffy had taken it upon himself to remind Ambrose to tidy up. He figured he had another week before sending him off to a barber.

With drinks replenished, Duffy, Walt and George gave the retired professor their full attention. Nothing could have prepared them emotionally for what they heard.

Ambrose began, his manner halting and unsure: "It was a Sunday. We had retired early. Sometime after midnight, I came back from one of my frequent trips to the bathroom. You boys are no stranger to that I'm sure. Sometimes Emily hears me go on one of my nightly adventures and she whispers something sweet. Other times I get up without waking her. That night, I got back in bed and noticed how still she was. Often, when either of us are that quiet and unmoving, we'll nudge each other, comforted by the other's sudden awakening. That Sunday night, Emily did not respond." Here his voice cracked. "She didn't wake up. I was a medic in the army in Korea and pretty much knew my way around death. I knew my Emily had died. I didn't call 911 right away because I wasn't ready for anyone to take her away from me. Instead, I moved her; gently rolling her over on her side so I could hold her close. Her thin arm fell across my chest, her hand which I spent forty-two plus years holding as often as I could rested on my right shoulder. Her head was on my left. It had been a long time since we'd held each other like that. I thought it was so like her to choose leaving me with little fuss or bother. I closed my eyes and begged God to please let me fall into that permanent sleep, too. I had no desire, no wish, no ambition and absolutely no reason to wake up the next morning. But I did," he sighed, his warm, blue eyes watering. "And that, my friends, is how Emily died."

This time Ambrose did not check his audience to see their reaction. Instead, he stared somberly at his refreshed Cuban Manhattan. What did I just do, he asked himself. Emily certainly would not have approved as she was never one to get too personal with mere acquaintances. In those few hushed seconds before anyone dared speak, Ambrose scolded himself. He had never told anyone about the night of Emily's passing and he wondered why he did now. Silently apologizing to her spirit which was always with him, he promised her it would cease to be a story for sharing. There was one small consolation, though. Normally, whenever Ambrose spun a yarn, his words would inevitably reach the ears of people beyond his targeted listeners. He didn't mind this. In fact, he rather enjoyed this manner of accidental oration. But this time, Ambrose was subdued and gentle; his voice low enough that Duffy had to lean in to hear him.

"Excuse me, gentlemen, I'm going in the back to give The Redhead a hug," Duffy said, breaking the silence, his eyes red. "A really big hug."

Ambrose looked up from his drink and managed a small smile. "Mr. Hart, you always seem to know the perfect thing to say."

Further lightening the heavy emotional moment, George Crowder asked, "So what are we supposed to do? You know, those of us who don't have wives on the premises."

As he was walking toward the office, Duffy replied, "Hug Walt. He needs it. Plumbers always need a hug."

Walt didn't hear Duffy's suggestion as his hypochondria had kicked in and he desperately wanted to ask Ambrose if Emily had complained of any aches or physical abnormalities prior to going to bed that fateful night. Did she have unexplained stomach or abdominal pains? (He was feeling quite at odds in that department.) Did she, perhaps, experience light-headedness? Did she have any pain in her arms? (His right arm had been bothering him.) All right, he said to himself, just ask him directly if there were any clues that hinted at the night's tragic turn. He thought it best, though, to offer some kind of condolence first. Clumsily he began, "Well, I..."

That's as far as he got. Ambrose held up a finger to shush him. "Walter, my friend, it has been my experience that in situations similar to this, when one begins a sentence in a halting manner with the exclamatory well, it means they are about to say something highly inappropriate or they are going to drag some tired old cliche out of retirement. Would you like to rethink whatever it is you wish to tell me?"

"Well, fuck it all, Ambrose," he shot back, surprising even himself with his angry reaction. "Sorry, professor, but we can't all be glib and wordy and witty like you. I put the word well in front of a lot of stuff. You probably thought I was going to say something like if you have to die, that's a hell of a way to go."

Ambrose looked thoughtfully at the plumber with the grizzled face and apologized for interrupting him. "And yes, if you must know, I did think you were going to say something like that."

Walt felt he had eked out a small victory in this conversational battle with his assertive response. "Well, I wouldn't," he said. "One time I said that when my sister's father-in-law died. Tony Romagna was eighty-seven and he passed peacefully with his family around him. Man, you really don't want to piss off a bunch of grieving Italians. Her asshole of a son, Serafino, works for me as a result."

"Again, I'm sorry for cutting you off." Ambrose said with a sincerity born from the guilt he felt for his being so detailed about the circumstances of her dying.

Walt rubbed his face. He decided to abort his mission to find out if there were any pre-existing conditions that lead to Emily's sudden death that mirrored his own imagined symptoms. Instead, he struggled to find the words to explain how he felt about Ambrose's great loss.

"Your story really touched me," he began. "I mean forty-two years of a happy marriage and all of a sudden it's gone just like that. I can't imagine the pain you must feel. But you know, you did have all those years. So how lucky are you? As I see it, because God didn't take you at the same time, you just have to make do and I think you can make do thanks to all the memories of those years together. I'll bet those memories can do a great job of keeping you steady and comforted during whatever time you have left before God has you and Emily meeting up again in heaven." Walter paused before mumbling a crude postscript: "Wherever the hell that is."

Ambrose spun on his stool and stared hard at Walt. The plumber's head jerked back and he said sharply, "What?"

The widower shook his head and smiled. "Nothing at all, Walter. You simply amazed me with your hard-scrabble eloquence."

George patted Ambrose on the back. Peeking around him, he addressed Walt as well. "When you guys feel the time's right to change the subject, let me know because I have a serious plumbing question for Walt."

By this time, Duffy had returned to his spot behind the bar. He'd heard George. "Before you guts start talking about leaks and old pipes —now I sound like a urologist — I have one question for Ambrose. The Redhead wants to know how old Emily was."

A tight-lipped grin took root on Ambrose's face. It slowly blossomed into a full smile. He realized Walt was right. Memories would sustain and comfort him until such time they meet again. One such memory came to mind. He recalled an evening when their best friends, Janice and Barnard, came over for Martinis. He could see them plain as day, seated in their living room. Emily wore her faux leopard skin high heel shoes. They were her favorite. While they usually covered a wide range of topics, this visit was all about age and aging, getting older and getting old. That's when Emily and Janice had decided to pick an age and stick with it. That's when he had adopted the Dowling calendar year of twenty-four months. That's when Barnard had told them they were all nuts.

Duffy patiently waited for his answer. Finally, Ambrose left his reverie and replied, "Emily was fifty-two."

# CHAPTER 3

# DID YOU HEAR THE NEWS TODAY

Katherine Gearon could not resist laughing whenever her lanky, six-foot two-inch husband attempted to work his way out of her sports car whenever the top was up. She knew that he also made light of the exercise; dismissing it as a shining example of awkwardness at its best. The car, a 2007 Mercedes SLK, was a ground-hugging, sleek little beauty; white on the outside with a saddle tan interior. On Wednesday afternoon, April 18th, lucky enough to find metered parking on Shattuck Avenue just a half block from Bar OSA, she was once again treated to the sight of the love of her life struggling to remove himself from the car she affectionately called Lillie. It was like watching Lillie give birth to a long-legged foal who, finally out of the womb, struggles to make himself upright.

After the meter was fed by her now steady on-his-feet husband, Katherine issued the couple's marching orders. Mike was to go directly to Bar OSA and secure two barstools while she scooted off to the nearby Walgreen's for hair coloring. "I won't be long. I know exactly what I want. At least, I think I know," she cautioned, giving him a quick, tender kiss; her way of thanking him for providing her with another light moment of entertainment.

Mike Gearon set off on a leisurely pace as the sights and sounds of this North Berkeley neighborhood never failed to delight. They had parked in front of a dance studio where a class of high-energy, tiny ballerinas in a colorful mash-up of tutus and tights had just let out. While harassed parents tried to herd their darling mini-divas into nearby cars, SUVs and vans, the giggly girls with their high-pitched voices and tireless energy continued to practice their dance moves on the sidewalk. He and Katherine were looking forward to being grandparents soon as their two recently married children had become serious about starting families. He wondered if they'd be part of this scene some day. Passing a drab mid-century, two-story building with age-worn, homemade signs advertising myriad services for body and mind that included chiropractic care, acupressure, acupuncture, massage, yoga and meditation, he wondered if it was all offered by the same person, perhaps the human equivalent of a multi-purpose Swiss army knife. Next came a compact, three-story apartment building that looked like it belonged in Santa Monica. He'd always thought Santa Monica was Berkeley with sand so it seemed appropriate. A row of small shops followed; one selling designer eyewear, another exotic but inexpensive women's clothing and a narrow smoke shop with an array of newspapers out front. Then came a small, been-there-forever post office, a jewelry store and Chez Panisse, the star of the block, if not the world when it came to fine-dining restaurants. Located inside an aging two-story Arts and Crafts house, the acclaimed restaurant and cafe not only attracted food lovers but also tourists who liked to stop and photograph the building and the posted menus. A large Monkey tree with a wide, dark-gnarled trunk separated Chez Panisse from Bar OSA. As the famous restaurant only served wine and beer, the tapas bar came in handy for those desiring a cocktail before going next door to dine. As such, they were perfect neighbors.

There was at first glance an ordinariness about Berkeley's Gourmet Ghetto. Mike Gearon was certain more than one visitor had come away from this eclectic avenue of splendid restaurants and unique shops unimpressed with the overall aesthetics of the neighborhood. But this part of town and for that matter the rest of Berkeley were a big deal to Mike and Katherine. A very big deal. They would argue all you had to do was look past that first glance to see the messy magnificence of a city built to embrace the myriad eccentricities that made it one of the more exciting and fascinating communities in the country. Certainly, the most eccentric. It's outré reputation was built in part by the enthusiastic welcome mat Berkeley put out for anyone who marched to their own drum. So it was, his spirit refreshed from the familiar sights of the short stroll from the car, that he arrived at Bar OSA eager to see if two stools at the inside end of the bar were free.

Opening the heavy door, he once again asked himself why it was so damned hard to open. As he'd been entering Bar OSA on and off for eleven years, it was a question that would go unanswered. This time it was washed from his mind thanks to Walt, who spotting him at the entrance, shouted enthusiastically, "Hey, Gearon, my man! Damn, I miss you and your buddy in the morning. Radio's not the same without you guys." The plumber greeted him with those exact words every time he saw him.

Mike Gearon, along with his partner, Frank Smith, had just retired from hosting a popular morning radio show called Smith and Gearon in the Morning. In the beginning, they had lobbied heavily to have management call the show Frank and Mike in the Morning as they thought using their surnames made them sound like a steak sauce or worse, a gun. He and Frank got nowhere and, as a result, after thirty-three years of Smithing and Gearoning their way through three hours of a highly rated show, no one except his family and close friends seemed to know he had a given name. Thus, he was and would always be Gearon to the plumber.

George Crowder was another matter. They'd known each other from his rough-and-tumble, football playing days as the radio station had broadcast the Raiders' games. Following his retirement, the articulate offensive linesman spent four years doing Raider reports during the season on their morning show. Thus, it was no surprise when he turned his 245 pound frame around and cheerily shouted, "Hey, Mike, how are you?"

"Fine, George. It's good to see you," he answered back.

While the Gearons themselves were not Inbetweeners, they too enjoyed the occasional late afternoon visit to Bar OSA. Their pleasure, however, came from catching up with their close friends, Duffy Hart and The Redhead, and that was their plan on this fateful Wednesday afternoon. Catching Elena Mendoza's eye at the far end of the bar, he pointed to the last two barstools; a signal meaning Elena was to put two napkins out to hold them. That done, he decided to visit with the Inbetweeners until Katherine arrived.

With his usual formality, his twinkling eyes and an accompanying dramatic wave of his rum-based Cuban Manhattan, Ambrose saluted the new arrival: "Greetings, Mr. Gearon, Walter here seems to be in a buying mood. Perhaps, he'll cover your first drink."

"I'm sure Walt appreciates you opening his wallet for him," he replied. "So what have I missed? With Duffy in attendance, something must be going on."

"You really don't want to know," George advised in a tone that seemed more like an order than a suggestion.

"Trust me, nothing important," Walt said all too quickly.

"Then I will tell you," Ambrose volunteered cheerily. "You see, I am having a birthday next Wednesday. Talking about it has taken up most of the afternoon. Now I'm afraid these gentlemen are most anxious to shift the direction of our conversation."

"Well, if I don't see you between now and then, happy birthday. I remember you telling me you're eighty," he said, noticing the sudden wide-eyed expressions on George and Walt's faces.

Duffy Hart held up his dish towel and waved it. "Yes, he's eighty, Mike. Please, just leave it at that," he implored.

Save for George Crowder, Mike Gearon rarely engaged the Inbetweeners. There were the occasional short visits and there were always cordial greetings and goodbyes as they all came and went from Bar OSA but extended chats were infrequent. That said, there were times when an Inbetweener, unable to find a spot close to the others, would manage to locate near the Gearons who always sat at the other end of the bar. From these experiences, Mike knew Ambrose could be a conversationalist nuisance, often frustrating, boring or tiring those around him. It was obvious he'd done so this afternoon. Even though Mike did not understand why, he sensed Duffy, Walt and George truly wanted to move away from discussing the professor's age, so he decided it was time he moved on as well.

"Okay. I, uh, am going to grab a couple of barstools down there," he said, pointing to the other end of the long bar, "Katherine is right behind me and I know she wants to talk to me about something really important."

"What's important?" Walt asked all too quickly. If he was lucky, it might be that she has a health issue. He might have admonished himself for entertaining such a morbid thought, but he'd come to terms with his hypochondria and the strange notions it put into his head. There was no guilt, just curiosity

"Who knows? I'm thinking it has to do with hair-coloring choices. But it might be all about tonight's dinner. Heady stuff, you know," he joked. Turning to leave, he remembered something he and Katherine had heard on the radio on their way there. "Oh, I almost forgot. I don't know if you guys heard..."

"Let me guess," Ambrose interjected, even though he knew he would be quickly voted down by a chorus of emphatic noes from his barstool neighbors. He was not wrong.

"What haven't we maybe not heard?" Duffy asked, wondering if that wasn't the weirdest question he'd asked recently.

"Dick Clark died today."

In later retellings of what happened on that quiet Wednesday afternoon that forever changed the lives of many of the bar's inhabitants, all would agree it was Mike Gearon's four-word declarative sentence that set it all in motion.

Appropriately, Ambrose was first out of the gate with a response. "I don't want to die on a Wednesday," he mused, his eyes staring into this drink.

"And just what the hell is wrong with dying on Wednesday?" snapped an already exasperated Walt Gillespie who was still upset at not knowing what felled Ambrose's spouse. "For Chrissakes, it's not like you are going to care,"

The professor's unconventional observation on the timing of one's passing even drew a response from the usually laconic George Crowder. "Look at this way, Ambrose. Let's say you do pop off on a Wednesday. The good news is you won't ruin anyone's weekend. Your friends and family will love you for it. Personally, I'd rather mourn on a Wednesday so I can watch TV sports on the weekend emotionally unencumbered. I'm sure I'm not alone in that thinking."

Shaking his head, Dowling sighed and said to the two men, "Gentleman, I may have spoken too hastily. That said, though, I do think Wednesday is a bad day to die. But then so are the other six. Personally, I would like to finish the week out and then peacefully expire, weekend sports notwithstanding."

Walt was not without his personal take on the news of Clark's death. "You know what's shocking to me? That it's Dick Clark. He was one of those guys who seemed like he never aged. Plus, you had the feeling that he'd always be with us. Kinda like Jack LaLanne in that regard. At least Jack is still around."

Ambrose put an affectionate hand on the plumber's shoulder. "Walter," he began with a sympathetic pause, "Jack went to the power juicer in the sky more than a year ago. In fact, he died just a few days after my Emily."

"No shit. Jack LaLanne is dead and it's been more than a year?" He was truly taken aback by the news.

"I'm afraid so."

"How the hell did I miss that? You know sometimes things happen when you're on vacation and you never hear about them. I remember when Pat Boone died. We were in Hawaii on the island of Maui. My brother-in-law rented this condo on the beach…"

"Whoa there, big fellow," George said. "Pat Boone isn't dead."

"Then it was the other Boone."

"Daniel Boone?" Ambrose asked with a smile.

"Could have been. When did he die?"

George did a quick Google check on his iPhone and replied, "September, 1820. Maui condo rates must have been a real deal."

"Perhaps you meant Richard Boone?" Ambrose asked.

"Might have been. It was awhile ago," Walt answered.

George consulted his iPhone again and laughed. "Awhile ago? Walt, it was thirty-one years ago."

"Yeah, well some things you don't forget," he said rather sheepishly. "Like Jack LaLanne pulling a rowboat of Victoria Secrets' models with his teeth in San Francisco Bay."

"A slight altering of the facts there, Walt, but I do like your version," said George, holding up his glass for a touch more of the white wine.

While Duffy topped him off, he addressed all three. "Look, guys, what matters here is that it is to their credit that we all were able to imagine Clark and LaLanne as two guys who would just keep on going. But it's Dick Clark we should be remembering here today. I still miss him not dropping the ball on New Year's Eve."

"And I'll bet he never had his teeth whitened," Ambrose tossed in.

"Whatever the hell is that about?" Walt asked.

"Emily commented on that youngster who now does it. I can never remember his name." Nobody seemed to know so he continued, "Anyway, she was convinced that nowadays you can't get a job in TV unless a recent teeth whitening is on your resume."

Duffy shook his head and marveled at the push and pull of their conversation. "Well, my final contribution to this unofficial Dick Clark memorial is to say I don't think there's anyone ready to step into the special category of appearing like they'll live forever."

"Hey, what about Regis Philbin," the retired football player said of his fellow Notre Dame alum. Born and bred in Oakland, Crowder guarded and tackled his way through Bishop O'Dowd High School and then did battle as a Fighting Irishman for four years before signing with the Oakland Raiders. What most people didn't know was, besides being an superb athlete, Crowder was an excellent student scholar who had attended Notre Dame on an academic scholarship.

"I wouldn't put Regis in the same category as Clark and LaLanne," opined Walt.

"How about Barbara Walters. She's still with us. So is Betty White," Ambrose noted.

"No, women don't count. They all outlive us," George laughed.

On and on it went. Between them the three had enough memories of Dick Clark to keep the conversation humming. While they chatted away, Mike Gearon headed for his end of the bar while Duffy sneaked away to tend to duties that once done would give him and The Redhead a chance to visit with the Gearons before the drinks-and-dinner crowd arrived; bringing with them a noise level that would deny them any chance at conversation.

Elena Mendoza was a handsome, strong-featured indigenous Mexican who began life in America cleaning houses with her older sister. The two were inexpensive, efficient and honest. One of these homes belonged to Duffy Hart and the Redhead who were so charmed by her determination to learn English, get her GED and eventually head off to a university, hopefully Cal, to pursue a career in environmental sciences, they hired her to work lunches even though it would be challenging for her due to her limited English. It was not a mistake. With her warm smile, charming shyness, fertile mind, intelligent dark eyes and eagerness to please, she so charmed the Bar OSA luncheon crowd that every exchange between Maria and a regular turned into an impromptu English lesson. What baffled Duffy was her ability to fake it when she was serving customers new to Bar OSA and unfamiliar with the menu. Later, when her English was good enough, she explained how she had assembled an inventory of generic responses by listening to the other servers. The food was easy as the menu was mostly in Spanish. Thus, whenever anyone asked about a certain plate, she would always answer, "It's one of my favorites." For wines, she had two replies. For reds, she would say, "It's a wine of complexity and character." Whites were easily handled by noting confidently, "It's dry, crisp and delicious. Perfect for our food."

In a remarkably short time, Elena was able to take the test for her GED. All things were possible in America, she thought giddily. She had many people to thank especially Mike and Katherine Gearon. They were Saturday lunch regulars whose patience and friendliness encouraged her to shelve her shyness when it came to speaking English. She loved talking to them about her challenges, ambitions and, more importantly, her progress.

She watched as Mike Gearon climbed aboard the barstool. There was no reason for her to step away from her cappuccino as she knew he would never order anything until his wife arrived.

"Maybe you get lucky. Maybe a pretty blonde lady will come in and sit there," she said, pointing to the stool next to him. It was an approximation of a line Mike Gearon had used on many occasions. Having it now served back to him, he realized the freshness date on the joke had expired. For Elena, it was stepping out there for her to kid with him like that. Impertinence wasn't in her vocabulary, but the word rude was and she worried she might have been. However, his wide grin set her at ease.

"Touché," he said in his broadcast baritone, his smile still intact.

Elena's quizzical expression told Mike it was time to fatten up her vocabulary. "Touché is a French word that comes from the sport of fencing," he explained, pantomiming sword play a little too aggressively with his left hand. If Katherine was there, she would have said in a motherly fashion, "Be careful, honey, you'll hurt yourself."

"It's something you say when your opponent hits or touches you. So when I used it just now, it was to let you know you said something funny and clever at my expense."

"Did I offend you?" she asked, trading in her usual smile for a worrisome frown, such was her concern.

"No, Elena, not at all. You merely reminded me that I have said the same thing to you way too many times. Plus, you did it in a clever, funny way. Believe me, I was not offended," he said a little too loudly.

"Offended? I can't leave my husband alone for ten minutes and someone has offended him. Okay, who was it? Point them out. I'll deal with the troublemakers." Katherine said in a less than threatening manner. In fact, her voice was brimming with warmth and cheer.

"Ah, the pretty blonde lady has arrived," he announced. "All hail the pretty blonde lady."

"So what's going on?" she asked, taking the barstool next to him. She settled in by moving her bottom this way and that; a provocative gesture that was still irresistible to Mike Gearon after thirty years of marriage.

"Elena just told me I have worn out one of my better lines when I come in here ahead of you."

"Oh, let me guess. It's the one about you having a feeling that a beautiful blonde will come in and sit next to you."

Both Elena and Mike nodded.

"And if you played your cards right, you might get lucky," she added saucily.

Once an acquaintance had commented on Katherine's voice, calling it silky and mellifluous. Then, laughing at himself, he added, "My god, I sound like a hyperbolic music critic for NPR." He explained he really thought her voice was downright sexy but that didn't seemed to be an appropriate choice of adjectives. Mike congratulated him on his discretion and Old World charm. Interestingly, the two words became like an ear-worm for Mike and he found himself often complimenting his wife on the silky mellifluousness of her voice. After a few weeks the ear-worm and the compliments lessened much to Katherine's delight.

"Are we each having a glass of wine or are we splitting a chilled tequila?" she asked.

They were not budgeting, nor were they cheap. Both were simply earnest about saving their cocktail appetites for one of Mike's Martinis at home. While not unusually large, this lovingly produced Martini would last them through ninety minutes of Midsomer Murders, episode 3 of season 14 to be exact. The British mystery series was set in the Cotswolds where every village had an adorable name like Piddling-on-Acton. In the series, they manage to knock off at least half the population of one those bucolic, thatched-roofed hamlets before a murderer is finally captured. The Gearons loved the series and always had a side bet going on how many murders each episode would feature.

"How about a chilled tequila,' he replied, spotting Duffy Hart heading in their direction. At the same time The Redhead bounced out of the office to say greet them.

"Hello, you two," she sang, giving Katherine a come-from-behind hug and Mike a quick kiss on the cheek.

This green-eyed, redheaded bundle of energy possessed an air of authority that somehow made her look taller than anyone she was addressing. Like Katherine, her sheer force of character gave her an attractiveness that was almost intimidating.

"Sorry, gang, I have to keep our visit short. I've got to get back to the office if I'm going to get out of here at a reasonable hour," she explained, her disappointment evidenced by a beguiling frown, one of a huge inventory of creative facial expressions that, if she were alive at the time, would have made The Redhead a major silent film star.

"Don't head back there just yet," Duffy said, now positioned across the bar from the Gearons. With a bemused grin, he said, "I cannot believe I am going to say this with a straight face. We have all been invited to the other end of the bar to attend an official... Yes, that's what they are calling it. The official Dick Clark Memorial."

# CHAPTER 4
# AN ODD BUT FITTING MEMORIAL

"And a hearty welcome to those of you from the distinguished east end of Bar OSA. You honor us with your presence. You have arrived at a providential moment," Ambrose declared. His usually ashen cheeks seemed puffier due to the reddening from the effects of a refortified Cuban Manhattan. Pointing to his two compatriots, he continued, "The plumber, the pro and the professor are just about to begin our memorial for Dick Clark. You are here because we decided it wouldn't be much of a thing if it were just the three of us."

Duffy, who was used to this kind of Inbetweener nonsense, called for attention by rapping his knuckles on the bar counter. "Guys, before you turn a portion of our bar into some kind of twisted variation of an Irish wake, I have a question. Truthfully now, no bullshitting. When was the last time any of you gave a single thought to Dick Clark?"

His sensible inquiry was answered by a muted choreography of shrugging shoulders.

"So why all the fuss now?"

Without offering an explanation, like two school children hoping to pass the blame, Walt and George pointed to Ambrose who had now turned his bar stool around to face the four new arrivals.

"Ambrose, you have had your nose in books for decades. Do you even know who Dick Clark is? Or was?" asked The Redhead with a snappish tone born of an eagerness to return to her office and dive back into the paperwork that needed completing.

Walt spoke up before Ambrose could respond. "Trust me, he knows all right."

"I didn't believe him at first, but his story checks out," George added, waving his iPhone, the holder of facts far and wide and more often than not error-riddled.

Katherine reached across the bar to take from Elena the two small glasses of a split, chilled tequila they'd ordered before being force-marched to the other end of the bar by Duffy Hart. She then handed Mike one. After the ritual of clinking glasses, each took a small sip. Mike was otherwise busy doing age math. He remembered being in high school when American Bandstand began. He had just learned Dowling had a nine year head start in life so he would have been in his mid to late twenties around that time. Mike supposed there was the possibility someone that age might be interested in watching a show where modestly dressed teenagers danced to the pasteurized, white bread hits of the day. He wondered, though, if that would hold any appeal to a young Ambrose Dowling.

It was as if he had read his mind. He hadn't, of course. The retired professor of English literature, having spent an obscene number of years in classrooms, lecture halls and seminars, was simply adept at guessing what his students were thinking by the faces they made during tests, lectures and discussions.

"Mr. Gearon, that scrunched-up look and the way your lips are moving, I'd say you're thinking, probably along with the rest of your gang, that I'm too old to have been a teenager when Dick Clark was hosting his dance party show."

They all nodded en masse.

Knowing what was coming, George Crowder felt compelled to warn the others. “Fasten your seat belts, everybody,” he said in a barely audible voice.

Clearly, I picked a fortuitous time to drop by Bar OSA, Ambrose thought. He was a giddy bundle as he knew there would be few, if any, who could pull a Dick Clark story out of their hat that was so rare, unusual and entertaining as the story he was about to tell. It was a particularly embracing moment as he was well aware that most of the time in Bar OSA he was barely tolerated; just some old codger to put up with. Today, though, the spotlight burned fever bright and he loved being in it.

“For a time, I dwelt in Utica, New York,” he began sonorously.

“Why can’t you just say lived in New York like everyone else in the frigging English-speaking world?” Walt barked.

Ambrose was not to be shaken by the plumber’s curtness. “If it pleases you, Walter, I lived in Utica, New York for a time. For those of you unfamiliar with this small community, it is in the Mohawk Valley and it’s twin city is Rome.” I do intend on milking this, he told himself, disregarding the disapproving look George gave him and the ire of Walt who had already heard it and wished for an edited retelling. “I was fresh out of university — Syracuse, if you must know — with a plan to go on to graduate school; a plan which eventually brought me here to Cal. In the meantime though, I landed a job as a cub reporter for the Utica Observer-Dispatch. One day, my editor, a fine, overfed gentleman by the name of Wellington J. Wheezer — yes, that was his real name — ordered me to head over to WKTV and interview the host of a new, locally- produced television program.” Here, he paused for dramatic effect. “The show was called Cactus Dick and the Santa Fe Riders.”

It got the reaction he wished; first a number of raised eyebrows, then a few gaping mouths and a generous amount of tittering.

"Do you mean to say Dick Clark, the World's Oldest Teenager, got his start as Cactus Dick?" Duffy Hart exclaimed, an image forming in his mind of the TV host wearing a 1950's East Coast producer's idea of a musical cowboy outfit. "So did you interview him?"

"I did. All five feet, nine inches of him," Ambrose stated proudly. "I added his height because people always seem to be curious about the long or short of someone famous. I'd like to say we kept in touch over the years but we didn't. This was around 1950 or 51. I think the dance party stuff came a couple of years later."

George tapped Mike Gearon on the shoulder. "Did you ever meet him?"

Mike shook his head. "What about you?"

"We probably breathed the same air a couple of times," he said. "A Super Bowl party, if I remember right. I think he was also at a Raider Game once as Al's guest."

Walt, a longtime season ticket holder, asked if that was Super Bowl II when the Raiders played the defending champion Green Bay Packers in Miami's Orange Bowl in 1967. Crowder was a starter for the Raiders who ended up on the wrong end of a very physical 33 to 14 game. While disappointed he and the his teammates didn't earn Super Bowl rings, he was resolutely proud to have played on a team that faced the Vince Lombardi-coached Packers for the championship.

George laughed heartily. "Oh, good God no! We were players. Gladiators in the Roman Coliseum were treated better than we were in those years. But I can tell you this; we managed to party hard on our own even though we weren't part of the official celebrations. No, the Super Bowl I'm talking about was in 1976 in Pasadena."

Walt raised his hand and shouted exultantly, "Hey, we won that one!"

Crowder got a kick out of people who made themselves part of the team with the use of the first-person plural pronoun. He never called them on it, though. Rather, he was understanding. In 1976, off the player's roster for six years, he remembered reacting the same way when the Raiders beat the Minnesota Vikings.

"So it was in Los Angeles where you and Dick shared some smoggy party air together," Ambrose said.

"Might have," he replied. "There were rumors that Clark was there. Of course, there were lots of familiar faces there. Most all of them thought they were celebrities but there were a few dyed-in-the-wool real ones. I will tell you who I did meet. Florencia Bisenta de Cassillas Martinez Cardona." He enjoyed saying her name, even adding a slight Spanish accent.

The Redhead and Katherine flashed beaming smiles. "That has to be somebody who is famous but goes by a different name," Katherine guessed, speaking for both.

"It sure as hell wasn't Cactus Dick," Duffy quipped.

"I'll give you a hint. She sang the National Anthem. By the way, Mike, you're benched for this game."

And for good reason as every 1960's and 1970's disc jockey knew the show business alias of Ms Martinez Cardona as it made for great on-air trivia. Mike stayed quiet while everyone else paused to think about the clue. No one went to their smartphones where the answer was just seconds away.

Walt broke the silence by blurting out, "Barbra Streisand."

"She's Jewish," Duffy pointed out with a laugh he quickly disguised as a cough. He was astonished the plumber would suggest her but he didn't want to insult him

"So?"

"So, if her real name is Florencia..." Duffy slowed to try and remember the second of her five names. "Okay, George, remind me. It sounds like placenta."

Crowder corrected him. "You're close. It's Bisenta."

"Anyway, Walt, I seriously doubt that she's Jewish with a name like that."

George decided another clue was necessary. "Okay, let's see if this helps. She also earned a doctorate in law at San Diego University."

"Gloria Allred," The Redhead joked, her green eyes twinkling. Like her husband, she was no stranger to quick responses; the bar business being an excellent training ground.

Ambrose realized they were slowly moving away from the real reason all seven were gathered at that end of the bar. This was to be a Dick Clark Memorial. He signaled for time out. "Ladies, Gentlemen and Walt, we are here to praise Dick, not to play a game of Super Bowl trivia. Now, George, please tell us who sang at the 1976 Super Bowl and let's be done with it."

"It was Vikki Carr."

"I haven't heard that name in ages. Is she still alive?" The Redhead asked.

Both George Crowder and Mike Gearon were of an age where that question came at them with stunning regularity. Whenever Mike encountered a former listener, they inevitably asked in some less than subtle fashion if his older partner were still alive and kicking. Fortunately, Mike could happily report that Frank Smith was in fine form. George had a tougher go of it as many of his former teammates had passed on and that news always put a dark cloud over the conversation. Like George's tolerating a fan's use of we when talking about the Raiders, neither of the men didn't let the alive-or-dead inquiry bother them as they often found themselves asking the same question on occasion.

"She is very much alive and still performing. Her voice is better than ever," George answered happily. He knew this because he and his wife had stayed in touch with her over the years and were about to head to Los Angeles to see her in concert.

Duffy glanced at his watch. He knew the atmosphere in the still lightly populated Bar OSA was about to change. Not a second after, like clockwork, the first of the early evening arrivals, two women in their mid-fifties entered the restaurant. In their loose-fitting blouses with fading colors, bulky scarves, oversized slacks that did not coordinate, dull brown sandals, long gray hair and no makeup, they were model representatives of what was a long-standing Berkeley fashion statement for many women. They waited by the door for someone to seat them. Duffy Hart's welcoming wave caught their attention. "You can sit anywhere there aren't people. You can even sit together," he said in a loud, friendly voice and a big grin.

Their reaction was predictable. First came a look of puzzlement which in seconds gave way to a smile and some light laughter as the two newcomers wrapped their minds around the fun of the second sentence. Something Walt apparently seemed unable to do.

"How come you tell them they can even sit together? They came in together, didn't they? Of course they want to sit together," he said as if lecturing a child.

Dick leaned across the bar and whispered, "Please, please, Walt, tell me you know I was just kidding around."

The oftentimes thick-skulled plumber sat erect and replied, "Of course, I know. You know how you talk about us always mentioning our age. Well, do you want to know how many times I've heard you tell people that?"

"Do you know why I do it?" Duffy asked. Walt shook his head. "It puts customers in a good mood and that usually makes them better guests," he explained, watching Elena describe some of the menu items to the two ladies. The ladies were like canaries in the mine; a clear warning that a storm of customers would soon descend on Bar OSA. Duffy realized the Dick Clark Memorial would end up being either an abbreviated ceremony or a very well-attended and noisy one.

Ambrose bounded off his barstool, a youthful move for someone a week away from turning eighty-two. "Let us begin," he said excitedly.

"I thought we had," Mike Gearon chuckled. "I now know more than I ever did about Dick Clark."

"Mr Gearon, that was just pre-memorial chit-chat. Now we begin to officially remember the man and as I seem to be the only one present who actually met him, who actually pressed flesh with the man, I feel I should kick things off."

"It's only appropriate," George remarked, smiling at the silliness of it all. Although, he had to admit, Clark was a rare form of celebrity. Perhaps, Ambrose might articulate that notion. He had his own idea but, he wasn't so sure he could put it into words.

Ambrose puffed himself up and said solemnly, "We remember Dick Clark…"

"Whoa, professor. You remember him. I don't," The Redhead interjected. She meant it to be funny, however it came out sounding harsh and critical; earning a quick look of disapproval from her husband who had more patience with the Inbetweeners. She attempt to put things right. "Okay, I'm sorry. It's a memorial, I know. Go ahead with the we stuff. I'm in."

Ambrose bowed and replied, "Thank you, Mrs. The Redhead. By the way, you do realize that's a very awkward nickname. Of course you do. But that's another discussion for another time. Right now we are remembering Dick Clark. So let me see, he was… What he was…" Ambrose paused. He thought a moment and, shaking his head, said, "To be honest, I am having a difficult time putting into words why I feel he's special."

Even though he was unsure he had the key to why Clark was such a unique personality, George Crowder attempted to come to his neighbor's rescue. Putting a beefy hand on Ambrose's narrow shoulder, he said, "Let me try. This may be a generational thing." He glanced at The Redhead. "I don't know. But it seems to me that no matter what decade I was in, Dick Clark was always there front and center. And you're right, Walt, you can include Jack Lalanne as one those ever-present celebs."

"For me, George Burns and Bob Hope were two that were always around decade after decade," Mike Gearon noted, taking a last sip of his half of a chilled tequila, marveling that it lasted as long as it did.

Then The Redhead jumped in. "While you guys are a little fatter in the decade count, I've got someone. How about Martha Stewart?"

"Yeah, Martha certainly qualifies," George said, chuckling. He slowly swiveled in his seat to look more directly at those standing near them. With his white golf shirt with a NFL Alumni logo and tan khakis, he looked like a coach addressing his team.

"Look, here's the thing: There's a temptation to say it's nothing more than another classic example of overexposure. That maybe we just saw too much of them. But I think it's more than that. Part of it was that throughout their careers, they seemed to stay the same, look the same and act the same. I think Dick Clark certainly qualifies for being in this unique group of people who, uh, seemed..."

"Ageless," Katherine suggested.

George pointed at her. "That's the word."

"Or overexposed," Ambrose added cynically.

"One more point. We always felt they'd be around forever," George said. "That's probably what makes this group unusual."

It wasn't eloquent, deep or even sufficiently explained, but Crowder's description of Dick Clark's unusual place in the world of famous people somehow passed inspection with everyone including The Redhead. Duffy knew that all this was just bar talk and it didn't have to intellectually fit or even make sense. What it was, he thought, was an enjoyable way to pass the time of day.

Fittingly, it was Walt Gillespie who guided everyone into the next phase of this ersatz memorial. Taking advantage of a momentary lull in the conversation, he put his glass of beer down, swiveled in his chair to face everyone and remarked casually, "You guys know the MEGA-Cash lottery is up to 460 million?"

The Redhead, whose patience was now worn thin as the white top she was wearing, asked, "What on earth does that have to do with the death of Dick Clark?"

"Mrs. The Redhead… Really, you must do something about that name," Ambrose began. "Anyway, Walter has not strayed from the subject at hand. Obviously, we can't end this memorial this by lighting a candle for Dick Clark as Mr. Hart, it seems, runs too tight a ship here to stock candles. Thus, we are going to do the next best thing."

Her green eyes showing a glimmer of temper, The Redhead, the one who watched over the bar's expenses, gave Ambrose a withering stare and asked sternly, "And just what is the next best thing?"

"We are going to buy a lottery ticket."

## CHAPTER 5

# DICK CLARK BY THE NUMBERS

"What is your given name?" Ambrose asked with a directness that might have caught The Redhead off guard had she not had a well-rehearsed response.

For the record, her first name is Caitlin. Born Caitlin Marie Conners, she was the youngest of four and the only girl. In her case, Mother Nature and Mother Nurture teamed up to produce a no-nonsense, tough-as-nails, but quite adorable Tomboy with a riot of fiery red hair and a head for numbers. According to her husband, that description of a young Caitlin still applied. She was simply taller with a figure that even in her early fifties still took his breath away. She was told she became The Redhead at birth, a title given her by her father after first seeing her in her mother's arms; a pudgy, blush-faced newborn with a joyous splash of raspberry-red hair. Growing up, her family and friends addressed her as Caitlin but always spoke of her as The Redhead. With her natural aloofness and being a back-office sort — someone happier with a computer than a bar towel — she rarely engaged Bar OSA regulars. Thus, she was known to them only as The Redhead; a sobriquet that over the years had turned her into a quasi-mythical personality. Regulars enjoyed the enigmatic role she played in the restaurant. Her husband often teased her by saying he would probably have to sell her as an asset should they ever put the place on the market.

Caitlin understood the fun of it as well and got a kick of being this mysterious ghost-like creature who occasionally haunted the dining room. Deciding Ambrose Dowling was not going to be the first patron among the Bar OSA loyalists to learn her real first name, she whispered in his ear the name she'd concocted for just such an occasion.

"Oh, you poor thing," he crooned sympathetically; a response not unlike others.

"Yes, it has been a heavy load to bear." With a benign smile and a soft sigh, she let the sentence hang there.

"That said, however, I can understand your parents wanting to name you after her," he remarked casually.

Caught off-guard, Caitlin stammered, "Wha... What do you mean? I thought it was a colorful musical instrument that uses gas or steam."

"Well, I suppose if you were a gassy, steamy baby who hummed a lot, that would make sense," he replied with his warm, engaging smile.

Observing this exchange, Duffy Hart said aloud to his wife, "I think you may have to change your nom de guerre."

"So you were christened Calliope," the former Oakland Raider observed. "That is very unusual. Though I am surprised you didn't know Calliope was the Greek mythological muse of epic poetry, the daughter of Zeus and supposedly the muse of Homer who wrote..."

"Thank you, I know what he wrote, George," she snapped, her cheeks reddening.

Hard to offend, he continued, "I think it's a great name but it must have been a tough one to grow up with."

It had been The Redhead's practice to tell strangers who had the effrontery to ask her her first name that she was named

Calliope. She chose it because it sounded like a ridiculous and silly name that no one would take seriously. Now here she was tripped up by a retired university professor and a scholarly lineman. Her husband was right. She should change her alias or, perhaps, drop the whole charade and expose Caitlin to the faithful regulars of Bar OSA. She just as quickly decided it would not be the latter. Maybe she'd dump Calliope and start calling herself Helvetia. Or was that a font, she wondered. No, that was Helvetica.

"If it isn't Calliope, my dear Mrs. The Redhead, then what is it?" a stubborn Ambrose asked, interrupting her reverie.

Caitlin thought about taking her new alias out for a test drive, but decided not to. This was fortuitous as Ambrose did know Helvetia was the female national personification of Switzerland. Instead The Redhead answered with a sweet firmness, "No, Ambrose. No. No. No. It will ruin a good thing. Don't you see? The mystery of me is an important part of what makes this restaurant so successful." Grabbing a menu off the bar, she held it up and pointed to a dish. "In some way, you might say I am like the salt cod and potato cazuela which, as you know, is so popular we can never take it off the menu. Now, let's get back to this silly memorial business."

Ambrose would have the final word on the subject: "I dare say putting yourself in the same company with your husband's incomparable salt cod and potato cazuela explains it all."

"I for one kinda like not knowing her name. Like she said, it's all part of the charm of the place," Walt remarked to no one in particular. Looking at The Redhead, he added quickly, "Sorry, Mrs. Hart, I mean your name. It's not polite to speak of someone in the third person in their presence."

This bit of grammarian etiquette coming from the man with the grizzled crewcut and the dirty plumber's uniform surprised them all, especially The Redhead who replied, "You're right, Walt, it is impolite. And I'm glad you appreciate the fun of it,"

There was a nascent liveliness in Bar OSA that would in short order send The Redhead scurrying back to her office and Duffy out amongst the tables to greet his customers old and new. Still, they and the Gearons were curious to know how the three Inbetweeners were going to put the finishing touches on their bizarre ceremony.

As he was the one who brought up the enormous amount of money in the MEGA-Cash Lottery, Walt decided he was the ideal spokesperson for this closing portion of the Dick Clark Memorial. Facing the small assemblage, he explained how the three Inbetweeners came to decide that a lottery ticket purchase would be a fitting inclusion into their remembrance of the life and times of Dick Clark, even though not a single one of them gave him much thought when he was alive. Also, not a single one of them entertained the slightest notion they could win the lottery.

"So we decided to honor Dick... Don't you think by this time into the memorial, we can call him Dick? Anyway, we brought you guys down to this end of the bar to join us by going in on a MEGA-Cash lottery ticket. We're looking for a dollar per person. Uh, that's a dollar per guy or couple as the case may be for you four," he said, pointing to the Harts and Gearons.

The Redhead threw up her hands. Looking at her husband, she said, "This is one of the reasons why I prefer staying in the office."

With a quizzical look, Mike Gearon asked, "Gentlemen, would one of you explain to me what purchasing a lottery ticket has in common with lighting a candle?"

"There isn't one," George replied. "But that's not the point."

"What is the point?" asked Mike.

The hefty former football player leaned back and said in a low but cheery voice, "The fact that there is none. This is just typical bar bantering; an admittedly weird but pleasant way to fend off boredom. I sense it's about to wind down, so stick around and enjoy the rest."

Duffy had moved to the end of the bar to allow Sam Calestri, a strapping young man in his late twenties with an ingenuous smile who had just come on duty, to serve the four or five people who had taken places at the bar. Standing next to Walt, Duffy said in a voice just loud enough for the his group to hear, "Why don't I go find us a candle."

Walt grabbed his arm. "Wait, wait. Our idea is a good one. Just hear us out."

Ambrose once again took center stage: "Gentlemen and ladies, it is our plan to find five Dick Clark-related numbers. Each one of us will pick one. Then we will purchase five dollars worth of tickets with five different mega numbers. They, too, will be Dick Clark-centric in that they will be based on the date he passed; twelve for the year, four for the month, sixteen for the week and eighteen for the day."

"You need one more," The Redhead noted with a smile. As she loved numbers, the lottery idea now had a certain appeal.

Ambrose counted on his fingers and asked, "Anyone know the time of death? The hour will do."

"How about the hour we all learned of his death," Mike Gearon suggested.

"I don't think so. It was the four o'clock hour which is also the sixteenth hour of the day. Both are in play."

"I see they are all even numbers, Ambrose. That should make you happy," George observed.

"I am ecstatic. Mr. Clark picked an auspicious date to expire."

Walt settled it. "This isn't going to sit well with you, professor, but how about seven for the seven people who came to his memorial today?"

A chorus of ayes rang out. Mostly because four wanted to leave.

Ambrose grudgingly agreed to the one odd mega number.

Duffy looked at his watch and warned them that the ceremony really had to end. "Look, you guys can stay here until closing, but The Redhead and I are working stiffs."

An impatient Walt leaned over and tapped George on the shoulder. "Go to that website where you found all that good stuff about him."

"You mean Wikipedia," George Crowder said, picking up his iPhone. The device disappeared into the folds of his large athlete's hands and vanished from view. "Okay, somebody take note of the numbers."

Duffy reached behind him and grabbed a piece of a paper and a pen. "You find them, I'll write them down."

George began in a stuttered rhythm: "Okay, let's see. Born November 30th,1929. You can get some numbers from that. Says here he knew he wanted to be a radio disc jockey at the age of ten. Oh, he hosted Bandstand in 1956 and it became American Bandstand in 1957. Then the show moved to LA in 1964. There are some even numbers here for you, Ambrose. Okay, Is that enough or do you want... Oh, here's something. He was married three times. That's a nice low number. If that means anything."

"High numbers, low numbers. I doubt in a lottery if it makes any difference," Duffy opined. "Okay, everybody, you heard the famous football player. Time to pick five numbers." Checking his quickly scrawled notes, he announced how it all would work: "I'll start it out. Then the Gearons, Ambrose, George and, finally you, Walt. That said, I hereby give my pick to The Redhead."

"I'll bet Dick Clark was a cute newborn. I pick his birth date, the 30th," she said without hesitation. "Put thirty down for us."

"Next up, the Gearons," Duffy said.

Mike and Katherine looked at each other. It was a happily married couple's look where no words needed exchanging. He pointed to her to make the selection. She shook her head and signaled her husband to pick one. She knew he'd pick the year Clark was born and that was fine with her.

"With apologies to Ambrose, I'm picking twenty-nine for the year he was born," he parroted as if he'd read her mind.

Duffy nodded to Ambrose who not surprisingly picked an even number. "I choose ten for the age he was when he decided to pursue a career as a disc jockey. Highly unlikely. When I was ten, like most other children, I had no ambition other than to figure out how to avoid eating broccoli."

"How do you spell broccoli?" Duffy joked. He looked to George for the next number.

"Seventeen."

"Seventeen?"

"Yes, seventeen," he repeated with a sweet sentimentality that suggested it might be a number of significant personal interest.

"Why seventeen, George?" Duffy asked gently.

"I'm guessing that's when he lost his virginity," he said. He saw no reason to tell them he, too, was that age when he and Joannie-Lynn Thomlison fumbled and tumbled on a beat-up couch in his parents' basement. His ardor and the resulting urgency was such that he wasn't actually sure he was where he was supposed to be to claim he'd actually done the deed. Nonetheless, it was officially recorded into his memory as the first time.

"Look, Mr. Crowder," Ambrose began to argue, "this was a man who right out of college became Cactus Dick on TV. That means he was a handsome young devil. I submit to you that equipped with those good looks and warm smile, some teenage temptress probably deflowered him in his sixteenth year."

The Redhead burst out laughing. "Ambrose, you're only saying that because you don't like it that George picked an odd number. And another thing: Girls are deflowered. Boys are... Oh, I don't know what happens to boys. Nothing good, I'm sure."

"Sorry, Ambrose, seventeen is duly recorded," Duffy announced. He then gleefully pointed to Walt for the final selection.

"Three," he blurted out with a second's hesitation.

"Three it is," Duffy noted.

"Aha, the number three as in married three times," George said, rechecking the Wikipedia site.

"We have that in common. If I'm lucky and well behaved, my third will see me out. If she doesn't wear me out first," he added with a lecherous grin.

"Okay, I've got five numbers and five megas. The numbers we chose are 3, 10, 17, 29 and 30. The mega numbers are 4, 7, 12, 16 and 18. I will go in the back and print them so we each have a copy. This is so utterly whacky, we'll probably win," Duffy laughed.

"No, let me do that," The Redhead said, reaching past George to take the note paper from her husband. "Katherine, come with me. We'll let the guys finish up their memorial." Then, looking up at the ceiling and waving, she added with a slight touch of irreverence, "Oh, and have a really groovy eternity, Mr. Clark."

"Don't forget to come back with the numbers," Duffy shouted after her.

The five men were now part of a crowded, bustling bar scene. Gone was the Renoir still-life atmosphere of the late afternoon. The bar was also clamorous; a cheery, chattery kind of noise that sometimes caused conversations to collide mid-point. The memorial, though, was in no danger of being interrupted because no one else seemed the slightest bit interested in what the five men were doing, including Sam Calestri who was in the vicinity making drinks, humming to the music of Manu Chao and seemingly oblivious to who was at the bar.

As he was standing in the aisle between the long bar and the tables, Mike Gearon was the one member of the memorial who fell victim to the happy crush of people coming into Bar OSA. Enough so that he decided the memorial can go on without him.

"You can't leave yet," Duffy shouted over the bar. "We have to pass the collection plate. Better, just leave a dollar on the bar." With that, he put a dollar on the table in front of Ambrose.

Just as quickly, the four others followed suit and suddenly there was a stack of five one dollar bills in a variety of conditions from mint-new and crisp to wrinkled and scribbled on. Ambrose scooped them up and waving them around, asking, "Okay, now who is going to buy this MEGA-Cash ticket?"

Their responses were surprising. George Crowder began with an admission. "I've never bought a lottery ticket before. I don't even know how. The odds of winning are so astronomically high, lotteries don't interest me."

Walter Gillespie simply didn't want to be put out. "I don't know a place convenient for me to stop between here and home."

Duffy Hart, of course, had a legitimate excuse. "Hey, guys, I'm on the job and the ticket has to be purchased by eight o'clock, I think."

Mike Gearon had had enough. "Why don't we each pick up our dollar and say this has been fun. Or better yet, leave it as a tip. Elena and Sam can use it."

Ambrose bellowed, "Nonsense! I say nonsense. We five will see this through. Dick wouldn't have wanted it otherwise."

Walt's reaction was immediate and loud: "Oh, fuck Dick."

"Ooookay, that's the end of it," Duffy huffed.

"I'm sorry, Duffy. I know how you are about swearing. It's just that Ambrose has this fancy way of speaking that sometimes bugs the shi... Well, it bugs me."

"Walter, I am truly sorry I upset you," Ambrose said. The sincerity of his apology was easy to spot. "I certainly don't do or say anything with the motive being to distress you. Now I have an excellent idea. Why don't I pick up the lottery ticket? I walk by a place that sells everything from lottery tickets to phone cards for Kuala Lumpur. When Mrs. The Redhead comes back, she'll give everyone the numbers and you can check late tonight or tomorrow to see how we fared. Or, of course, you can ignore it altogether as the chances of winning are seventy trillion to one. Perhaps even more."

Walt patted Ambrose on the shoulder. "I've just had a bad day. Nothing serious but I think I ended up taking it out on you. But sometimes you really can be a horse's ass." Walt poked him gently and added, "Only kidding, professor."

"And peace comes once again to Bar OSA," Duffy said. "I'm going to track down The Redhead and get our numbers." Just before her walked away, he asked, "Can I safely assume we've just said 'amen' and the Dick Clark Memorial has come to an end?"

The three Inbetweeners and Mike Gearon solemnly but discordantly murmured, "Amen."

Walking backwards toward the other end of the bar, Duffy gave them the traditional priest's blessing with his right hand while silently mouthing "Dominus vobiscum." With the memorial officially over, Dick Clark, like Lady MacBeth, was now the poor player that struts and frets his hour upon the stage and then is heard no more. At least in the minds of the Inbetweeners.

Walt surveyed the room and seeing the full bar and mostly occupied tables, he commented, "You know, it's a good thing we dumped out of that. Otherwise we'd start drawing attention to ourselves."

"Nonsense, Mr. Gillespie. We are all at an age where we are pretty much invisible to those around us," Ambrose remarked.

"Speak for yourself, big guy," Walt countered, not at all ready to accept the professor's premise; a premise he felt deep down probably had some merit. He just didn't want to accept it.

"Walter, I speak for all of us," Ambrose responded. "I put it to you that any one of us could sit here stark naked, chugging Andalusian Sidecars while singing the Cal fight song in Cantonese and not draw the slightest attention to ourselves."

Crowder burst out laughing. "Professor, I'll be more than happy to hold your clothes if you're serious, but don't strip down on my account as I happen to agree with you."

"Thank you, Mr. Crowder. I suppose if I were really serious about proving my theory," he said, looking around the room, "I certainly would not include singing the Cal fight song in Bar OSA."

"Not a good idea, even in Cantonese," Mike pointed out, picturing the entire bar on its feet in full voice in any number of languages cheering on the California Golden Bears.

Mike Gearon, like George Crowder, felt Ambrose's premise that older people in general were often photoshopped out of society for no other reason than they were of an advanced age was pretty much on the mark. He wondered though if some seniors didn't volunteer themselves into social exile. There were ways to stay in the game, he thought. That explained, in part, why he was standing there in well-fitting jeans, saddle-tan Ecco shoes with argyle socks, a sea blue button-down shirt and a decades old linen jacket that had recently be relined in pink. He finished it off with a gold patterned pocket-square that he'd purchased in Rome and treasured. More than the clothes themselves was the fact that he wore it all with a nonchalance, an ease that grew from the fifty plus years he spent working in a medium that often thrust him into the public spotlight, sometimes more than he wished. To his credit, he didn't dress to look younger. Being well-groomed, well-attired and fit was enough.

As it turned out, the debatable subject of seniors' visibility or lack thereof had no legs. The Inbetweeners seemed of a mind to break it up and head home. This they would have done had not Mike Gearon insisted he now get his dollar's worth of lottery fantasy. So even though the amens were said, it was obvious the Dick Clark Memorial would continue.

# CHAPTER 6
# MONEY CHANGES EVERYTHING

The three Inbetweeners stared at Mike Gearon as if he were speaking another language. Because of their obvious puzzlement and his growing uncertainty that he could not easily explain what he meant, Mike was hesitant to repeat himself. But he did.

"I said I wanted to get my money's worth of lottery fantasy."

"Aren't we amusing enough" George Crowder teased, taking a last sip of his Albarino.

"Trust me, I have gotten more than a dollar's worth of amusement from you guys. No, this is about something else," Mike replied just as Duffy Hart returned from his back office with copies of the Dick Clark-related lottery numbers.

"Walt, how much did you say was in that MEGA-Cash lottery?" the restaurant owner asked as he began handing out the notes.

"$460 million," he replied. "I don't know what it will be by eight tonight when they draw the numbers. Probably more."

"So what kind of payoff am I going to see for my huge investment?" Duffy asked.

George laughed and said, “Realistically? Twenty percent of nothing.”

“I don’t know exactly, but it ain’t going to be $92 million,” Walt said, ignoring the former football player’s comment.

“You’re right about that,” Mike Gearon said, jumping into the conversation even though it strayed a bit from what he wanted to discuss. “Just for the sake of argument, let’’s figure the amount is $460 million and the winners take a lump sum instead of annual payments. That means they’ll get about half or a little more than half of that. Let’s say half. Divvy up 230 million five ways and you’re looking at…”

“46 million! Whoa,” the craggy plumber yipped, rubbing his hands together. “I can handle that.”

Mike held up his hand. “Keep those greedy thoughts in check. I’m not through yet. Now you have federal taxes to pay and they can reduce your winnings by 28% to around 40%,” he reminded them all. “There may even be more ways they cut in to it. Maybe there’s a state tax. I’m not sure.”

Quietly doing the math, the plumber muttered, "So that leaves us…”

“I figure we’ll each get $7.69. On a one dollar investment, that’s an excellent return,” George joked, clearly enjoying his cynical insertions into the conversation.

“Very funny. Anyway I figure we each would end up with somewhere between 24 and 29 million,” Walt said. “That is still a very tidy piece of change.”

George leaned in and looked around Ambrose at Walt. “Of course, the odds of winning that jackpot are one in God knows how many million. That’s why I don’t buy lottery tickets. Except for offbeat memorials like this.”

Odds were not something Walt dealt with on a regular basis. This was confirmed when he replied, “I’m guessing it’s like the odds of being struck by lightening.”

Once again, George dove into his iPhone, clicked on the Google icon and found his answer. "Walt, those odds are one in 700,000. It says here a big lottery win like that is one in 175 million. You care to know what the lottery odds actually look like?"

"Yeah, go ahead. Thrill me," Walt mumbled.

"I just spotted this on the search results, so bear with me," George mumbled. After a quick scan, he continued, "Okay, this is really good. It says here a Washington D.C. statistician..."

Ambrose stopped him by putting a hand on his arm. "Excuse me, but why do we need to know the statistician is from our nation's capital?"

"Because it is important to the story," George explained. Walt marveled at how calmly he handled the professor's peskiness. "So this statistician has 175 million brand new one dollar bills delivered to his house in two semi-trailer trucks. Now one bill is marked as the lucky bill. Find it and you win. All the bills are laid out end to end. According to this story, the line of bills would stretch from his home south to Orlando and Disney World, Then they would stretch all the way across the county to Disneyland. From there the bills would extend to Portland, Oregon and across the country to Portland, Maine and then back to his home in Washington D.C.."

"Whew, that's quite a distance," Walt said. "I doubt the money would stay out there too long."

"Why do I sense that isn't the end of the story?" Mike said.

"Because it isn't," George replied, his eyes still trained on the Google info. "It says here that there are still enough dollars left in one of the trucks to stretch around that same loop a second time. This will make you feel good, though. You have a better chance of winning the lottery than being attacked by a shark."

"I assume you don't mean the two-legged variety," Duffy said.

Ambrose was clearly delighted with the former Oakland Raider's information. "Mr. Crowder, while I'm not sure if any of that is true, I thank you for your fascinating description of what I would call impossible odds. Personally, I'm very comfortable with the knowledge that I can't possibly win. I'm not sure how I would deal with all that money. More to the point, I worry about how it would deal with me," he said with an obvious shiver.

Shoving the Time's crossword puzzle in his coat pocket, Ambrose signaled he was ready to call it a day. George looked at his empty glass of wine and wondered if he wanted another. Sensing Crowder's indecisiveness, Duffy held up his hand with his thumb and index finger measuring out a splash size. George nodded and pushed the glass toward him. Seeing that George was staying put, Walt ordered a half-pint of beer, otherwise known in Bar OSA as a baby Stella. Ambrose watched as the re-fueling started and decided he, too, had more time to devote to the afternoon's nonsense. Pulling the puzzle out of his pocket, he placed it back on the bar. "Mr. Hart, I think it is best that I have something tamer than a Cuban Manhattan. I'll join Walter here in a baby one of those. Otherwise, who knows how I will spend the five dollars you are entrusting to me."

"Mike, what were you trying to tell us before we got on that winnings and impossible odds kick?" George asked. "I know it's something about getting more bang for your buck. So what's the bang you're looking for?"

What Mike Gearon did not tell them was that on some Saturdays he and Katherine bought a five dollar Super Lotto quick pick from a small product-packed, donut/deli/odds-and-ends store just off College Avenue in Berkeley. The purchase was part of a ritual; a ritual like countless others that are fashioned by couples doing couples' things. These practices can run the gamut from silly to romantic, prosaic to poetic. This particular rite meant a five dollar outlay which the Gearons considered money well-spent. After all, they might win and even if they didn't from Saturday afternoon to Sunday morning when they read the numbers in the paper they would enjoy many moments daydreaming about how they would handle such a windfall. Interestingly, they only played the California lottery when the jackpots were under fifteen million. Their thinking was the total amount that eventually would find its way into their checking account would be small enough that they could keep secret the fact that it was a lottery investment. Thus, they would avoid all the negative aspects of being lottery winners. On Sunday mornings with coffee and the paper, they had what they called the Reading of the Lotto. Mike found the winning numbers in the paper and read them off to Katherine who would confirm they came nowhere close to winning. Even so, they always closed the ceremony by saying aloud, "We are still the richest people in the world."

What he did tell the Inbetweeners was this: "There are two things at play here. Firstly..."

Ambrose's hand went up, shushing him. "Mr. Gearon, your use of firstly is laudable," he enthused.

Walt poked Ambrose. "Will you let the man talk. This isn't some frigging college exam he's taking."

"Maybe we ought to wrap this up," Mike suggested, mildly frustrated with himself for having started this conversation in the first place.

"No, no," said a penitent Ambrose Dowling. "Please continue."

"All right. As I see it, there are only two reasons to buy a lottery ticket. The first is obvious. You can't win if you're not in. Impossible odds or not, there will be a winner eventually and it could be you. Secondly, it allows you to fantasize or daydream about what you'd do with the money. Of the two, this is the most important reason because that's about all you're really going to get for your purchase; the fun of fantasizing and daydreaming."

"So you're saying that's what we ought to be doing? Talking about what we'd do with the money," George said, answering his own question.

Mike shook his head and mumbled, "That's pretty much it."

"Do you buy lottery tickets?" Walt asked.

"We do on occasion."

"So what do you fantasize about?"

"Lots of things. Most of them are not very romantic. Katherine and I talk about helping our son and daughter and their spouses with their student loans. Maybe help them get a house or condo in this crazy market. For us, we would travel more and maybe fix up the house. We also have this growing list of people who can always use a little help. Money would go toward that as well."

Walt looked puzzled. "Give me an example."

"Sure. We have a friend, a colorful, glib Irishman who fell on tough times financially. He was born, raised, educated and worked in Manhattan. The island is in his blood. If we won the lottery, we'd see to it that he gets a plane ticket..."

"First class, I hope," Ambrose interjected.

"No other way," Mike said, grinning. "Anyway we'd send him back to Manhattan for an extended visit all expenses paid."

"Aha," Ambrose sighed, "now you'd like do the same with our group."

"What? Send you all back to Manhattan?" he asked jokingly.

"No, of course not. If you were able to do that, so would we, as all of us would be knee deep in U.S. currency," Ambrose chuckled. "What I mean is you'd like us to talk about what we'd do to with the 24 to 29 million that Walt figures each of us would pocket."

"That's pretty much it," Mike said, feeling like a recreational director trying to get children to participate in some silly game. Nevertheless, he carried on, suggesting Ambrose begin. "What would you do with your winnings, professor?" he asked.

Ambrose Dowling shied from the question, leaning back as if it were a missile headed in his direction. "No, don't start with me. I'll say something incredibly silly and then if we win, I'll be bound by it."

Spotting his wife and Katherine heading in their direction, Duffy announced their arrival by asking the Inbetweeners to please keep their fantasies aboveboard. This was an appropriate warning as Walt had this bawdy response he'd remembered from a movie comedy that he'd always wanted to use if asked about what he'd do with newfound wealth. The trouble was nobody ever asked him so this was to be a debut of sorts. It involved the winner signing to a long term contract a blemish-free, wrinkle-free, youthful hooker with full pouty lips and the talents of an acrobat. He thought it would be a guaranteed laugh-getter. While it might earn a good-natured groan, it had nothing at all to do with his real desires as he and his third wife, Jeannie, while no longer blemish or wrinkle-free but equipped with full pouty lips and the moves of an acrobat, enjoyed a robust and imaginative sex life. In fact, she was his fantasy.

The Redhead had changed tops and was now wearing a loose-fitting men's white dress shirt over her black Capri pants. Katherine wore tights that pretended to be form-fitting jeans and a black, high-collared knit top, her blonde hair pulled back into a ponytail. Thanks to their trim figures, bright smiles and confident manner, both women could wear clothes their peers had abandoned years ago. While they could still turn heads, no one in the room admired them more than their husbands. Both men's eyes were trained on their spouses as the they marched back into the wackiness of the Dick Clark Memorial, a ceremony they thought was finally over.

"Welcome back, ladies," Duffy said as the women positioned themselves on either side of Mike Gearon. The Redhead never went behind the bar as she figured, quite rightly, only bartenders skilled in the craft of making cocktails should be there. She also refused to call them mixologists, a term slowly gaining popularity in some of the hipper establishments.

"So what did we miss?" Katherine asked.

"Your husband has us talking about what we'd do with our lottery winnings," George explained.

"And you're just in time to hear all about it," her husband replied.

The Redhead said, "I know one of you is probably going to pull out the time-honored line about securing the services of the world's most expensive hooker."

Duffy pounded his fist on the bar and said, "Honestly, how did you know I was going to say that?"

"It damned well better not come from you," she said with a sly smile.

"I can assure you there'd be no expensive hookers for me," Walt boasted, just a bit disappointed to learn his debut joke was an old chestnut. "Jeannie is my one and only. Maybe I'll just open a running account for her at Victoria's Secret so she can surprise me each night when I come home from fixing people's broken pipes."

"Each night!" exclaimed George Crowder. "Obviously there's nothing wrong with your pipe."

Mike Gearon was not without a comment either, but Katherine, knowing full well what he was thinking, nudged him. Instead he said, "Ambrose, don't shy away from it this time. What would you do with all that money?"

Before he could reply, The Redhead interjected, "Wait, I'm curious. How much are we talking about per winner?" Her husband provided the dollar amount which clearly impressed her. "My, that is a lot of money. So, Ambrose, what would you do with a stash like that?"

"I honestly don't know that I would keep it," he stated.

"That's a very Berkeley answer," Walt remarked.

Ambrose looked over at him and grinned. "So Mr. Gillespie, would you care to give us a very El Cerrito answer?"

"Sure. I got twenty-five to twenty-nine million ways I'd spend it," he said greedily. "My business would go. That's for sure. No more plumbing. Jeannie and I would probably move to some double-gated community far from here just to put miles and security between us and my sister's in-laws."

Ambrose was genuinely puzzled. "What on earth is a double-gated community?"

"Just that," George said. "You enter one gate to get into the main section of the housing development and then within that sanctum is another smaller, more exclusive gated community."

"How utterly horrid," Ambrose remarked.

Katherine, too, was wary of suddenly having such a huge amount of money. She took that moment to offer her thoughts: "You do hear some really strange stories about lottery winners. How friends and relatives the winners hadn't seen or heard from for years suddenly come out of the woodwork with their hands out."

"I heard about a guy who won a couple of million and as soon as he got the check, his wife divorced him and took half. It was downhill after that," Duffy said, adding to the growing list of woes that seem to befall lottery winners.

"What he needed was a prenup that kept his bride from splitting if he suddenly fell into a fortune." He looked at Katherine and The Redhead who were glaring at him. "Okay, maybe that's not such a good idea."

With the exception of Walt and The Redhead, everyone else seemed to get behind Katherine's central theme that winning a lottery might not be all that good of a deal.

"There are aspects of it that give one cause to worry," Ambrose remarked.

"My thought is if you made that amount of money by working for it, people pretty much leave you alone," George Crowder opined. "Not so with instant money."

"George, there may be something to that," Duffy said. "Lottery wealth is different from earned wealth, even inherited wealth. It's lucky money, funny money and for some strange reason anyone remotely connected to the winner believes they are entitled to a share."

"Imagine all the sales' pitches you'd get from people aching to put your money to work with them and for them," noted Mike Gearon. "Now those are shark attacks that defy the odds."

"While money might buy you many things, it won't make you wiser, smarter, cuter or younger," Ambrose observed, purposefully not looking at Walt lest he should take it personally.

Walt retorted with a snorting chuckle, "Hell, if you got a ton of money, you don't need to be smart, cute, younger or... What was the fourth one?"

"Wiser."

"Yeah, wiser" he echoed. "Money trumps all that."

Mike Gearon, who started it all, had contributed little to the discussion on the cautionary aspects of winning a lottery. Feeling he ought to participate, he said to one and all, "Walt, you just reminded me of one of life's indisputable truths."

"What's that?" he asked.

"Money changes everything."

This barebones cliche drew shrugs and nods from Ambrose and Walt but, judging from the smile on George Crowder's face, it was downright inspirational. Off-key and in a gravelly voice, he began to sing, "Money changes everything..." Fortunately for any ears within listening range, they were spared hearing more. "It was a Cyndi Lauper song from the early eighties. I remember it because it was just about the same time salaries in the NFL started rapidly climbing rather than just inching up. Money certainly changed that business," he said.

"Not to mention totally screwing up higher education," added the professor.

"What about health care," noted Walt who with his hypochondria loved his doctor visits.

Ambrose would have the last word. "Interesting, isn't it. While this discussion has not been without substantive content, it has been for the most part cliche-ridden. There is a hint of banality to it. However, here's the irony. Take one of our boilerplate comments like 'money changes everything,' turn it into a song lyric and it suddenly becomes noteworthy and, I should add, makes a ton of money for the songwriter."

Mike Gearon, flanked by Katherine and The Redhead, was just about to toss in a thought or two Ambrose's caviling comment when he noticed that The Redhead was turning redder and redder.

## CHAPTER 7

# THE REDHEAD TAKES CHARGE

"People, listen to yourselves," The Redhead exclaimed, her tone that of a veteran teacher admonishing her third grade class. "Why do you even bother buying a lottery ticket for this MEGA.... uh, this MEGA..." Her scolding lost some of its punch as she finished in a faded murmur, "Whatever the heck it is."

"MEGA-Cash," Walt replied with a meekness all of them were suddenly feeling.

"Thank you." Looking at them, she was once again ready to issue an earful. "Let's get one thing straight. You are not going to win. Now having said that, except for Walt who must have the shopper's gene and thinks winning would be a greedy hoot, the rest of you sound as If the only thing you'll end up winning is an IRS audit or maybe a root canal. But, you know, I suppose in a way that makes sense. This way when you learn tomorrow you've lost, you'll all feel a great sense of relief."

Katherine Gearon was so keen on Caitlin Hart's dressing-down, she raised her right arm skyward with the palm of her hand facing The Redhead for a congratulatory high five. Even though she had a large inventory of cute gestures, Mike Gearon couldn't remember ever seeing his wife give anyone a high five. Is a fist bump next, he wondered.

"Caitlin's right. We do sound more like whiners than potential winners," Katherine remarked.

"So here's the deal." The Redhead began. "Let's wrap up this Dick Clark Memorial by pretending we won the MEGA-Cash lottery and we have divided it five ways. So now that each of us is in possession of, let's say for fantasizing sakes, twenty-five million dollars, what are we going to do with it all?"

Ambrose pursed his lips and looked curiously at the bar owner's take-charge spouse. Needing clarification, he asked, "Mrs. The Redhead, is that a we as in 'what are we as individuals going to do with our money,' or is that a we as in 'what are we doing with the money as a gang of seven?'"

Caitlin Hart folded her arms and looked up at the ceiling as if she were giving his question serious thought. Finally, she announced coolly, "Oh, most certainly the latter."

It took Walt several seconds to react because he was always confused about which was which when former and latter were used in combination. Once he figured it out, he said with surprising vehemence, "No way, no how, lady."

George Crowder was more circumspect. "I'm not going to try and second guess you as I suspect you have your reasons. Just how do you seeing it all working out? Fantasy-wise, of course."

"Give me a moment to think that through, George," she replied. "What I have in mind is not really complicated, however, explaining it requires a delicate touch and I've always been weak in the delicate department. Let me think how I can best present it."

Katherine, always smiling, cheerfully noted, "While I haven't the slightest idea what Caitlin's thinking, I am certain it will be fascinating. As I see it, the real goal here is to just enjoy chatting about how five lucky lottery partners would handle 125 million tax-free dollars."

While she made no indication she was looking for an immediate response, Walt jumped in and said, "That's easy, Mrs. Gearon. The money is divided into five equal shares. That's it. We all go our merry way. End of discussion."

Ignoring him, she continued, "The Redhead, in my opinion, is trying to think outside the box and maybe with a little altruism thrown in for good measure. At least that's the way I see..."

Duffy's wife put a hand up and shushed her friend. "Thank you, but that's all the filler I needed in order to get all my ducks in order. Now I'm ready to quack."

"Trust me, you have our undivided attention. Except for maybe Walter," Ambrose said.

Clearing her throat, The Redhead began with a direct question: "First off, are we all agreed we are talking about something that will never happen?"

An approving nod, two yeses, and a pair of uh-huhs confirmed those in attendance were all of one mind.

"Of course, just because we all agree on, let's say, my rather imaginative unorthodox way of handling the winnings — even though we know it can't possibly happen — doesn't mean it can be disregarded should for some odd reason, some quirk of fate, it actually works." With that, she looked around to see if everyone understood her.

"Now you guys have a pretty good idea why we chose not to write our own wedding vows," Duffy said.

Before she could react, Walt spun around on his barstool to face her. "Let's see if I have this straight. We all agree to do what you want to do with the money. Then if for some reason we really win, we're stuck with that agreement. That means I can't walk away with my $25 mill and say, 'Sayonara, everyone, and don't try to call. Our phone number in that double-gated community is unlisted.'"

"I suppose you can, Walt. Certainly, no one would stop you. But why not listen to what I have to say and then decide."

"Well, it's all for fun anyway," he remarked. "Knock yourself out."

The Redhead moved away from the Gearons and walked to the end of the bar where she could address the small gathering without being bumped or jostled by incoming and outgoing customers. Putting her hands on the bar, she studied them for a moment before speaking. A loud cough from her husband was a clue that she'd better start orating or the memorial was history.

"I am not an actuary. However, I do know the lifespan of the American male is somewhere in the mid to late seventies. That means one of you is already living on borrowed time." She looked directly at Ambrose who gave her no hint at what he thought of her comment.

"76 years and two months. That's fresh off the Internet; an up to date 2012 statistic, " George Crowder reported after once again diving into his iPhone for on-the-spot information.

"Thank you, George. Except for Ambrose, the rest of you are closing in on that number or are already there. Now that isn't to say you can't all live well into your eighties and nineties."

"Sure is nIce of you to think we could," Walt mumbled.

"But, I doubt it," she said matter-of-factly.

Before she could utter another word, Duffy interjected, "And here, gentlemen, you have my lovely wife at her most sensitive. Imagine what she'd have said if she hadn't give some thought as to how to delicately deal with the male aging issue."

Aware she was blushing which seemed to make her hair even redder, Caitlin knew she had a great idea which was, regrettably, based on their advanced ages. Hell, she thought, they ought to be able to deal with it, tactfully presented or not. Scowling at her husband, she decided to proceed in her own prickly fashion. "Look, I'm sorry, but I'm really trying to make a point here and it's a good one."

"As I am the eldest here, I will speak for the others," Ambrose said, foam from his half pint of beer lining his upper lip. "Don't worry, Mrs. The Redhead, little if any offense was taken. I might add, though, you have piqued our curiosities."

"All right, here's the thing: You all have lived to a ripe old age where routine is important. You have your favorite restaurants, hopefully this one, your favorite TV programs, your favorite just-about -everything. From where I stand, you all seem reasonably content with your lot in life. You have, as they say, been there, done that. I'm pretty confident none of you has a long shopping list of boys' toys that you covet, Ferraris, Rolexes, Brioni suits, a fractional ownership in a jet and four hundred dollar haircuts are probably not must-have items. I'm betting you all have been or continue to be successful. While I'm not privy to this kind of information, I doubt if any of you have money problems. You all seem happy and satisfied with your own ideas of what is enough. Now what you don't have is a lot of..."

"Please, don't say it," Duffy pleaded.

"...is time."

Duffy tossed his bar rag in the air. Catching it, he exclaimed, "Here we go."

"No, don't interrupt," she commanded. "What I am trying to get at is with fewer years left, you don't need a lot of money. Certainly not twenty-five million dollars. Most of it will just go to relatives, some of whom you probably can't stand. So I have an idea. Each winner takes home two and a half million to do with whatever they like. Spend it, save it, burn it... It's fun money. The other twenty-two and a half mill you leave in the pot." Reading from a cocktail napkin she'd been scribbling on, she said, "That totals $112,500,000."

With laudable patience, George asked, "And what do we do with all that money?"

The Redhead beamed, "Ah, I am glad you asked. All five winners which is really seven if you count Katherine and me, which you damn well better do, form a group that donates money whenever, wherever to whatever and whomever we deem worthy. An unorthodox kind of charitable foundation. And because this has all been inspired by the fact that Dick Clark died today, perhaps we can call ourselves the Clarkists."

Mike Gearon shook his head. "No, that won't work. It sounds too much like a religious order."

"How about the Clarkistas?" Katherine suggested.

"Kat, that sounds like a rebel group from a Latin American country or people who makes coffee drinks," her husband said.

Duffy raised his hand. "I've got it. We'll call ourselves the Dicks."

There was silence. Well, as much silence as you're going to get in Bar OSA at that time of evening. At the end of the bar, each took a turn in reacting to Duffy's suggestion.

"I cannot conceive of a more appropriate way to end this nonsense. And I would have put up money that it would come from my husband," Duffy's wife said.

"Perhaps, my dear, but may I add that I found it rip-roaringly funny," Ambrose responded, the beer foam still clinging to his upper lip.

Walt laughed his way through his response: "Hey, I love the idea. Hell, if we don't win, maybe we ought to form a bowling team and call ourselves the Dicks."

George had another idea: "No, we stick with The Redhead's idea and if we win, we'll sponsor a public television show. Imagine hearing the announcer say at the top of the program: 'Birds of Zambezi comes to you tonight thanks to viewers like you and through a generous grant from the Dicks. And then it shows a photo of all seven of us."

"I think we've pretty much run this whole thing into the ground," Katherine said. "Not that it hasn't been enjoyable."

When Duffy Hart did something that he might classify as witty, mischievous or cleverly off-color, he stamped it with an impish look that stayed on his face for awhile.

Coming from behind the bar, he joined his wife and the Gearons. He was going to now officially close the Dick Clark Memorial in his inimitable style: "This has been a classic afternoon of... What did you call it, George? Banter. This one definitely ranks in the top five of my bar banter experiences. Now, because I have made very little in the way of income from this, I am officially putting another amen on this memorial with an observation made earlier by my radio friend here. Mike said and I quote, 'Money changes everything.' I will add to that money also changes everyone. But the good news is we Dicks will never find that out. Now The Redhead has work to do and I am going to greet customers who are actually spending money." With that, he and his wife wife worked their way to the rear of the bar; she making a beeline for their office and he stopping here and there to welcome the newly arrived drinkers and diners.

Walt and George were the first to leave. Both let everyone know they too thought this was one of the more entertaining afternoons and both wished Ambrose a happy birthday should they not see him before next Wednesday. Ambrose accepted their good words and assured them he would purchase the lottery ticket on his way home. Neither seemed to think it was necessary. As proof, both left their lottery numbers on the bar.

## CHAPTER 8

# THE BAR BANTER AFTERMATH

"What an odd afternoon," said Katherine, her head still full of the antics of the last hour. While anxious to pull out of her parking spot on Shattuck Avenue, she waited patiently as an older man on a beaten-up ten-speed appeared in her side mirror. Clad in baggy corduroys with a bicycle clip on one pant leg, a weathered sweater, contrasting scarf and battered bike helmet, the hoary gent slowed as he neared the driver's window to peer disapprovingly into the car. Katherine paid him no mind as she turned into traffic behind him. To further show his apparent disgust for automobiles, their drivers and anyone younger than he was, he stayed right in the middle of the slow lane forcing her and a procession of cars behind her to inch toward Vine Street where, if all went well, he would go straight through whilst she turned right. Katherine was neither frustrated nor angry about what was happening. She was used to it as the Berkeley and Oakland streets were now peppered with all types of cyclists, good and bad. Among the latter were the grizzled gents with their old clothes and old bikes who rode to among other things make a political statement, the Lance Armstrong-wannabes in their colorful skin-tight racing outfits who biked like they were in the Tour de France and some college students who freewheeled down the hilly streets seemingly ignorant of the fact that people in very big, bicycle-crunching machines actually crossed the intersections they blithely zoomed through. There were, of course, myriad types of car drivers, many of them just as irritating, particularly the ones who don't know their cars come equipped with turn signals. However, because cycling as a form of transportation was relatively new to the Bay Area traffic scene, the cyclists were the latest to feel the ire of those with whom they shared the road. This public scorn was in some ways justified because so many of them exhibited a blatant disregard for stop signs, stop lights and traffic laws in general. At least that's what one would glean when the topic of bikes and cars came up in conversations in Bar OSA.

Not taking her eyes off the road, Katherine continued talking to her husband. "I'm sorry we didn't get a chance to visit with Duffy and Caitlin, but I'm glad it turned out the way it did. I must say bar banter certainly has its entertaining moments."

Mike turned to admire his chauffeur, marveling at her patience as he was still quietly seething at the incivility of the coot on the beater of a bike. Letting it go, he told her that he, too, enjoyed the afternoon's silliness. "Caitlin certainly showed us a side we rarely get to see, " he noted.

"I think sometimes people are just as surprised by the real you as opposed to the radio guy they were used to hearing. Believe me when I say I appreciate that you don't feel compelled to always be on."

"I suppose there is quite a difference between the radio version of me and this cute pile of romantic charm sitting next to you."

A determined driver, Katherine only allowed herself a quick glance at her passenger. "No you don't, Mike Gearon. I know that voice and I know that lecherous smile, and I know where you're headed with this romantic charm business. So let me tell you that tonight it's Martinis, Midsomer Murders, pork chops and early to bed. Besides we have a busy Thursday."

"You can't blame me for trying, Kat, obsessed as I am with your astonishing beauty and seductive powers." Then with an abrupt change of tone, he asked, "If romance is out of the picture, can I have a baked potato with my pork chop?"

"Will that cool your ardor?"

"It could."

"A baked potato ranks right up there with me in the romance department?"

"No, no. There's a big difference. The potato is comparable only if there's butter, bacon bits and green onions on it. I should add that I prefer you with nothing on."

She stole another glance at her husband, this one warm with affection. "Maybe tomorrow night?" she asked sweetly.

"Oh, yes indeedy," was his enthusiastic response.

"I wonder if Ambrose will remember to buy that lottery ticket?" she asked aloud.

"Who knows? Who cares?" he replied, reaching to turn on KQED to hear All Things Considered. Before he turned the volume up he offered what would be his final comment and their final thoughts regarding the MEGA-cash lottery, the Dick Clark Memorial and the damaging side effects of money: "Remember when I said money changes everything. I want to amend that. The real problem, Kat, is too much money changes everything."

George Crowder could not remember ever not feeling achy or sore. Battered from years of football, his body regularly sent woeful signals from a variety of sources; shoulders, back, neck and sometimes body parts unknown to him. To ease the pain which followed him into retirement, he relied on powerful prescription drugs and occasionally too much alcohol. Debbie, his wife, put up with him until she couldn't. With the threat of separation hanging over his head, he was determined to repair himself and ultimately their relationship. To his thinking, it was remarkable that he never had a concussion. Fortunately, his fertile brain was still intact; a healthy body part ready and willing to help him. As he was a good and decent man even in his drugs and drinks' days, Debbie didn't hesitate to support him when he told her with gritty determination, "I can change. I can get a handle on this, but I need your help." With her by his side and on his side, he did get a handle on it.

During his professional football days, he along with two other Raider players invested in Oakland properties which he now managed for the group. One property was an eight unit luxury apartment building in the thriving Rockridge neighborhood. With a son in Manhattan and a daughter in Santa Monica, he and Debbie had sold their Oakland Hills home and just a year ago moved into the light-filled, airy top-floor unit where he now sat reading the New York Times on his iPad.

"I'm home," Debbie yelled from the foyer. "Sandra was late and I had to wait for her."

"Sandra is always late," George stated factually. "You really ought to talk to her."

Debbie, with another former Raiderette, owned a small boutique on College Avenue called Moms of Rockridge that catered primarily to the Stroller Brigade, a term the shop owners gave the mothers of children who were young enough to still require pushing or carrying around. There were indeed lots of them in the neighborhood and the shop thrived.

"Did you meet up with Tom?" she asked, giving him a welcoming kiss.

"No, he canceled. So I drove to Bar OSA and had a bottomless glass of wine..."

"Let me guess. Duffy was behind the bar."

"Yes, but they were sensible pours," he reassured her. "Anyway, after that I made a quick meditative stop at Stonehenge on the way home."

Stonehenge was his code name for Newman Hall, a Catholic church near the Cal campus. Home to Holy Spirit Parish, the church's stark, ascetic features and the plain stone altar had reminded him of England's historic site. One afternoon during a particularly low moment in his life, he was walking by Newman Hall when a parishioner recognized him and asked if he'd stop and sign something for his brother who was a huge Raider fan. Standing on the steps, he remembered his days as an altar boy and how he loved the elaborate and grandly-costumed High Masses and other ceremonies that required the services of a young, devout lad draped in a red or white cassock and a starched white surplice. Now he was a lapsed Catholic; not having been to church since his days at Notre Dame and not giving much thought to it. That day he decided to step inside Newman Hall. It was a rewarding visit as the spacious nave of the quiet, unpopulated church provided him a comfortable place for spiritual contemplation and prayer; exercises that helped either ease his physical aches or put him in a state of mind to tolerate them. He reasoned it was a darnn sight better than sitting in a doctor's examining room with only your underwear to keep you warm. Plus, it was considerably less expensive, even considering the generous donation he always left.

Debbie sat across from him and stretched her legs. A pretty woman, dark-haired and dark-eyed, she asked, "So who was at Bar OSA?"

"You remember Ambrose?" She did, indeed. "He was in rare form. Also Walt... I can never remember his last name. Starts with a G. But I did find out today he's a plumber. I might have some work for him. Oh, and Mike and Katherine Gearon were there."

"How are they? I miss their company."

"After this afternoon they are probably like me still wondering what this afternoon was all about," he laughed. "I think Ambrose may have been the ringleader." He shook his head. "No, it was really Mike Gearon who started it all."

"What did he do?"

"He told everybody that Dick Clark died today."

"Blame the messenger, huh," she laughed. "I did hear about his death on the radio."

With that, George explained to his wife in detail how seven completely sane people managed to consume a hour of the day by taking part in what he considered one of the most bizarre bar conversations in recent memory. He defended the use of the word recent because he was certain there were equally quirky, alcohol-fueled experiences during his Raider days but they now resided in a foggy portion of his memory.

Debbie was laughing out loud. "And Ambrose had everyone participating in a Dick Clark Memorial? Oh, I wish I could have been there. I will say though that The Redhead's idea on how to use lottery winnings is very clever. The Dicks! That is sooo funny."

George put his iPad on the coffee table and prepared to rise from his chair. Debbie knew she'd hear a crack or two as the big man's joints went to work. "Hey," he said, halfway standing, "Skyfall is at the Elmwood Theater. You want to have a quick hamburger at the bar at Wood Tavern and then go see it?"

"Deal," she exclaimed. "I like this new Bond. He has rough edges. Kinda like you. Scarred handsome by experiences. By the way, did you really put a dollar toward that lottery ticket?"

"I did."

Debby's smile widened. "Wow! Now that's a first."

"Trust me, it's also the last."

With that short exchange, George and Debby Crowder thought no more about Dick Clark, Bar OSA or the MEGA-Cash lottery.

"Hi honey!" Emanating from the kitchen, Mrs. Gillespie's voice, while earsplitting, was full of cheery affection. And ardor, thought Walt. When he was greeted in this fashion where the second syllable of honey was held for two or more seconds, he knew it was definitely a mating call. Walt wondered what she had on.

This immediately caused a stirring and he smiled smugly knowing he was up for it, even though tonight was the rubber game of the Giants-Phillies' series at AT&T Park and he was anxious to watch it on TV. He thought if she suggests a pre-dinner romp, then both were possible though he might miss an inning or two. Walt knew if his forty-nine year old wife, Jeannie, was still in her work clothes, the evening's format could include a long shower for two and then some pre-dusk love-making followed by dinner on trays in their media room watching the game on their wall-mounted big-screen television. Jeannie, an aesthetician by training, was indeed in the sexiest part of her uniform. She worked four days a week in the cosmetics department of a Hilltop Mall department store in San Pablo. This Wednesday evening, Jeannie was squeezed into grey tights and a silver-pink, racerback tank top that fit comfortably under her loose-fitting, at-work tunic. Missing was the tunic, thus revealing Jeannie's stunning figure. She was of medium height but that would the only time one could apply the word medium to describe anything about her. She was tiny-waisted, full-breasted with shapely hips and long legs made even longer thanks to her taupe, open-toe shoes with dangerously high heels. Jeannie, a brunette with a cheerleader's cute-as-a-button face, was Walt's third wife. Twenty years his junior, they found each other on an Internet dating service. Neither one of them had puffed up their profile. In fact, Walt was achingly honest with his as he felt that after two failed marriages, truth in advertising was the only way to go. Even his photograph showed him at his worst. Obviously, Jeannie had no need to be anything other than honest. While her physical appearance resembled a Vargas model come to life, she was something else entirely. Sweet-natured with a nurse's capacity for TLC, Jennie was fully aware of the realities of marrying an older man and was confident that when or if the time came that her husband needed care she could happily supply it. Now five years into the marriage, Walt gave daily thanks that this gem of a women chose him; a hypochondriacal, big lump of a man who came home dirty from his day's labor. They were an odd but uniquely compatible pair. Both were San Francisco Giants' fans, die-hard, season-ticket holding Oakland Raider fans and both loved flea markets; he always on the hunt for antique fishing gear and she on a constant search for old movie posters. Neither of them had children, so adult toys were affordable as evidenced by the two Harleys and the fully equipped bass-fishing boat in the garage.

Walt threw his keys on the table in the entry, took a quick look in the mirror, determined he looked good enough for the mission ahead and strutted into their open-spaced kitchen and family room. He threw on a smile that widened when he saw Jeannie by the sink, rinsing out a glass. My God, how lucky am I, he thought for the second time in just two minutes.

"Hey, beautiful, your happy plumber can be cleaned up in less than five..."

The sound of the front doorbell stopped him mid-sentence. Jeannie gave him a look of exasperation and threw her hands up as if to say, "I'm not expecting anyone."

Walt returned to the foyer and peered through the front door peephole. There in all his elemental ugliness stood Serafino "Fino" Romagna, looking even uglier through the magnification of the glass. He was moving back and forth in time to whatever music he was listening to through his earbuds.

Walt opened the door and with clenched teeth, asked, "What do you want, Fino?"

His sister's stepson's predictable response was, "Huh?"

"Pull those things out of your ears," Walt ordered.

The young man shifted his stance and his attitude. Staring defiantly at his uncle and boss, he slowly removed them. "Yo! You wanted your truck. Right?" he snapped, tossing him the keys. "You told me to drop it off here after fucking work. By the way, I did fifteen minutes overtime. A half hour more if you include bringing your truck here."

"How are you getting home?" Walt asked, ignoring the assault of vulgarity.

"Rico is picking me up. He'll be here in… Hey, Uncle Walt, I really gotta pee."

Walt moved aside to let him race to the powder room just off the foyer. Fino closed the door but even that couldn't stifle the sound of what Walt's urologist would call a very healthy flow. That was another reason he couldn't abide him.

Walt returned to the kitchen and noticed that his wife had changed into baggy sweatpants and one of his old sweaters. When she learned who was at the door, she immediately switched outfits because whenever Fino was around he was unable to keep his eyes from wandering from one end of her body to the other. Plus, he had an inventory of expressions to send the message to his uncle's wife that he thought they should pair up if only for her benefit of experiencing a younger man.

That Wednesday evening, Fino wandered into the kitchen while checking that he'd zipped up his fly, a gesture he hoped she noticed. "Yo, Auntie Jeannie, how's it?" he asked.

"I'm fine, Fino," she replied with just a glance in his direction and no note of affection in her voice.

Fino was not, as Walt would have you believe, a physically ugly man. Rather, he was broad-shouldered and trim where a man needed to be. He was vain enough that he'd had his Gillespie Plumbing shirts and blue work denims specially tailored. Fino was a taller knockoff of his father who sported a rough-hewn but appealing face with jet black hair. The difference was Fino was filled with a youthful sullenness and his physicality reflected this surliness, making him very repulsive indeed. Or so Walt thought.

"Okay, so look," he said, climbing aboard a stool by the kitchen island, "I have no idea when this little shit…" He glanced over at a disapproving Jeannie and mumbled, "I mean Rico. Look, I have no idea when he's going to be here, so how about a beer or something?

We can have a family bonding moment." He tried smiling but it came out looking more like a smirk.

For the second time, the doorbell rang. Walt looked at his nephew and with a sigh of relief said in a surprisingly friendly voice, "Looks like the beer will have to wait. I'm sure that's Rico. You better get going. Besides, I can't afford your overtime." He knew Fino would have added every minute he was in his house to his timesheet.

There were two reasons Walt tolerated the antics of his obnoxious nephew. The first was his love for his sister, Margaret, and his strong desire to keep peace in the family. The second was Serafino "Fino" Romagna, despite his unpleasantness, had turned out to be an excellent plumber.

Fino gone, Jeannie said she wanted to change out of her nun's outfit; a term that described anything that did not cling tightly to every curve. While they changed, Walt told her about his unusual afternoon at Bar OSA, the Dick Clark Memorial and the silly dollar investment in the MEGA-Cash lottery. Out of his dirty work clothes, he was just about to put on a US Open T-shirt when, in a voice sweeter than the heady scent of a gardenia, Jeannie suggested they shower together. The large man turned in her direction to see his wife in the process of removing her sweatshirt which was now off her body and high above her head. "Is that okay?" she cooed, peeking under the shirt. "We'll probably miss a couple of innings of the Giants' game, you know."

Walt's jaw was still capable of dropping after five years of wedded bliss and it did so once again. Letting his shirt fall to the floor, he of the hairy chest that inspired Jeannie to call him her teddy bear walked toward his wife and with a loving, hungry smile said, "What game?"

Ambrose was the last to leave. He moved slowly and carefully as he was aware of how dangerous a fall is for a man his age. After all, I am eighty going on eighty-two, he chuckled to himself. What a grand afternoon, he thought. Full of himself and some tasty alcoholic drinks, he had decided to splurge on Japanese takeout. Next door to Bar OSA was a food court that was home to Kirala where he picked up salmon sashimi, vegetarian gyoza, two pieces of shrimp tempura and two pieces of unagi sushi. Then it was another three block stroll to the small liquor store where he purchased the group's lottery ticket.

Ambrose's apartment was a strenuous uphill, four block walk from Shattuck; a stroll he classified as exercise. The three-story apartment complex consisted of twelve units. His was a front corner apartment with a filtered view of the Bay. It was an agreeable place to live as most of the tenants had been there for more than fifteen years. The landlord was friendly, accessible and kept the building and grounds in fine shape. Ambrose and Emily were the senior residents having lived there twenty-five years when she died a year ago. He never once thought of moving because Emily was a constant memory; more a spiritual companion, in fact. She still kept him company and where better than the place they shared for twenty-five years of their marriage.

So it was he sat down to dinner in the small dining alcove off the living room with a setting for two. He was full of stories tonight and couldn't wait to share them with her. As he ate, he told her of the special time he'd had at Bar OSA. He saved the unagi sushi for dessert. Heating it up in the microwave, he returned to the table with the warmed eel and finished his report to Emily. "It's a strange thing, my dear," he said aloud, "but through all this social silliness, I felt an real affection for those with whom I was whiling away the afternoon. It was a rare time and I am thankful for it." After bussing the table, he returned and picked up the two dinner mats he'd set out. "Always be neat," he muttered to himself, with just a trace of sadness in his voice. Glancing back at the empty chair where his wife normally sat, he shook off the sudden tic of grief and said, "I shall sleep comfortably tonight, Emily. I was at the top of my game today."

He sunk into his favorite chair in the small living room. One wall was a sliding glass door that opened on to a substantial balcony. The wall opposite was floor to ceiling shelves filled with books. On the table next to him was a Penguin Classics' edition of Anthony Trollope's Phineas Finn which he read until his eyes were heavy.

Both the bed and his heart for one year had shared the same emptiness. Emily was missing. His bedtime habits, however, remained the same. He turned down both sides of the bed and plumped up her pillow just as he had done for so many years. Getting into his side of the bed, he turned onto his left side and whispered, "Sleep tight." Then he closed his eyes and wished for a quick escape into sleep. This night was different, though. His one last thought was of the MEGA-Cash lottery. He assured himself that with the odds being one in 170 million, he would have no need to explain himself tomorrow. How embarrassing would that be?

## CHAPTER 9

# THE MORNING AFTER

At six-fourteen Thursday morning, April 19, 2012, Walter Gillespie's alarm made a low, almost mournful sound. He'd purposely set it for for that specific time because KCBS radio had a sports' report every fifteen and forty-five minutes after the hour. The extra sixty seconds gave him enough time to disarm the alarm, get out of bed, scoot into the bathroom and turn on the radio; all without waking Jeannie who had no need to rise early that Thursday morning. Contrary to the low opinion he held on the state of his health, he was remarkably spry for a sixty-nine year-old. Making this speed run from their master bedroom to their spacious, recently remodeled bathroom was made even easier because he was also a quick riser; able to shake off the rough edges of sleep in an instant. This morning, he was anxious to hear the final score of the Giants' game which had gone into extra innings, both teams scoreless. He and Jeannie wanted to stay with the game but their lovemaking and linguine con vongole dinner had so sapped their energy they called it quits in the ninth inning. He was elated when he heard the sports' anchor report the Giants won one to nothing in eleven. That's all he needed to know. Had he continued to pay attention to the radio, he would have next heard a news story about a lottery, but now that he knew the score he had tuned out so he could give some time to his back and what might have caused it to stiffen. He'd recently read on-line that sometimes faulty organs can cause an achy back and that was worrisome. It never dawned on him that his back might just have been complaining about last night's sexual gymnastics. To Walt's credit, he somehow managed to keep his health concerns to himself, thus not alarming or, to his thinking, disappointing Jeannie. As for the lottery news? He gave no thought at all to the lottery or the one dollar investment he made at Bar OSA the previous afternoon.

Neither did the Gearons, the Harts or the Crowders. By Thursday dusk, if questioned about hearing any news of a lottery, their answer would be no and why do you ask. It was testament as to how washed from their minds and memories were the details of their Wednesday afternoon gathering. Thus, there is no need to dive deeper into their morning routines.

Professor Ambrose Dowling is another story, however. After his morning ablutions — his expression of bathroom time —he tuned his small kitchen radio to KCBS to hear the news while he had his usual breakfast of a glass of half orange, half cranberry juice, some plain Greek yogurt and one slice of buttered wheat toast. Normally, he would listen to the classical music station. This morning he understood why as he found the news station's repetitious traffic and weather reports tedious. As he rarely went anywhere he couldn't walk or take the bus, he didn't need traffic reports and as regards weather forecasts, he reasoned it was just a matter of sticking one's nose out the window. Just as he was about to switch stations, though, he heard the news anchor mention there was no MEGA-Cash winner and a record amount of money would be in the pot for Saturday night's drawing. Ambrose gave a huge sigh of relief. Of course, the odds were such that he really had no need for concern, but he worried anyway. As to the lottery ticket he purchased by accident? He would get around to checking that later in the day. Right now, his sights were set on his usual Thursday morning outing. It was actually an outing performed every weekday morning but it was Thursday when he spoiled himself.

The retired professor's destination was a short three block walk. Today, like most mornings, he ran into the same mix of dog-walkers, students and other pedestrians who hit the streets the same time he did. There were many waves and crisp hellos. Ambrose wouldn't have minded some conversation, but they all at one time or another had been a victim of a Dowling delay; a sidewalk visit that just went too long, so while they still greeted him warmly, they keep moving.

Alfred Peet opened his first coffee house at the corner of Vine and Walnut in April of 1966. Two decades later, when they moved into the neighborhood, Ambrose and Emily started going there. Since Emily's death, Ambrose was a weekday morning regular, always ordering the coffee of the day with two sugars and some lo-fat milk and the New York Times. Thursdays, he treated himself to a Caffe Freddo and a large blackberry-raspberry scone. He was so faithful to this routine, he rarely had to order; the friendly Peet's crew just set to work as soon as they spotted him coming through the door. While table-sharing was just fine with Ambrose, on Thursdays he enjoyed being alone so as to better savor the fruit-filled scone and the funnily-named ice-blended coffee drink with whipped cream. This pleasant April morning, he found an empty window table near the entrance and quickly claimed it. Most of the regulars knew his habit and left him alone. But not Leonard Saxby, a tall, rail-thin black man with a handsome face and short curly grey hair. Having just retired from the Berkeley Main Post Office, he was a recent member of the Bar OSA Inbetweeners and so known to Ambrose. Leonard came equipped with a permanent smile and cheeriness. He was a rare visitor to Peet's, preferring the coffee shops in the downtown area near his old place of work, the Berkeley Main Post Office which was located in a much-loved, historically important building. Built in 1914, the post office's design was loosely based on Brunelleschi's Foundling Hospital with its gracious, arched lines. Leonard loved the building and even though he was retired, he found himself staying close.

Spotting him through Peet's window, Ambrose quickly moved the other chair to a neighboring table. Knowing from experience he would be subject to the standard Saxby greeting, he warned himself not to lip-synch it when he heard it.

"Hey, my man, we're still here!" Leonard boomed, his voice a magnificent bass.

Ambrose loved listening to him and if it were any day but Thursday he would have welcomed him with open arms. This day he just looked up, smiled warmly and agreed with Leonard that indeed they were still amongst God's living creatures.

"Wish I could join you, Ambrose, but I'm just here to get a coffee and go. I have a doctor's appointment and she's just up the block. Nothing serious," he explained. "Hey, speaking of things close by, did you hear the winning Super Lotto ticket was bought in Berkeley."

"No, I didn't."

"I don't know who the winner is. All I heard on the radio was that the winning ticket was purchased at some liquor store in north Berkeley. It's a big jackpot. $188 million!" Leonard leaned down to continue, a gesture that comforted Ambrose whose neck was stiffening looking up at the tall man. "Ambrose, let me ask you. Who in his right mind wants that kind of money? Suddenly your life is full of reporters, lawyers, financial advisors, tax experts, CPA's, hangers-on, bad-ass relatives and God knows who else. Now what I'd really like to win is something like $188 thou. That I could put to good use all by my lonesome," he said with a huge laugh as he went off to order his coffee. No one enjoyed what Leonard had to say more than Leonard himself whose sonorous laugh ricocheted through the crowded coffee shop.

Ambrose returned to his Cafe Freddo and scone. Both were delicious and he would take as much time as he wanted finishing them. It wasn't as if he had a busy schedule. Or any schedule for that matter. Still, he liked to give some form to his days and this Thursday there were two items on his to-do list. Prominent on his mind were the goings-on in the latest chapter of Phineas Finn. The political machinations were such that he had decided to contact a former colleague and see if he would like to discuss it over a wine sometime in the afternoon. The other matter was the lottery ticket he purchased. He'd not thought about it much until Leonard Saxby brought it up. Aware of the impossible odds, he still felt he ought to at least find out what the winning numbers were. How does one go about doing that, he wondered.

With a final long sip of his Cafe Freddo, Ambrose assembled his waste and headed toward the exit. Tossing it all in recycling, he noticed the front section of the San Francisco Chronicle on a long counter. They must publish lottery results, he reasoned. Picking it up, he opened the paper to check the table of contents. The lottery results were in the lower right hand corner of page two. He was surprised by the number of games. Just as he was about to read the Super Lotto Plus numbers, a man tapped his shoulder.

"Excuse me, that's my paper. I just put it down to pick up my coffee." The pleasant voice belonged to a man in his early forties. Of medium height, he was well-groomed and expensively dressed; his hair trimmed, shoes shined and nails professionally manicured. As well-turned out as he was, he wore it all with as much ease as the casually dressed man in a tired brown sweater, jeans and sandals standing next to him.

"Oh, sorry. I wasn't planning on absconding with it," Ambrose chuckled. "I was curious about some lottery numbers."

"You seem to have found them," he said, pointing to the section that Ambrose was reading.

"I'm only interested in the Super Lotto numbers." Ambrose patted his coat pocket and realized he'd left his pen and notepad at home. "Damnation, I have nothing with which to write them down."

The man grabbed a napkin, pulled a Cartier pen from his inside coat pocket and instructed Ambrose to read the numbers to him.

"Let's see, they are 3, 10, 17, 29 and 30. The mega number is 16," Ambrose recited. "You know, I think I may have the mega number."

"Good for you. Maybe you won a few bucks. Better yet, maybe you won it all," he said, handing Ambrose the napkin. "How much is the jackpot?"

"188 million dollars."

The man whistled softly. "Well then, I certainly hope you win it all."

"I don't know that I would want that to happen," Ambrose said impulsively, closing the Chronicle, folding it neatly and handing it back to him. "Anyway, thank you, kind sir, for your assistance."

"I'm puzzled. If you don't mind my asking, why would you buy a ticket if you don't want to win?"

"Oh, it was a ceremonial purchase. Something of a whimsy actually," Ambrose replied dismissively. He had no intention of going into any more detail.

The man laughed heartily and said, "Now I know I'm in Berkeley."

"One can deduce by your fashionable attire that you are a visitor to our uniquely liberal and completely zany city."

"I am. From New York. Manhattan, actually," he answered. "I'm a huge fan of Peet's coffee. They have one in the Financial District. I thought as long as I'm in the Bay Area, I would make a pilgrimage to the original store."

Ambrose extended his hand and introduced himself. "I am one of Peet's more faithful regulars. Have been since 1987," he noted proudly.

"Sebastian Meyer," the man said, reaching into his pocket and extracting a business card which he handed Ambrose. It seemed an automatic gesture. "Meeting a Peetnik from the original store is quite an honor. But I must say, as a venture capitalist, I find your indifference to winning millions to be..."

'Blasphemous?"

His laugh was hearty. "That's as good a word as any, I suppose," he said, checking his watch, clearly an expensive instrument. "I have to run. I'm meeting two app developers, a game inventor and then back to San Francisco for two more meetings and a deposition that might get testy."

Ambrose replied, "I'm pretty busy myself. I have some reading to do, all pleasure, of course. Then there's the Time's crossword to battle. After that, I'm hoping to meet a friend to discuss Trollope's Phineas Finn after which we might hit a movie and then a cocktail before heading home.

The money-loving venture capitalist studied Ambrose for a moment. "Tear up that lottery ticket, professor. You're rich enough and you've certainly earned your day." Then with a sudden change of tone, he said joylessly, "Unfortunately, I am still paying for mine."

Ambrose was surprised but also clearly impressed by Meyer addressing him as professor. "How did you know I educated bright young things?"

Shrugging, he replied, "A number of reasons. This is Berkeley. The way you're dressed. Plus, nobody but a professor, probably of literature or English, uses the word damnation and then goes to lengths to not end the same sentence with a preposition."

"My God, Mr. Meyers, with those deductive powers, you should change your first name to Sherlock," he exclaimed

The venture capitalist shook Ambrose's hand and made for the exit. Before leaving he turned around and took a last, wistful glance at the busy, original Peet's and its colorful, diverse clientele. I can picture myself here some day, he thought. Maybe after a few more deals and divorce number three gets worked out. That latter thought didn't particularly sound grim to him as Sebastian Meyer was a whiz at deals and divorces.

As Ambrose strolled home, his mind was awhirl after his most recent encounter at Peet's. It was curious, he thought, that in the space of twenty-four hours, Leonard Saxby, Sebastian Meyer and The Redhead, three people unrelated to each other, brought up the Jesuitical concept of what you have is enough. At least he thought it was Jesuitical. He had a Christian Brother friend who could set him straight. He was aware, though, that Brother Malachy wasn't too keen on the Jesuits and might be reluctant to give them credit for such a worthy tenet. He hoped he was right because he loved the word Jesuitical and loving saying it. As to the principle itself, he and Emily were always comfortable with the idea of enough except for books. Covetousness was not in their nature. What would I do if I was suddenly rolling in dough, he thought. Then he laughed out loud at the idea. His plan was to go home, confirm that they lost the lottery and then get on with his day. While he fumbled with his keys to the small apartment lobby, he started mumbling.

"Ambrose, are you having trouble with the door?" Mrs. Patton asked. She was a plump widow in her sixties who lived on the ground floor. With two full grocery bags, the dowdily dressed woman was standing right behind him on the apartment steps

Startled, he spun around and uttered, "What? Oh, it's you, Mrs. Patton..."

"Ambrose, why do you insist on calling me Mrs. Patton? Please, call me Posie," she said sweetly, and to Ambrose's ear, flirtatiously. He felt she'd shown a keener interest in him since Emily passed away.

"Yes, indeed. Well, Posie, you caught me struggling with my keys."

"And talking to yourself again."

"Yes, I tend to do that."

"It sounded as if you'd lost something."

"I have. At least I think I have. It's a lottery ticket."

Opening the door, Ambrose scurried inside and held it open for Mrs. Patton who moved sideways to accommodate her heft and the two big grocery bags. Once inside the small foyer, the two of them were brought closer together by the small size of the area. Taking advantage of the forced intimacy, Mrs. Patton said, "Let me put these groceries away and I'll come up and help you look. Of course, if I find it for you, we have to split the winnings." She began to giggle, a girlish chuckle that seemed more fitting for a teenager.

"We would no doubt end up splitting nothing, Mrs. Pa... Uh, Posie. You know the enormous odds on these games of chance. Anyway, I'm sure it will pop up."

She moved close and he took a step back. His neighbor had a fondness for perfumes. Perfumers go to great lengths to create agreeable fragrances and when their scents are tactfully applied, the results are nothing but pleasing to one's nose. Mrs. Patton, though, was free and easy with her perfumes and when they were mixed in with the myriad other body lotions she liberally applied, the results were less than pleasing.

This particular morning, all Ambrose could smell was a heady combination of cats and mothballs.

"I have some left over cog au vin," she whispered seductively. "I can always bring it up to you."

"Now isn't that a coincidence. I just made the same dish. I'm positively swimming in the stuff," he said, moving his keys from one hand to the other so as to hold the handrail while climbing the stairs to his apartment. "It's always good to see you, Posie."

He complimented himself on his inspired thinking. Coq au vin! Maybe I'll give it a go sometime. Entering his apartment, he looked around and wondered where he ought to start in the search of the elusive lottery ticket. Once found and deemed worthless, he could breathe a second and final sigh of relief.

# CHAPTER 10
# DIVINITY IN ODD NUMBERS

"Dante missed a bet," Ambrose said aloud as he opened the door to his apartment. He felt the Italian poet should have added a tenth circle of hell in his Inferno for people like him who keep losing thing. No, I'm being too harsh, he told himself. Maybe we just deserve a few centuries in Purgatorio. Fortunately, he didn't have to search long for the Super Lotto Plus ticket as he could see it from the entrance to the living room. The top edge of the distinctive ticket was peeking out of Trollope's Phineas Finn, nestled between pages 234 and 235 to be exact. He was forever recruiting strange bookmarks and that's what had happened to the group's lottery ticket.

While it was not a ticket for the MEGA-Cash lottery, Ambrose still felt this one belonged to all of them if for no other reason than by moral default. He pulled the Peet's napkin out of his coat pocket and headed for his chair. His plan was to first check the numbers, confirm they lost and then reread a portion of the book before calling his friend to meet for a conversation about it. After sliding the ticket from the top of the book, he unfolded the Peet's napkin and placed it atop Phineas Finn on the side table. Holding the ticket, he began looking from one to the other. In a split second, he realized he had in his shaking hands a temporary bookmark worth a king's ransom.

The lucky numbers staring up at him were 3, 10, 17, 29, 30 and the mega number 16. Even though Sebastian's six looked liked a five, he clearly recalled telling him the mega number was sixteen. He remembered thrice-married Wally chose the number three for the number of Dick Clark marriages. He selected ten for the age Clark was when he knew he wanted to be on the radio. Seventeen was George Crowder's peculiar pick. The former football player speculated that the TV star might have given up his virginity at that age. Ambrose suspected it probably applied to George's coming of age. Michael and Katherine Gearon picked twenty-nine for the year Clark was born and... Here is where his memory failed him. He knew Duffy and The Redhead selected thirty but he couldn't remember why. Maybe it was his birth date month. He continued to stare at the five numbers, gathered in a most entertaining fashion at Bar OSA the previous afternoon. For possibly the twelfth time, he checked first the ticket and then the napkin to confirm the six Dick Clark-related numbers. "How can this be?" he asked aloud. It was a question that needed no answer and he quickly dismissed it. What it was was something that had to be dealt with right away. Regarding that, his feelings were decidedly mixed.

"Emily. Emily. Oh, Emily," he cried out. "You were always the more resolute and decisive of the two of us. I wish you were here to offer counsel. I know I should be up and dancing for joy for having won such an inglorious amount of money, but here I sit bound to this chair as if I'd been strapped to it. Of course, I know why and you'll agree. It is change! That's what it is. I am afraid of change. Oh, I definitely am, my dear. I still miss you terribly, but I have in the past year or so become accustomed to my life as it is. I like it. I cherish it, in fact. Besides having you to talk to, there is a routine and an ordinariness that is most comforting. I don't really have any wants and as for charity, as you know, we've never been keen on throwing money at something. I guess that's why we always volunteered instead of sending checks. So here I am, almost eighty-two, and I will soon be in possession of many millions of dollars. Perhaps, that's just fine with others, but quite frankly, it puts me off. Emily, I am going to sit here quietly and think about what I want to do. I know that's exactly what you'd tell me to do."

Ambrose Dowling did just that. With the valuable lottery ticket in his hand, he sat in his comfortable, old easy chair and slipped into his version of a meditative state for a little more than an hour The quiet hour of contemplation had done the trick. It had given him a plan, a direction, and he was more than happy with it. Most important, he was certain it was what he wanted to do. With a new energy and enthusiasm, he realized the first thing he had to do was find out what one did with a winning ticket. He turned the card over and laughed. Who on earth can read this small print, he wondered. He'd misplaced his magnifying glass and was in no mood to resume the hunt for it, so reading those instructions was out of the question. So what now, he thought. Smiling, he said aloud, "Who better to tell me than Mr. Google." Slowly lifting himself up from his chair, Ambrose walked to the small dining room table and opened his new MacBook Air to begin his on-line education on lotteries; specifically the one he'd just won.

Late Thursday afternoon, Bar OSA was just as quiet as Wednesday. Duffy Hart was not surprised by this lull as the 2012 tax deadline date was just four days prior and most restaurants saw fewer diners for a time after that. It would not last long, so it wasn't worrisome. What was unsettling and very troubling was The Redhead's sour news that just that morning the landlord called her and announced an obscene bump in their rent beginning in January, 2013 when their lease was up. It could mean only one thing. Someone with deep pockets and a desire to be in the heart of Gourmet Ghetto wanted the location. Their landlord-tenant relationship had started out adversarial, much of it due to the building owner's boorish insistence that he and his pals were somehow entitled to unlimited free meals and drinks in the Hart's establishment. In her blunt manner, The Redhead had let him know otherwise. But by never missing a rent payment, keeping the place in working order, rarely requiring his involvement and occasionally, though begrudgingly, treating him to a lunch or dinner, they managed to keep him off their backs for nine years. While each had a college-age child from a previous marriage, Bar OSA was the baby Duffy and Caitlin conceived together. Only nine, they wanted to see this youngster flourish and grow for another ten years before letting it go. That now seemed problematic.

By four o'clock, there were three Inbetweeners chatting up a storm. Duffy was happy to see them eating and drinking instead of nursing drinks. None of the Wednesday crowd was in attendance. The Redhead's surprising news had dispirited him to the point where he was In no mood to kibitz with this bunch. Instead he kept himself busy at the other end of the bar by wiping in clockwise circles the corner end of the bar, using an old rag he kept in a nearby drawer. This was his thinking rag and no one else dared use it. Whenever something weighed heavy on his mind, he put the dull, threadbare cloth and his mind to work. He'd told The Redhead this exercise was inspired by watching the Jackie Gleason Show as a kid. He loved the comedian's character, Joe the Bartender, who wrapped up each skit singing and wiping down the bar. His favorite character, though, was Crazy Guggenheim who he loved to impersonate. He'd still be doing it if The Redhead hadn't told him Crazy Guggenheim's fame didn't make it into the Third Millennium and he ought to let it go.

Sometimes Duffy Hart used the time with his rag to give himself a pep talk. And that's what he did on this Thursday. He managed to convince himself that in the eight and a half months they had to plot and plan before the lease came to an end, they would find a way to work it all out. Little did he know that the answer to his problem had just walked into Bar OSA looking remarkably like Ambrose Dowling.

The retired professor stopped for a moment to converse with the trio of Inbetweeners. Duffy hope that whatever they were hashing over would be of enough interest to keep the professor firmly docked at that end of the bar. He'd had quite enough of him on Wednesday. Now it appeared he would have yet another dose of him as Ambrose broke away from the Inbetweeners and headed in his direction. He could have escaped into the office but he'd given Elena the rest of the day off. He was stuck.

"Good Afternoon, Mr. Hart," Ambrose said formally, taking a barstool across from the circling rag.

"What are you drinking?' he asked. Unable to disguise his snappishness he increased the speed of his wiping.

"Is something wrong?"

Duffy shook his head. Returning his thinking rag to the drawer, he said almost cordially, "Sorry, I was just dealing with a small problem. Well, actually a big problem. Listen, Ambrose, do you mind if I set a few conditions on the conversation we're about to have?"

"Certainly not. This is your establishment. You don't have to admit the inebriated, you can eject people in flip-flops, tank tops, even men with bad toupees or combovers. You are the..."

Unable to keep from laughing, Duffy held his hand up and shushed him. "Okay, okay, So here's the deal, no talk about birthdays, Dick Clark's passing or skipping birth years."

Nodding, Ambrose surveyed the wall of alcohol, all in decorative bottles. "I think, perhaps, both of us might benefit from a drink of some sort. How about a Margarita for me. No fancy tequila. Just well stuff. And salt, please."

Duffy made two. Handing one to Ambrose, he lifted his glass and said, "To your good health."

"And yours. Which if it isn't topnotch right now, it soon will be."

Duffy shot him a puzzled look. "You usually don't pop in on Thursdays. What gives?"

"As you didn't mention numbers specifically in your list of no-no topics, I'd like to visit that subject for a moment. As you know, I have always been fond of even numbers. It was Pliny the Elder who wrote, 'Why is it that we entertain the belief that for every purpose odd numbers are the most effectual.'"

"Pliny the Elder is also a cult beer from Russian River Brewing Company," Duffy said, pronouncing Pliny with a hard i, a sound offensive to the the professor's ear but preferred by the beer set.

He was about to correct Duffy but decided to let it go. "I sometimes use the Roman statesman's comment to defend my affection for even numbers. However, that has all changed. I have now learned that odd numbers for some occasions can be most effectual and, as Shakespeare so wisely noted in The Merry Wives of Windsor, 'There is divinity in odd numbers, either in nativity, chance or death.'" Holding his glass up, readying it for a congratulatory toast, he continued, "In our case, Mr. Hart, the divinity is in chance." He reached forward and tapped Duffy's glass which sat on the bar.

"You realize if The Redhead were out here now, you'd be cut up in little pieces and added to our paellas as a substitute chorizo."

"She is intolerant of the art of the dramatic?"

"So where are we headed with all of this?" he asked tetchily.

"I'm sorry but I have to do this my way," Ambrose insisted.

"You're paying for that Margarita, you know. All right, have at it."

"As you know, I was entrusted with purchasing our Dick Clark Memorial lottery ticket. When I got to the store to buy it, I took one of those forms you use to fill in your own numbers. I was diligent. I double checked that all five rows were correct. Then I gave the clerk the form and our five dollars. He gave me a ticket and off

I went. However, I erred. I mistakenly filled out the form for Super Lotto Plus. You can imagine how distraught I would have been had we won that lottery.

"You obviously aren't distraught. So I'm assuming we didn't win."

"We didn't. Therefore, I don't have to report my mistake."

"Ambrose, you just confessed to it. I'm confused."

While Duffy watched, the retired professor reached in his coat and withdrew from the inside pocket the Peet's napkin containing the winning numbers. Unfolding it, he laid it on the bar with the numbers facing Bar OSA's owner.

"What are these?"

"Those, Mr. Hart, are one of the five sets of numbers we selected yesterday afternoon."

"What are they doing on a Peet's napkin?"

"When I tell you, will you swear to me that you will be restrained in your reaction. Perhaps, you might run back to your office and share the news with The Redhead. However, I would appreciate you being as normal as you can be out here amongst your loyal patrons."

The warning given, Ambrose leaned in and whispered, "They are the winning numbers of Super Lotto Plus."

"And they are our numbers?" he whispered back, a huge knot forming in his stomach.

"They are."

"How much did we win?" The knot tightened and his heart began to race.

Ambrose rose from the stool, walked to the edge of the bar and standing next to Duffy whispered the amount in his ear. Stomach knotted, heart racing, the bar owner eyes now widened. Otherwise, to his credit, outwardly he was much himself even though he was experiencing a wide range of emotions. Moving away from Ambrose, his mind bouncing from one thought to the next at breakneck speed, he opened the drawer that held his thinking rag. He looked at it for a second and then tossed it back.

"Hey, Duffy, we need refills down here." The voice was loud but friendly. The closest Inbetweener to them was holding up his empty beer glass and waving it.

Clearly shaken by Ambrose's startling news, Duffy shouted back, "Be right there."

He picked up the Peet's napkin and handed it to Ambrose. "I'm alone out here for another few minutes. Can you go back to our office and tell my wife the news. And, Ambrose, this is very important. No dramatics, no long-winded explanation. Just give her the facts. Otherwise I can't be responsible for what she'll do to you before you get to the best part."

While Duffy tended to the three thirsty Inbetweeners, Ambrose walked into their tiny, cramped office. The Redhead, in a bulky Cal sweatshirt and jeans, was working on the computer. Sensing movement behind her, she turned and seeing Ambrose, snapped, "What are you doing back here?"

Speaking quickly and unemotionally, he replied, "I am loathe to present this to you in such a blunt manner, but your husband instructed me to be brief."

"Thank God," sighed The Redhead. "So what is it?"

"I am here to tell you we won the Super Lotto Plus lottery with the numbers we picked yesterday. The prize is 188 million dollars. It is, by the way, the second largest in Lotto history." What a shame, he thought, to have to report this extraordinary, life-changing news that also came with a rich backstory in this Twitter-like fashion. No wonder he detested the social media site.

Caitlin spun around and looked up at the gray-haired gentleman who nervously stood there fearing she might think this some awful joke and have at him with her famous temper.

Her face, though, told another story. Gone was her trademark redness. She was ashen and appeared almost timid. Caitlin asked tentatively and almost rhetorically, "You... You're not kidding?"

"No, Mrs. The Redhead, I am not," Ambrose said cheerfully. He wondered if this is how genie feels after making someone's wish come true.

When Sam Calestri arrived, Duffy told him to apron up and finish the Inbetweeners' orders as he had business to tend to in the office. As soon as Caitlin saw him, she jumped up from her chair and threw her arms around him. They held each other silently for enough time that Ambrose felt he need to issue a loud ahem. Just then they separated and both looked at Ambrose.

"How? I mean I thought you bought a Mega-something lottery ticket?" she asked, still incredulous at the thought they'd won all that money.

"By mistake, he bought into the wrong lottery which, as you can see, turned out to be the right one," Duffy explained to her. He suddenly had a thought. "You know, Ambrose, I suppose you could give us our dollar back seeing as we didn't participate in the MEGA-cash game which we would have lost anyway. That makes the Super Lotto money all yours."

"Nonsense, it's all of ours," Ambrose Dowling replied. He was surprised Duffy would think he would feel otherwise. "Now Mr and Mrs. Hart, I have had sufficient time to deal with this sudden change of fortune. It's only fair to give you time to do the same."

Shaken by the good news, Caitlin sat back down. "Then you want us all to share in the winnings?" she asked even though he had made it perfectly clear that that was his intention.

"The ticket belongs to all of us, Mrs. The Redhead," he replied.

She looked up and whispered sweetly, "It's Caitlin."

The professor was taken aback. "Your given name is Caitlin."

"It is and it's only fair that you should know it."

"You know, Dylan Thomas' wife was named Caitlin. He bragged he had her in bed ten minutes are they met."

The Redhead looked at her husband. "Whatever you are thinking of adding to that, pass on it," she said sternly but with a smile she couldn't erase since hearing the news of their good fortune.

It was decided the other partners needed to be, in The Redhead's words, rounded up ASAP. It was also decided they would not share the news with them by phone, e-mail or text. They realized they couldn't meet at Bar OSA; it being too public a place to share the kind of news that would elicit reactions that were best exhibited somewhere private. To that, Duffy had an inspired plan. He knew the manager of the Berkeley City Club and was certain he would give them a private room for their meeting. The Julia Morgan-designed building, an elegant, Moorish beauty with old fashioned style, was nearby and all three agreed they couldn't pick a more appropriate place. Once the room was secured, they set about finding the others. Caitlin caught Katherine Gearon at home. After hearing the unusual and ambiguous invitation, she reluctantly accepted but only after several unsuccessful attempts to learn more. Five-thirty was the designated time and she promised she and Mike would be there. Caitlin assured her that her husband wasn't up to any of his tricks. Duffy had George Crowder's mobile number and rang him. The joint-sore former football player was at the chiropractor's which was on Telegraph Avenue, just a mile from the club. While the doctor continued to adjust him, he listened to Duffy's unusual invitation. Like Katherine Gearon, he, too, was skeptical. Only after hearing Duffy swear there was no nonsense afoot, did he agree; explaining that he was in sweats and would have no time to change but he'd be there. Next up was Walt Gillespie who made it exceedingly easy for them as he had just dropped into Bar OSA and was happily chatting away with the Thursday batch of Inbetweeners. Duffy had no problem getting him to come to the Berkeley City Club as Walt was interested in getting the plumbing contract and this would be another chance to chat with the manager. He never gave a thought as to why Duffy wanted them to meet there.

## CHAPTER 11

# AND THE GANG'S ALL HERE

No sooner had Duffy parked their battered but beloved Toyota van across the street from their destination, than Ambrose stepped jauntily out of the back with an ease that impressed both the Harts.

Pointing to the impressive Berkeley City Club, he shouted over the traffic, "I contend that if this were Julia Morgan's only design, she would still be included in the pantheon of the world's great architects."

"Spoken like a true homer," Duffy muttered, putting a hand on Ambrose's back and guiding him as they jaywalked across busy Durant Street.

The club with its appealing Moorish influence opened in 1930, the same year Ambrose Dowling came kicking and screaming into this world. While they were the same vintage, Ambrose didn't recognize his years but he considered the club to be old and charmingly historic.

Having just been buzzed in, Duffy, Caitlin and the professor stood in the ornate lobby near the front desk. The air was heavy, pronounced and aromatic. Ambrose wondered if they might have some secret spray which gave the place such a distinctive ambience.

He truly loved everything about the building, inside and out, particularly its uncanny ability to take him back in time. As he looked around, he took in a deep breath which did not go unnoticed.

"Hey, are you all right?" Duffy asked with concern.

"Oh I am," he said dreamily. "Whenever I come here, the first thing I like to do is inhale the past. Just think, Mr. and Mrs. Hart, you are breathing the same air that is no doubt perfumed by the exhalations of the many ghosts that wander the hallways."

Scurrying down the stairs to greet them was Bryce Allen, the nattily-attired, good-natured general manager who had just heard Ambrose's colorful explanation of what he considered merely the club's stuffy atmosphere. Laughing, he said to his arriving visitors, "Don't let him fool you. Those aren't ghosts. They are just some of our older members."

All three were known to him as Ambrose Dowling dropped by frequently, and at one time Bryce worked for the Harts at Bar OSA. "You're in luck, gang. The members' lounge is free for a little more than an hour. I won't need to get in there until a little past six-thirty to clean up for a scheduled seven o'clock function," he said, giving hugs to both Duffy and The Redhead. As Ambrose was a resolute handshaker, Allen reached over to greet him. "Can I get you any drinks or refreshments?"

"Sparkling wine and maybe some mixed nuts or, better yet, your truffle popcorn," Duffy said. "I know you have Gloria Ferrer. How about two bottles? We'll need seven glasses." Dropping his voice, he leaned in and added, "Oh, Bryce, we'd like to be left alone."

Bryce wagged his finger. "Ah, now what could that mean. Are we maybe making plans to buy a second restaurant? If so, remember me, please. Don't get me wrong, I love it here but I really got a kick out of working for you two. It was a very special time."

"One restaurant is tough enough, sweetie," Caitlin chuckled. "Actually, we're here to plan a surprise party for Ambrose."

The GM studied the three. Perplexed, he said, "I know it's Berkeley and we do things differently but I still have to ask. Why is the guest of honor with you?"

"He's paying for it," Duffy joked.

Bryce fooled with his paisley yellow and blue bow tie. Then, pretending to zip his mouth, he said, "Okay, I get it. Whatever you're up to is top secret and that's how it shall stay. I'll bring the goodies myself and keep the staff away."

"We can't thank you enough for this," The Redhead said warmly.

Glancing at his watch, the manager pointed to the wide carpeted staircase that lead to the members' lounge. "Look, you have ten minutes before your meeting gets started. Let's go up and visit for awhile. You can kick me out when the others get here."

As they started for the stairs, Duffy noticed Ambrose walking in the opposite direction down a darkened hallway. Bryce tugged Duffy's sleeve and explained the professor's defection: "He'll find you. First he has to do his rounds. It's something he does every time he comes in. His first stop is always the pool."

Ambrose preferred visiting the pool when it was empty. He thought it unbecoming and a bit creepy to sit in the small, raised spectators' area and watch complete strangers doing laps. Peeking through the door's small window and seeing no one splashing about, he entered and took a seat. What a glorious sight, he thought. Even his nose approved. The club was extremely diligent in its care of its indoor treasure. The long, decoratively-tiled pool resided under a colorful ceiling with high, turquoise arches. The walls were ochre and appropriately-spaced classical columns lined one side. The water was always a temptation even though he wasn't much of a swimmer. He and Emily had often talked of joining the club if for no other reason than to use this opulent natatorium. He remembered an evening in the early seventies when they were at a banquet of academics. It was, for the most part, a restrained affair, almost to the point of boredom. However, one colleague, a freshly minted Nobel Laureate, had too much to drink and wandered off to go skinny-dipping. He was followed by six or more of his acolytes which included two women. Ambrose heard from a witness later that the award-winning scholar was heard boasting that his member was as big as his brain and the naked swim would allow this select group to see that he was made of truth. Unfortunately, the club had turned the heat off that day and the shockingly cold water took all the bravado and more out of him. It was only two days later that this same professor publicly decried the antics of a Greek fraternity for a stunt that paled in comparison to his own mischief. None of this was mentioned in the scientist's carefully sanitized memoir.

Ambrose continued his sentimental journey with stops that included Julia's, the comfortable and clubby restaurant where the dinning staff was busy readying the place for dinner. The Dowling's had enjoyed many hours there, always as guests of members. He next poked his head into the smallish Berkeley Room, then the larger but still intimate Venetian Room before heading to the members' lounge which did double duty as a library.

Spotting him, Duffy called out, "We're almost ready to begin, Ambrose."

Ignoring him, Ambrose walked through the lounge and then left onto the club's outside terrace which looked down on their parking lot and the Berkeley Free Clinic. They were contrasting but good neighbors. The terrace was his last stop. Satisfied with his tour of the place, he returned to the far corner of the lounge where the Harts, Gearons and George Crowder were huddled around a large refectory table. There were two opened bottles of sparkling wine and bowls of nuts and popcorn. Seeing him, The Redhead poured Ambrose a glass of the Gloria Ferrer.

"We seem to be missing someone," Ambrose said, nodding hello to the new arrivals while taking a seat across from them. "Mrs. Crowder couldn't make it, George?" he asked.

Still in his sweats, the large man replied, "Store duty. So, professor, I'm told we're all here at your behest."

"Indeed," he replied. "And I promised not to waste your valuable time. Where's Walter?"

"I'm here," the plumber said loudly, stomping rather than walking into the room. He was in his usual Gillespie Plumbing attire "So this guy with a bow tie directed me up here. He said we're planning a surprise birthday party for him," he said, pointing an accusing finger at Ambrose. "Please tell me that is so not true."

"It is not true," the professor replied. "That said, though, I promise to make your visit here worthwhile. And if time permits and you wish to discuss some sort of celebration for me next Wednesday... Well, I can hardly refuse."

Sitting down, Walt examined his whereabouts. A quick glance said it was too formal for him but there was something inviting about it. At the end opposite the entrance was a wall of old books separated in the center by a large, ornate fireplace. There were scattered sitting arrangements and a piano in one corner. The library's colors were dark, vibrant and rich. It wasn't his cup of tea and that was what he was about to tell the rest when Duffy called for order and introduced the professor.

Ambrose Dowling surprised everyone. He did a marvelous job of editing, and in a matter of two minutes had fully explained his mistaken purchase. He was just about to announce to them that they were all rich beyond their wildest dreams when Walt interrupted him.

"So how much did we lose in the Super Lotto drawing?" he asked.

"One hundred and eighty-eight million dollars," Ambrose answered dramatically and with a huge grin. That said, he sat down and waited for the resulting hoopla.

Instead, Walt threw his hands up. "Hey, no big deal. No one was expecting to win anyway. Consider yourself forgiven, professor. Now why are we all here?" he demanded to know.

Ambrose looked utterly confused. He whispered to Duffy who sat next to him, "What doesn't he or the rest understand?"

"You didn't hear him. He asked how much did we lose."

"Oh! I see," he exclaimed. Standing up again, he looked at the beneficiaries of his mistake. "Excuse me, everybody. I think some awfully good news got lost in translation and, no doubt, from my being somewhat hard of hearing. You see, I thought Walt asked how much we won."

There was silence. No one dared speak. They were all hesitant to fully embrace the notion they'd won as Ambrose had not made it absolutely clear yet and they were frightened they may be wrong.

Walt was the first to address their collective fear. Staring at the white-haired, gentle man, he asked nervously, "Are you, uh, trying to say we might have won?"

"Mr. Gillespie, I'm not trying to say we might have won. We are definitely the winners of the second largest Super Lotto Plus pay-out in its relatively short history. I say short because it is younger than I am." He pulled out his Peet's napkin and waved it about. "I have the numbers here if any of you care to see them. Of course, the only numbers of real interest are one, two eights and a whole lot of zeroes."

"That's a paper napkin. Where's the lottery ticket?" George asked.

"I have a safe deposit box at the bank across the street from Bar OSA. I put it in there before coming over here. It is safe and sound and hasn't been ironed."

"Why on earth would you iron it?" Walt asked. And why is it, h thought, that Ambrose always adds some smart-ass comment to everything.

"Because it clearly states on the back of the ticket not to iron it," he dutifully explained.

If a TV game show producer were directing the next few minutes, there would have been such manufactured enthusiasm that

Bryce and his staff would have been forced to descend on the lounge with pleas to stifle their riotous behavior. As it was, Walt, George and the Gearons, having just learned they were instant multimillionaires. would have had the producer tearing his hair out as their reaction to this astonishing news was somewhat passive and unnervingly unemotional. The reason was simple. They were struck dumb; their respective brains grappling with the myriad questions created by the news of their instant wealth.

Duffy coughed loudly and got everyone's immediate attention. They seemed to welcome the call to order, hoping it would be followed by instructions as to how to proceed. Duffy didn't disappoint.

"The Redhead and I have had a chance to let the reality of all this settle in," he began. "I can see you're all working your way through it. It's a lot to take in, I know. We have an idea and I hope you give it some consideration. Next Wednesday, as you know, is Ambrose's eighty-second birthday. We plan to close the restaurant that day for lunch. We'll open at four instead of the usual noon. I won't have to call anybody in except for a couple of kitchen guys to prepare the food. Then I'll give them a break. I propose we all meet at eleven-thirty at Bar OSA. We'll get a cake from Virginia Bakery. After all, it's supposed to be a birthday party. This will give us a chance to talk about how we want to go about approaching the lottery people."

Walt was not enthusiastic. "I don't get it. What's all this about a birthday party. We go to the nearest lottery office tomorrow and tell them we won. They cut five checks and we're out of there. What's the problem."

Walt was beginning to get to Duffy who had the patience of Job. Maintaining a smile, he replied, "It's not as easy at that."

"Why the hell not?"

"I can answer that," Mike Gearon said. They were the first words either Gearon uttered since coming into the members' lounge. "I'm speaking for Kat and me here. We'd like to figure out a way to go about this without drawing any attention to ourselves. We're not comfortable with the public knowing we are lottery winners."

George agreed. "Speaking for Jeannie and me, I side with Mike and Katherine. We're going to need a plan."

"We're in pretty much the same boat," Duffy said. "There's a lot to discuss, a lot to think about. That's why I'm suggesting we all take the next few days and think about it. Then Wednesday we'll decide on how to go about claiming our prize. We have plenty of time."

Walt was exasperated. He wanted his share and he wanted it know. "So how much do you figure we'll each get?"

Ambrose put a hand on Duffy's arm. "Let me answer that." He stood up, harrumphed and then harrumphed again. He decided this was as good a time as any to tell them of his own plan. "Please remember these are strictly ball park figures. If you opt to take the cash option..."

"Of course, we're opting to take the cash option," Walt snapped.

"Then figure you will probably get about fifty-two to fifty-five percent of the total. That amount would be taxed at around twenty-five percent by the Fed. There is no state tax. Divide what's left into four and you will each receive somewhere around eighteen million dollars or so. I could be off several hundred thousand dollars or more."

Mike Gearon was the first to question the professor's use of pronouns. "You said four. There are five of us."

Ambrose decided to face the rest at eye level before explaining. Taking his seat, he placed his hands on the table and stared at them. Funny, he couldn't remember not having age spots. He remembered Emily didn't like it when he called them liver spots. Raising his head, he looked at the rest of the Dick Clark Memorial participants; all of them curious about what this eccentric man was going to say.

What he did say was said with genuine affection. "I do want you to know that I am truly ecstatic we won the lottery. I am very happy for all of you and now, after giving considerable thought as to how I want to deal with my share of this good fortune, I am extremely happy for me. More to the point, I am content and being so has provided me the assurance I am doing the right thing. And what is it I plan to do? I will tell you on one condition. You respect my decision and you don't try to convince me otherwise. "

Six bobbing heads told him he would not hear otherwise.

"Good. Firstly. to make it official, I would like Mr. Hart to return the dollar I invested in this madcap, wondrous adventure."

Duffy reached into his pants' pocket and pulled a small wad of bills out. He took a one dollar bill from it, unfolded it and handed it to Ambrose. This was all done with some ceremony which Ambrose appreciated.

"Thank you. I suppose to be absolutely fair each partner should give you a quarter, but I'll let you settle that amongst yourselves," the professor said. After putting the dollar in his jacket pocket, he continued, "This passing of the buck means I am now no longer part of this syndicate, and I must say that is a great relief to me."

Walt was having none of it. "No one in their right mind gives up millions of dollars. Absolutely no one," he emphasized. "But I suppose if anyone is going to do something as crazy as all that, I'm glad I'm part of the group benefiting from it."

"Nicely put, Walt," Mike Gearon muttered with a disapproving frown.

Ambrose ignored their testy exchange. He was too busy trying to put words together to explain his obviously baffling decision. Just wing it, he told himself. Some of your best classes were sessions that lacked preparation. That's when the true professor in him came out.

After a short silence and realizing they were waiting, he jumped right in. "I'm afraid this will lack the eloquence you have come to expect from me. However, I will try my best to help you understand my decision. A decision, I might remind you, that also affects all of you as Walt so greedily put it." He took a sip of this champagne and searched for a good beginning. "Yesterday, when I told you I feared money would change me, you may have thought I was being flippant. I wasn't. Such a huge amount of money requires diligence. You can't just sock it away and forget about it. And I don't have the time, energy or ambition that spending it, saving it or giving it away takes. Therefore, it is best for me to not have it all. My circumstances are such that I am quite comfortable. I live rather well. Nothing grand, mind you, but I have enough." He glanced over at Duffy's wife. "There's that infamous E-word, Cai... Uh, Mrs. The Redhead. You remember bringing it to our attention yesterday. The truth is I have what I want or need. There is my beloved fiction. There is my daily routine which is a pleasurable mix of leisure, intellectual stimulation, a fair amount of physical exercise, occasionally the warm company of others and enough time for reflection and prayer. None of this requires a large financial outlay."

George spoke first. "So you're going to just walk away from millions of dollar?"

The professor nodded. "From millions of dollars? Yes, George, I certainly am. However, it is not my intention to walk away empty-handed. I am submitting a fee for having been the purchasing agent of said winning lottery ticket. I am charging each of you twenty-five hundred dollars."

"Whoa! That's ten thousand dollars," Walt exclaimed. "Seems like an awful lot for just stopping by a store on the way home."

The former Oakland Raider finally had enough of Walt's pettiness. Actually, everyone was fed up with him but it was George Crowder who called him on the carpet for the inappropriateness of his remarks. "Just where the hell is your head? Do you realize if Ambrose wanted to do, he could claim the Super Lotto prize for himself and he wouldn't owe us anything more than the dollars he didn't use to buy a MEGA-Cash ticket."

Walt was clearly embarrassed but his pride kept him from apologizing. Instead, he tried to improve on his surly reaction. "Look, I thought he was asking us to pony up twenty-five hundred right here and now. Hell, how do we even know he has the winning tickets. All I see is a stupid napkin."

Pulling his iPhone out of his pocket, George said, "Let's take care of that right now." In a matter or seconds he was on the California Lottery site and in another few seconds he was reading off the winning numbers. "Walt, do you want to look at that napkin again. From what Ambrose has said we are all going to be very rich. Well, maybe not rich in the context that some people are today. But to my way of thinking, we have a whole hell of a lot of money coming our way. And if Ambrose wants a check from me right now. I'lll write it. Then I will be all over you until you cough up your share before you leave this club."

Ambrose rose once again and extend his arms as if he were blessing the assemble. "Gentlemen, gentlemen, please," he implored. "There's no need for fractiousness. There's no need for any check-writing. When you get your money, I will get mine. Besides, I am asking for a lot more than ten thousand dollars."

Mike Gearon raised his hands and shouted, "Hooray for that."

"To be exact, I would like ten thousand dollars for each year of my life."

Once again Walt did the addition. "That's eight hundred and twenty thousand dollars. You want two hundred thousand and change from each of us?"

Mike Gearon and George Crowder glared at Walt. Mike asked, "You have a problem with that, Walt? Before answering, please consider how much more is coming your way with Ambrose only taking that paltry amount."

"Look, I, uh... It's only that Ambrose and his antics get to me sometimes," Walt clumsily explained, withdrawing into himself.

"How did you come up with that figure?" Mike asked. His wife nudged him and he knew why. Sometimes he slipped into what she called his radio interview voice. This was one those times.

"Well, Mr. Gearon, because it is less than a million it is not so intimidating. And it seems manageable. I might treat myself to a cruise of two. Should I need special care at some time in the future, I will have enough to cover it. And if anything's left, there is one distant cousin and there are a few former students who will be surprised to find themselves in my will."

"So how do you want it? Twenties, tens and fives?" George Crowder joked.

Duffy checked his watch. He and Caitlin needed to get back to Bar OSA. Rising, he said, "Everybody okay with next Wednesday at eleven-thirty?"

The vote was unanimous. Duffy warned them that until Wednesday, it was important to keep the good news to themselves and to keep in mind all they were doing next week was attending Ambrose Dowling's birthday party. Finally, he thought it wise everyone share their contact information.

As they began to file out of the members' lounge of the Berkeley City Club, Ambrose once again called for their attention.

"I just want to say that gifts are not required. However, I am registered at..."

Mike Gearon cut him off. "Say goodnight, Ambrose."

# CHAPTER 12
# SECRETS AND CHANGE

Of secrets, Victor Hugo wrote, or was once heard to say, probably in a bar after too much absinthe, “No one ever keeps a secret so well as a child.” If this is indeed the case, the seven in attendance at the Berkeley City Club gathering were able to summon the better side of their inner child, remaining tightlipped until their meeting on the following Wednesday at Bar OSA.

Of change, the Latin elegiac poet, Sextus Propertious, probably in a mournful mood over an overly starched toga, wrote, “Never change when love has found its home.” Indeed, love was alive and flourishing in the homes of the four remaining lottery winners. Thus, it was inevitable that in the time before the Wednesday luncheon meeting at Bar OSA, each couple — the Crowders, Gillespies, Gearons and Harts — would discuss amongst themselves just how the tumult of change from claiming many millions of dollars would affect their otherwise harmonious hearths.

After the Berkeley City Club gathering, two of the winners still had to inform their spouses. As soon as he got home, George Crowder spilled the golden beans to his wife, Debbie. His spouse’s exuberant reaction upon hearing the news more than made up for the mystifying coolness and passivity of the others. She whooped and danced and kissed George and then whooped and danced and kissed George before repeating it for a third time. After finishing her celebration ceremony, she sat cuddled up next to him on their oversized sofa. The former offensive lineman gently kissed her forehead and told her that she still had her Raiderette moves. No such compliment would head in his direction as he had said goodbye to his gridiron moves a long time ago. Now that she had calmed a bit, George asked her if she was up to dealing with the public glare of winning a lottery. She assured him that after years of dealing with the sometimes feral behavior of fans of professional football, she could easily handle whatever challenges a winning lottery can dish out. He then explained what was to happen next Wednesday at Ambrose's birthday party and asked if she wanted to come along. Debbie rose and then resettled herself in her husband's ample lap. She answered sweetly but firmly, "No. You go find out how to get the money and I'll stay here and figure out how to spend it." She then gave him a sultry kiss that lingered long enough to send a blatantly seductive message in his direction; a message that didn't come these days with the same frequency as when they were younger and more physically able to handle the rigors of the ensuing romantic exercise.

When he was finally free to speak, with a voice turned gravely from Debbie's surprising, amorous smooch, George asked, "Uh, are we just necking around here or do we want to take this further."

Debbie gave him a quick peck and whispered with a breathless urgency, "I'll be right back. Don't you dare move from this spot." With that she jumped up and sashayed to the bathroom. How funny it is, she thought, that after a certain age, even spontaneity required careful preparation.

George, on the other hand, was armed and ready. All it took to rouse him to action was a combination of that kiss and catching a glimpse of what he called her incredibly sexy behind. He felt fortunate, grateful and just a touch proud that at his age he needed no help from the drug manufacturers who specialized in rigging moments like this.

Oh, that the evening could have been that easy for Walter Gillespie. When the City Club meeting ended, after first approaching Bryce Allen with a business card and the promise of a huge discount on their first plumbing repair should they choose to try him, he drove home barely keeping to the posted speed limit. Once there, he quietly entered the house through the garage. As anxious as he was to share this phenomenal news, to shout it from the rooftops so to speak, he knew the one person that had to be left in the dark was his nearest and dearest. It was not going to be easy, though, because he knew Jeannie would be wearing something skimpy, tight and utterly provocative. This meant any resolve to stay closed-mouthed would quickly vanish with her welcome-home kiss and a few seconds of his compulsive ogling. Why was it important that his wife not know about their good fortune? The answer is as you suspect. While being loving, caring and a temptress to boot, Jeannie Gillespie was also an unapologetic chatterbox. When her cosmetics' department colleagues weren't busy waxing, plucking, painting, dusting, caking and powdering their customers, they were busy telling tales and dishing dirt. It was well known that Jeannie was one of the best. For that reason alone, Walt decided she could only know when everything was settled and they were headed off to the bank to make the biggest deposit of their lives. Fortunately, that evening, Jeannie was on the treadmill, thus allowing him to keep his shaky resolve a while longer. That taken care of, he turned his mind to yet another problem and that was how this disparate group from Bar OSA was going to go about claiming their lottery winnings. What nagged at him was their seeming reluctance to collecting the money. It was obvious to him that next Wednesday he had to do everything he could to convince them to march lockstep to the local lottery office just as soon as Ambrose blew out his birthday candles. Besides, there was a Corvette he was anxious to buy.

Plus, Jeannie was making noises about them getting a Tesla sedan. They'd sell the Harleys, of course. With all that money, why tempt fate, particularly at their age? Fun times ahead, he said to himself, his mood brightening considerably. Grabbing a bottle of Semper Idem Pale Ale from his well-stocked fridge, he headed toward their media room admiring the label of his latest favorite beer. "What the hell," he said to no one after taking a swig of the pale golden ale, "I could buy the damned brewery."

Had Walt examined the bottle more closely, he would have discovered the popular Oakland-based brewery was owned by the son and son-in-law of one of the Dick Clark Memorial attendees. Kevin Gearon and his sister's husband, Raphael "Raf" Conners, were the operating partners of Semper Idem Brewery. Because they were located close to Jack London Square, they felt their brewery needed a name that would connect it to the famous author. Their problem was other breweries and wineries had pretty much emptied the coffers of London's more recognized stuff. When they were just about to give up, Kevin's mother, Katherine, suggested he search through her book of Jack London short stories. There he found a title character named Semper Idem. Even though the story was bloody, gritty and gruesome; more life-crushing than life-lifting, he realized he had found the brewery's name. Latin for always the same, it was up to his sister, Caroline, to work it into something positive. Caroline had just left a large, old-school San Francisco PR firm to start her own agency and Semper Idem Brewery was her first client. It was a complete family affair as the other brewer was Kevin's wife, Jansis Canning. Katherine and Mike Gearon had done their part by putting a few bucks into the venture to get it up and brewing.

Driving along busy Oxford Street on their way home from the Berkeley City Club, the mother of Kevin and Caroline, tapped her passenger on his knee and out of the blue asked, "Hey, are you going to want me to trade in my car for something bigger?"

Her husband, whose responsibility as copilot was to keep any eye out for bicyclists and pedestrians who enjoyed wearing dark clothing, glanced at his wife. "Why do you ask?"

"Because we're going to have the money to do that, you know. Now I want you to think of our next car as you would a pair of pants or a shirt. It's obvious small doesn't fit you. Medium probably won't work either so a large might do the trick. I'm ruling out extra-large because they are usually those gigantic SUV's that tiny women with blonde ponytails and big attitudes love to drive." Patting him again on the leg, she added, "That said, though, I really would miss the fun of seeing you getting in and out of my little darling."

"Kat, I love this car. As far as I'm concerned, your little darling can see us out."

"You can't fool me, Mr. Gearon," she laughed. "You just don't like the car buying process."

"I would refuse the lottery money just to avoid it."

Katherine shuddered. "I would too. I'd rather have a root canal."

"I wouldn't refuse the money for you doing that."

"Oh, thanks!"

"Think nothing of it, my sweet." His tone more serious, he continued, "What we really have to think about between now and Wednesday is how to get our hands on the money with the least amount of publicity. Ideally, without any at all. Any idea would be much appreciated."

When someone uttered Think about this, please, Katherine Gearon did just that. More often than not, whoever asked was inevitably pleased with her response. This time she just nodded to her navigator and quietly hummed the rest of the way while he kept his eye on potential road hazards.

When they arrived home, she watched his always entertaining exit before pulling the car into the garage. "Michael," she called out while gracefully easing her way out of the sports car, "there must be one or two among us who would be more than happy to announce themselves as the winner."

"Right now, I can only think of one."

"Let me guess. Walt?"

"You got it."

"Then why not let him claim it. Let him get his fifteen minutes of fame and when the spotlight dims, he can send us all checks for our shares."

"That's worth considering," he said, opening the front door to the house for her and hearing the familiar beep, beep, beep of the house alarm. "How you go about doing that is…"

"Don't say above my pay grade," she pleaded. "That seems to be the response du jour for questions people can't answer. I'm hearing it everywhere."

"Well, in this case it is," Mike replied, entering the four digit code that disarmed the system. "I know this much, though, you can't just go around handing out millions of

dollars willy-nilly to individuals. There are taxes, laws, more taxes, regulations, then even more taxes and then taxes on top of that. Oh, and throw in lawyers and CPA's. I'm kidding but I might not be that far off base.

Katherine followed him into the bedroom where the two quietly changed. Both knew what the other was thinking. It was only a question as to who would broach the subject first. This time it was Katherine.

"Are we being silly about all this?"

While he continued to change, she sat on his side of the bed, hands folded in her lap. Mike knew he need not reply as she going to first try and answer the question herself which she did: "I mean we are soon going to have… What did Ambrose say? Maybe eighteen million dollars once taxes are paid. Could be less, could be more. My God, who cares! Whatever it is it's still a humungous amount of money. I know we live in an age of mega-millionaires and billionaires who probably think that eighteen million is a paltry sum, but to me it's a ton of money. It's certainly more than we could spend in our lifetime. Honestly, Michael, I find it intimidating and a bit scary."

"Frankly, so do I," Mike said through a baggy long-sleeve T-shirt he was donning. "Odd, isn't it?

"What's odd?"

"You know how you and I tell each other that we are the wealthiest people we know?"

"We are," she affirmed. "So what's odd about it?"

"We never factor money in when we talk about our true wealth, our real riches. Money plays no part and never will," he replied. "Maybe that's why this enormous chunk of change is causing this uneasiness."

"Yeah, but there are some benefits. With the kind of money we're about to get, you can waste all the dental floss you want. You really do take more than you need for a good flossing. Wait. I have a better example," she exclaimed before he could defend his extravagant method of oral cleanliness. "We won't have to fly coach anymore."

"I don't use that much floss and besides we don't fly coach now."

"I know, but it's always such a struggle for you when you book a flight using mileage," she said. "You should hear yourself moaning and groaning your way through the torturous process. Then we might be in business or first class but we're on flights that are anything but direct or convenient. Now we can give all that mileage to charity."

He joined her on the bed. Taking one of her hands, he kissed it. After a whirlwind courtship and almost thirty years of marriage, he still loved the feel of her skin and how her hand fit so well into his. "Kat, I do agree with you. We are being silly, but it's a silliness born out of a real concern."

"I'm wondering whether one of those concerns might have to do with how extraordinarily happy you have been since leaving the morning show. It's amazing how easily and quickly you made the transition from being a popular local celebrity to a happy and fulfilled..." She looked to the ceiling for the right word.

"Nobody?"

"You'll never be that," she laughed, squeezing his hand. "Look, I'm just thrilled you have the same kind of joy and enthusiasm for this quiet and private life of ours that you had when you were on the radio. When you and Frank called it quits, I worried about how you would handle it."

"I worried, too. However, I can tell you in all honesty that I am perfectly content, I am madly in love and, while I have a head crammed full of astonishing memories, I truly don't miss what was. To sum it up, I absolutely, positively cherish this insular life of ours." That said, he gave her a high five. Her second of the day, perhaps her life.

Unlike George and Debbie Crowder who were headed to bed, Mike and Katherine rose from theirs and headed for the kitchen. While he made a vodka Martini for both of them, they continued to talk about their difficulty in coming to grips with the reality of a small fortune headed their way.

While Mike sprayed the fresh-from-the-freezer glasses with a mist of dry vermouth, he listened as Katherine mentioned one important life-altering consequence of having so much money. "I was just thinking about how this will impact our relationship with the kids and their mates? I fear it will change it and I'm not sure for the better."

"It will affect our relationship with everybody, Kat. We will no longer be plain old Mike and Katherine Gearon. We'll be known as Mike and Katherine Gearon, lottery winners. Money will be a constant topic and not always a pleasant one."

"We'd have to tell them," she said.

"Tell who?"

"The kids."

"Of course, we would." Putting the sprayer down, he faced her and asked, "What is it you like to say whenever you're in a particularly buoyant mood?"

She sat erect and, like a student eager to provide the correct answer, replied chirpily, "I would not change a thing about our lives. Then you usually say I wouldn't either. Or else you nod or grin or give me a kiss or something."

"Kat, this is going to change everything."

Martinis made, they headed for the living room where they spent the first part of their evenings at home. The medium-sized TV was hidden away in a beautiful Oriental cabinet. Mike opened it, grabbed two remotes and joined his wife on the sofa. Before turning on the television, Katherine signaled she had more to say.

"Looking on the bright side, my dear, imagine all the things I can tweak without having to think about whether we can afford it or not," she remarked.

"What sort of things?"

"Well, for example, my dining room chair seat needs repair — you can't sit on it with your weight — and all the chairs need recovering. And, uh, let's see... Oh, I would love to replace the furniture on the terrace and sometime in the near future we're going to have to replace some windows frames. Plus, I could go absolutely crazy in the garden. You want some more?" she giggled.

"No, that's enough for now," he said, an idea beginning to take shape in his mind. "So we're talking about tweakable cash?"

"Well, they are tweakable expenditures, to be sure. Nothing big, you understand. I know part of our annual income is the money we earn from investments and so we don't want to start spending down that principal. So I guess the eighteen million would provide me with more than enough tweak money." Katherine paused, thought over what she just said and then burst out laughing. "Oh my heavens. I can't believe I said that out loud."

By the time she'd finished talking, Mike's idea — a plan inspired by her use of the word tweak — had taken shape. He knew exactly what they should do. After Katherine heard the dramatic details of his plan, it was no longer what they should do. It was what they were going to do.

Katherine picked up her Martini and raised it in a toast. "Michael, people are going to think we are out of our minds."

"We are," he chirped, clinking her glass and taking a sip of the cold vodka drink. "That's the beauty of it. We are wonderfully and happily out of our minds. By the way, thank you for saying tweak. It put everything into focus."They clinked again and settled in to watch a rerun of Inspector Lewis.

Duffy Hart and The Redhead did not have the luxury of a sustained conversation. They dealt with the lottery win in snatches; a chat here, a chat there while they tended to business at Bar OSA. By the day of Ambrose's birthday lunch, they still had not come to any decision as to how they would handle their share of the lottery loot. They knew, though, they were definitely averse to the publicity associated with a big lottery win.

# CHAPTER 13
# WHAT? NO CANDLES?

A thick overcast awaited anyone in Berkeley and Oakland who chose to get out of bed and step outside to face whatever Wednesday, April 25th, 2012 had planned for them. While the day got off on a gloomy note, by midmorning the dark grey cloud cover had thinned, small areas of sunshine appeared and moods brightened. One of those who now sported a lifted spirit was Duffy Hart who with a skeleton kitchen crew was busy preparing the food for Ambrose Dowling's birthday luncheon. He selected dishes from the menu that could be served at noon with little effort. His plan was to give his two kitchen aides a midday break with instructions to return at three. Until then, he would be a one-man restaurant team catering to the others so they could plot and plan in complete privacy.

Duffy Hart was easy-going, funny in a droll sort of way and totally unflappable; qualities which worked extremely well in operating a bar and restaurant. Perhaps, though, what distinguished him from others in the profession was in the course of a typical day, you'd often find him, depending on the need of the moment, hosting, serving, bussing, bartending, cooking or fixing things that often went wrong. No job was beneath him and he wouldn't have it any other way. What he did not like nor did he have a talent for was the clerical side of running a restaurant. While The Redhead wouldn't be caught dead removing an empty, messy plate of potato bravas from a table or serving up a salty Margarita, she enthusiastically embraced routine office chores like filing, billing, taxes, invoices and payroll. They were a match made in heaven.

"Caitlin, it's almost noon," he yelled into their small office from the kitchen. "Do you think I should run across the street and get flowers for the table?"

"We're fine," she shouted back. "I don't know that they'd be noticed. This crowd has only one thing on their minds."

"I presume it's the same thing that has dominated most of our thinking for the past week?"

"If you're talking about the root of all evil, then yes it is, my darling."

"Ah, but don't forget, my dear, along with your brilliant head for numbers and the fact that you possess negotiating skills honed to perfection by your mastery of tact…" Suddenly, he remembered he wasn't alone in the kitchen and wisely decided it was a sentence not worth finishing.

Caitlin, of course, could finish it for him as they had earlier talked about their lottery share putting them in a unique position to purchase the building. Still, she wasn't going to let him get away with that smart-alecky remark about her supposed mastery of tact. After a pause that seemed more a deadly silence to Duffy, she answered back, "How interested are you in seeing our up until now marvelous sex life continue?"

While the two young men helping him prepare the lunch spoke mostly Spanish, their English was good enough to understand what Caitlin asked. Ernesto and Luis glanced at her husband with close-mouthed grins and waited to hear his reply.

"Honey, I should remind you that there are three of us here in the kitchen."

"Are you confused about whom I am talking about?" she shot back.

That sent his two co-workers into a fit of laughter. They high-fived, fist-bumped and danced in place a bit before returning to their cooking duties.

"You're a big comedy hit out here," he shouted.

"I'm sure I am," she replied. "So what were we talking about? Ah, the flowers. No, I don't think we'll need them. We have a decorated cake coming from Virginia Bakery. That'll make it look festive. By the way, I called Kat and she and Mike are going to pick it up on their way here."

Everyone was on time except Ambrose Dowling. Even though the former professor knew his birthday celebration was merely a cover for a clandestine meeting to decide just what to do with whatever was left over after the feds took their healthy share of $188,000,000.00, he still wanted to make an entrance worthy of a guest of honor. He was certain he'd be welcomed with open arms. After all he was the one who mistakenly purchased the Super Lotto ticket, and then by bowing out of the lottery, further sweetened their already substantial shares.

His dress rarely varied, but for this occasion Ambrose decided to add a Cal Bear blue and gold tie which proudly displayed two distinctive gravy stains that joined the design during a retirement dinner some three decades ago. He remembered his wife, Emily, telling him that the stains were a sign that he'd finally become a card-carrying member of the Cal faculty as she'd never seen anything but food-stained ties around the necks of his colleagues. Clutching the winning lottery ticket in his right hand, Ambrose pulled opened the heavy door to Bar OSA. His smile widened and his heart swelled as he heard the happy sound of twelve clapping hands coming from the undecorated round table in the rear of the dining room which Duffy had expanded to comfortably seat seven. The Redhead pointed to the empty chair to her right and beckoned him to come join them. His other neighbor, George Crowder, pulled the chair out for him.

Ambrose had already rehearsed what he would say upon arrival. Arriving at the table, his left hand fumbling with this tie, he first nodded hello to everyone and then magnanimously announced, "You all certainly have my whole-hearted approval to blurt out a short verse of Happy Birthday in whatever key suits you and then get on with the real business of the day." Then he held the lottery ticket high to prove there truly was important business to conduct.

"Nonsense," shouted George Crowder just as magnanimously. "There's plenty of time to celebrate your eighty-second. Most of us pray we'll reach that number some day. And that some day is coming sooner rather than later for a couple of us." Looking at Duffy, he asked, "How long do we have this fine establishment to ourselves?"

"'Til three," he replied. "Then our kitchen crew and wait staff start showing up and it's business as usual."

"I don't know if there's ever going be such a thing as business as usual if you consider why we're here," a somewhat dour Caitlin mused while reaching for a toasted piece of a baguette topped with bocquerones and anchovy.

Taking his seat, Ambrose gave her a pensive look and said, "Do I detect a sour tone in that response, Mrs. The Redhead? Certainly, you are not already lamenting the future which now seems gold-plated."

Putting her montaditos back on her plate, she replied, "No, I am not." Realizing her snappish response got everyone's attention, she continued, "Look, I know we've made a game out of my name, but now that we're among friends, please use my first name. By the way, George and Walt, it is Caitlin." Then, turning to Ambrose, she leaned in close enough to almost make him swoon from the exotic scent she was wearing and whispered, "Ambrose, if I hear Mrs. The Redhead one more time..."

"Mrs. Hart, it will never pass my lips again," he whispered, quickly crossing his heart but not hoping to die. By the way, as long as we're talking about names, I was always curious about your husband's right and proper first name."

"That's easy. It's Duffy," Caitlin replied matter-of-factly. Nudging her husband, she asked if he wanted to tell them the story behind it or should she.

"I will," Duffy said. "My father was an attorney and he was able to make partner in his small firm thanks to his mentor, Chester Duffy, who was one of the two senior partners. He was so appreciative of the man, he named me after him.

Stories told by Duffy Hart always came with a punchline. This one was no different. Usually his wife supplies whatever extra material is needed, but in this case, Mike Gearon stepped in. "And who was the other partner?" he asked as he'd asked on any number of occasions."

"Edward Dinwiddie. Dinwiddie Hart would have been hard to live with."

Wiping the oily remains of a beef en adobo montaditos that didn't completely make his mouth, George backed his chair out and slowly rose to address the group. "Okay everyone, while Dinwiddie.. I mean Duffy pours Ambrose some of this wonderful cava, I want everyone else to raise their glasses in a toast to the professor who we have learned in true Berkeley fashion marches to his own drum. That eccentricity combined with a confusion or dottiness which eventually affects all of us after a certain age…"

"I hate to break it to you but we are all at that age," Duffy interjected while pouring the pricey Spanish cava into Ambrose's champagne flute. Noticing the disapproving look on his wife's face, he quickly added, "I mean the men, of course. The women here are mere babes in the woods."

"Nice recovery, Duffy," George quipped. "Anyway, thanks to this literate bundle of Cal Bear wit sitting next to The Red… Uh,

Caitlin and me, we are all newly minted multimillionaires and I know we're all itching to talk about it. For now, though, I propose we celebrate the most senior member of this gathering."

"Here, here. I couldn't agree more," Ambrose remarked.

George put his hand on the professor's shoulder and continued, "I assume you've prepared a speech. So to give some order to this afternoon's proceedings, I propose that..."

"Who made you jury foreman?" Walt abruptly asked, his manner typically belligerent and bullying. Maybe a little too much of both considering the heft and threat of the person to whom he had directed the question.

His brusque manner didn't faze George in the least. Glancing across the table at Walt, the six-foot, four-inch former football player merely grinned. Taking his time to answer, he finally mouthed, "I did." Others in similar situations might add more words to their response in order to give it more force or weight. But not George Crowder. With his drawn-out, well-practiced iron firmness that had been a big help when he was the Raiders' team leader, those two little words were all he needed.

The plumber winced, but not because he was cowed by George's blunt reply. He was puzzled by it. To Walt's thinking, he was just ribbing the big guy and he wondered why George didn't laugh it off. The reason is easily explained. Walt's life-long problem was he was incapable of delivering a jest without it sounding confrontational. His size, scowl and scrappy manner didn't help matters either. Thus, as he'd done so often in the past, he finished off this last attempt at a joke by muttering, "Sorry, okay? I was just kidding around."

A disappointed Ambrose threw up his hands in mock disdain and uttered, "Oh darn! What could have been an entertaining conversational dustup quashed after a two sentence exchange."

George, who was still standing, looked down at Ambrose and shook his head. "You are definitely a weird one, professor."

"Is it wrong to root for a snappy contretemps at one's birthday party?" he asked, taking a sip of the cava and wondering when it might be polite to ask his host for a Cuban Manhattan.

"Hey, Ambrose, if you like cussing, drinking, teeth-baring relatives with high-decibel voices and the occasional thrown plate or dish of food, I'll get you an invite to one of my sister's in-laws' family shindigs. Hands down, they're better than any reality TV show," Walt said with a half-chuckle.

Every party needs an icebreaker. George's attempt to put some structure to this particular celebration had merit, but what this group needed was something more organic and spontaneous. Walt's remark did the trick. Soon everybody was weighing in with their own experiences with family celebrations gone awry. It soon became a contest of Can You Top This. If they handed out awards after the story-telling wound down, Walt Gillespie would have been declared the winner with his preposterous but hilarious stories of boisterous family gatherings. Caitlin Marie Hart, nee Connors would have been a close second with a sequence of tales of confrontation, all of them involving an uproarious drunken uncle named Barney whom she later discovered was not a relative at all but just a guy in the neighborhood with a nose for a good party.

It was a now a happy, garrulous crowd with words flying in every direction across a table of colorful and lively salads, even livelier wax-green pimientos, tasty bocadillos, montaditos and plates of olive-oil drenched jamon serrano with grilled onions. Somehow it all got eaten in a timely manner even though one wondered when they had time to chew as it seemed the myriad conversations never slowed. After a time, Duffy cleared the table and returned to the kitchen to bring out a customized version of what Virginia Bakery called their Cal Graduation Cake. It was a flat cake rimmed with blue and gold icing. Atop the cake in blue icing was the word Cal and just above it the number 82. In another three weeks, the cakes will be in high demand as the university graduations get underway.

Duffy held the whimsically-frosted cake high and at an angle so everyone could admire it. Now when a birthday cake usually makes its entrance, it's a cue for any and all to begin singing. Typically a lone tentative voice kicks it off and then two to three notes later everyone else joins in. This birthday celebration was no exception with Mike Gearon's baritone voice, not all tentative, attacking the first note

Ambrose was delighted and clapped through it all. He was touched the Harts went to the trouble of ordering a cake for him and a beautiful one at that. Still, he couldn't resist a little mischief. As Duffy placed the cake in front of him, he commented, "I realize eighty-two candles are cumbersome. They are also tedious to put on the cake and time-consuming to light and, I daresay, I don't think I have the lung capacity to blow them all out especially if they are the type that keeps lighting back up. That said, Mr. Hart, I don't begrudge you sticking to your obviously very strict no candle policy."

Caitlin decided to make the Hart's official response. She tugged on Ambrose's sleeve to get his attention. "Ambrose, if we had candles anywhere in the building, you would have gotten one for your Dick Clark Memorial a week ago. That would have meant you wouldn't have bought that lottery ticket. And that would have meant you'd be celebrating your birthday by yourself today, probably at Peet's where they'd put extra whipped cream on your Cafe Freddo to honor the day. But I'll bet they wouldn't put a candle on it."

After his wife's gentle scolding, Duffy asked the professor, "Can I trust you with a knife?"

"Speech! Speech! First a speech." This out of the blue exhortation, while not unusual at events like this, surprised everyone at the table because it came from Walt. His appeal to Ambrose to orate away, though, was somewhat disingenuous. Walt figured they'd never get around to the business of the lottery until Ambrose ran out of words and what better way to do that than by having him putting them all in one speech.

And that's exactly what Ambrose did. Pulling his chair away from the table, the eldest of the gathering slowly rose. Keeping one hand on the table's edge to stay steady, he turned to Duffy and said, "As regards your inquiry about the knife, Mr. Hart, I suggest you slice and serve while I will share a few thoughts. Then as they say, it's off to the races."

Noticing Ambrose's use of the table as a support, Caitlin suggested he might be more comfortable sitting down.

"That's very thoughtful of you, Mrs. Hart, but I'm quite all right standing. While teaching, I fell into a nasty habit of propping myself against my desk or lectern. More out of laziness than anything. I'll be fine."

"Okay, who wants cake and how big a slice?" Duffy asked.

The orders taken, Ambrose set off on his birthday speech. Looking around the table and seeing he had everyone's attention, even Walt's, he began: "Thank you for making this birthday so very special. I truly appreciate the..." He paused to consider what it was he appreciated. He decided to be honest. "...the attention. Yes, I appreciate the attention. I'm a glutton for it. And I thank you, Mr. and Mrs. Hart for hosting such a fine party. And thank you, Walt, for insisting on a speech. It shall be short, I assure you."

"Hey, take your time, professor," Walt replied, surprising even himself that he meant it.

"I love stories and as a professor of English literature, I particularly love them when they are well told. Oh, and preferably in English," he added with an impish grin. "I have been blessed in that I have been able to make a decent living immersed in the world of literature which is simply a hoity-toity name for well-told stories."

"Preferably in English," Mike Gearon noted.

Ambrose pointed to him and heartily exclaimed, "Exactly, Mr. Gearon. Now looking around the table, I think it's fair to say that all of you also feel blessed that you work or worked in fields you love."

Walt, whose head was down trying to discreetly look at a suggestive text his wife had just sent, glanced up and said, "Whoa, you including plumbing, Ambrose?"

"And why not?" the professor asked.

"It's more a business than a calling. The reality is it stinks. Literally and figuratively."

"Ah, but you love it, don't you?"

"Believe it or not, I do," Walt replied. "But once my share of the lottery is in the bank, that's it. I am hanging up my plumber's snake."

Duffy, ever the handyman, looked up from cutting the cake. "Hey, I'll take it."

Ambrose called for order with a loud ahem. "We are straying, ladies and gentlemen, and I know you want me to be as brief as possible. Allow me to explain my reason for mentioning stories." Waving his arm around, he continued, "We are all part of an extraordinary narrative. Perhaps in the future, bits and pieces might find their way into local lore, but given all our unorthodox approaches to money, the real story, the truthful accounting, will never be told. Last Thursday was as strange a day as they come; the silly barroom banter that lead to a Dick Clark memorial, the ridiculous thinking that a lottery ticket can take the place of a candle... Thank you for reminding me of that, Mrs. Hart, and a sincere mea culpa for my candle criticism. Oh, and we have Walt to thank for bringing up that lottery with almost half a billion dollars at stake. Then, of course, we have Mike Gearon to thank because if he never mentioned Dick Clark's passing, we'd all have just finished our drinks, wandered home and that would be that. But it's something else entirely now, isn't it? There is money, scads of it, to be collected and distributed. As I have already bowed out and wished anonymity when it comes to my involvement, I suppose I must take credit for the first alteration of this extraordinary tale. I'm sure there will be more revamping of the story as you get on with the business at hand. My plan was to leave now and let you work it all out. I can't do that, however, as I am really, really curious to know what form the story will take when you finally decide what it is you each plan to do. To that end, I have decided to stay. I shall be quiet. I shall offer no comment. Believe it or not, Ambrose Dowling can keep quiet. On one condition, though."

Duffy was just finishing up the small serving of cake he served himself. "What's the condition, professor?" he asked between bites.

"I'd like to trade in this excellent cava for a Cuban Manhattan."

## CHAPTER 14

# WHERE THERE'S A WALT, THERE'S A WAY

Even the prickly plumber agreed the oddball birthday salute to an eighty-two year old retired professor whom they hardly knew was a good bit of fun. Even though the party portion was at an end, the mood remained buoyant with everyone happily chatting away while Duffy made drinks for the table; one of which was Ambrose's Cuban Manhattan. The rum cocktail was a small price to pay for his promise to stay quiet through the all-important business portion of the afternoon's get together at Bar OSA.

"Don't talk lottery stuff yet, okay?" Duffy pleaded as he started bringing an assortment of drinks to the table.

Wiping some of the blue frosting from his lips, Ambrose said, "I assure you, Mr. Hart, not a word about the lottery has passed from anyone's lips since you've been gone. Certainly not mine as I have taken a vow of silence regarding said topic. For the rest of the afternoon, I shall be like a Trappist monk. Besides, my only interest now is in taking my sweet time, no pun intended, to enjoy this delicious cake. As you know, it's awfully hard to talk with your mouth full."

"This is the perfect time then to take another big bite of cake, Ambrose. You can wash it down with this," he said, placing the Cuban Manhattan next to the larger than usual slice of cake. "And you can thank me by remembering your mute button is now on until the end of the meeting."

"There's no way he can go the distance," Walt observed. In response, Ambrose waved to him and then with his thumb and index finger pretended to zipper his mouth.

"A fat lot of good that will do," Walt laughed.

Taking his seat, Duffy took a sip out of a bottle of DogFish Head 90 Minute IPA. "Okay, this meeting is officially called to order. We have a lot to talk about and all of its good because it's about money. Lots of it." Surveying the guests, he asked, "Who wants to go first?"

The plumber did. Frustrated and a little angry, Walt Gillespie wanted to jump up and ask why all this fucking around; his indelicate way of describing what he considered their overly cautious approach to claiming their winnings. He wanted to tell them to stop all the bullshitting, drink up and follow him to the local lottery office which was in Hayward (He'd already checked.). Two things, though, kept him from doing that. Firstly, he was uncomfortable starting things off on such an antagonistic note. He knew no matter how hard he ranted and raved, it truly wouldn't move things along at all. Not with this gang. Secondly, he'd just received another provocative text from Jeannie and he knew he'd better reply or she'd just keep at it and the texts would get even naughtier. So instead of volunteering to go first, he stood up, waved his smartphone around and made for the other end of the room, grumbling, "Sorry, I have to deal with this. Only be a minute."

"Go ahead, we'll wait," Duffy told him. "We have plenty of time."

"No, get started. I'll just be a second," he replied, figuring they would just go on blathering about how conflicted they were about having cold hard cash suddenly being dumped into their respective laps. He was, quite frankly, frustrated by it all.

Duffy shrugged and asked again, "I'll start over. Who wants to go first?"

"Actually, I do," Mike Gearon said, eagerly raising his hand.

Radio had taught him that while timing wasn't everything, you are one lucky person if you have a keen sense of it. Mike did and he recognized that Duffy had just given him the opportunity to tell the others what decision he and Katherine had reached as regards their involvement in the lottery. Or to be more precise; their choosing not to be involved.

His volunteering to go first was welcomed by the others as it prevented what would have been a period of awkward silence. A silence inspired by, as Walt had correctly assumed, the fact that the Harts and the Crowders, even after a week of discussing the myriad side effects of winning a lottery, were still unsure and undecided as to how they were going to deal with their shares. Thus, Mike Gearon's opening statement was providential.

"The floor is yours, Mr. Gearon," Duffy said with an air of mock formality. "Yikes, no sooner do I get Ambrose silenced than I begin to sound just like him."

Ignoring his self-deprecating remark, Mike announced, "Katherine and I have decided to sell our share of the lottery." He paused to check everyone's reaction and then asked with a half-smile, "Anybody want to buy it?"

"! do," shouted Duffy, jumping up and pretending to make for the cash drawer. "Let me get a dollar. Will you take four quarters?"

"Nice try, Duffy, but it's going to cost a bit more than a dollar."

Ambrose was now kicking himself that he promised to remain close-mouthed through the meeting. He had no idea things would get off to such a bubbly start. Neither did the others at the table. Duffy and Caitlin each wore that expression married couples wear when they wonder whether one or the other was privy to what was happening. George Crowder's reaction was to exhale loudly and then mumble, "Wow."

"What did I miss?" Walt asked, returning to his seat after having elicited a promise from Jeannie to hold off on sending any more texts, particularly the bare-breasted selfies.

"The Gearons are selling their share of the lottery," George explained to him.

"Yeah, sure," Walt scoffed. "Okay, I'll play along. How much?"

The former football player shrugged his shoulders and replied, "All we know so far is that the price tag is more than a dollar."

Now a bit confused about what he'd walked back to, Walt looked over at Mike and asked him directly what the selling price was.

"Four million dollars," Mike replied. "Of course, that's a tax-free four million. So depending on the buyer's accountant and what magic he or she can do regarding gift taxes, the buyer might be more like five and a half million or so out of pocket. Oh, and you also pay my share of what's owed Ambrose."

Jumping in, Katherine added, "Remember, though, the share is worth possibly eighteen million or even more, so when you do the math, you can see it's a pretty terrific deal." Realizing that what she just blurted out was something everyone was keenly aware of, she reddened from embarrassment. "How silly of me. Of course, you know," she mumbled.

Not one to pass up an opportunity to have a little fun, George said, "Uh oh, we're getting double-teamed. I think they're desperate."

Joining in the fun, Duffy added, "Maybe we can talk them down to three and a half mill? It's still a damn sight larger than their original investment."

George added, "They'll probably want the money put on a prepaid debit card."

Walt was now thoroughly confused by their humorous exchange. He figured that somehow the meeting must have gotten off on a light-hearted note with Mike Gearon joking around. He wouldn't put it past him. After all, joking around was what he did for a living for so many years. Still, he thought the former broadcaster sounded pretty serious and businesslike when he rattled off those numbers. Confused, he was reluctant to say anything because he didn't want it to seem he'd been taken in by their horsing around.

Fortunately, he didn't have to ask as Duffy did it for him. "Mike, all kidding aside, what's the deal? We have to get a lot settled this afternoon."

"We aren't kidding," Mike insisted. "Katherine and I want to sell our share for four million dollars. It's as simple as that."

Nonplussed, the former Oakland Raider groused, "Sorry, Mike, but it's not as simple as that."

"No, of course it isn't, George," he agreed. "Nevertheless, we are dead serious about selling our share."

"Why?" asked Walt.

"Right now, I think a more relevant question is how, not why."

"Okay then, how?"

Mike pulled out a piece of paper from the inside pocket of his linen sport coat. Unfolding it, he looked over an array of numbers that all began with a dollar sign and more zeroes in them than he had ever worked with before. Holding it up, he said, "I think I have worked out how we manage this."

"Mike, let me have that please," Caitlin said, reaching across the table so he could hand her the paper. "I'll run off a few copies so we can all follow along. I'll bring pencils if people want to make notes."

He handed her the paper. "That's a good idea, Caitlin. You'll see it's pretty self-explanatory."

"I'm curious. Why are you selling your share?" her husband asked. "And why just four million?"

To explain Mike's opaque response to his friend's two questions, it might be best to first provide some background on a majority of our players. While outgoing and social, the Gearons, the

Crowders and, to some degree, the Harts were also insular couples. They were not, as the word can often imply, small-minded or parochial. Rather they simply preferred their own company over others. They were, as George once said of his and Debbie's partnership, lovingly hermitic. While successful in their chosen careers which had put them in the public spotlight, both Mike and George much preferred that portion of the day when they were home in the company of their wives. It is, perhaps, the reason both adapted so well to retirement. Over the years, and there were a lot of them, the three couples fashioned distinct and somewhat eccentric lifestyles. Theirs were happy and satisfying existences, but difficult to explain to others. So it was that Mike, realizing he'd have a hard time explaining how he and Katherine had come to terms with how to handle their lottery winnings, decided on an obfuscated response that did contain a smidgen of truth.

"Mark Twain said a well put together unreality is pretty hard to beat. Kat and I agree with that bit of Twain wisdom. We're both confident four million will be sufficient to keep our unreality in good working order for some time to come," he said.

Walt's reaction was predictably gruff. "Yeah, it's fucking unreal all right." Seeing the disapproving frown on Duffy Hart's face, he quickly added, "Okay, I know. This is a no-swearing zone. Sorry, but it's still unreal."

Before George could coax Mike into further explaining himself for no other reason than it would be fun, The Redhead reappeared. As she distributed copies of Mike's scribblings, she said to him, "I spotted something you may have overlooked."

"I think I know what you're talking about. Kat and I discovered it on the way over here. It's a problem but maybe there's a way to work around it," he replied, looking over his page full of numbers.

Pushing himself away from the table, George emitted a groan as he slowly, painfully rose from his seat. "You people mind if I stand for a minute? I've been sitting too long and my back is acting up." There was no hint of complaint in his voice, no looking for sympathy, no frustration with what was a chronic situation. He was just letting them know why he was going to stand.

Hearing that, however, Walt began to wonder about that slight discomfort he was feeling on his left side. It wasn't going down his leg so sciatica could be ruled out. His hypochondria was such that he wondered if he ought to stand as well. But how would it look, he thought. Sensibly, he stayed seated and once Mike Gearon started talking, he lost all interest in his supposedly aching left side.

Mike had remained seated while he detailed what he thought The Redhead had discovered. "The problem Caitlin no doubt spotted was if we sell our share which is a quarter of the lottery amount, it throws a wrench in the works because with only three people showing up to claim the money, the lottery will divide it into thirds. That gives everyone extra money whether they bought our share or not."

Caitlin's red hair bobbed about as she nodded in agreement. "One practical solution is either the three remaining partners each buy a portion of your share or whoever buys it brings a partner along to keep the group number at four," she explained. "For instance, if you bought it, Walt, you could bring your wife... Uh, I'm sorry, I don't know her name."

Walt reddened and said without hesitation, "Her name is Jeannie and that's not a good for instance."

"Gotcha." she said, wondering what awaited him when the money poured in.

Mike decided a quick review of the how and why of what he'd presented to them would be appropriate and maybe appreciated. "Katherine and I came up with this idea of selling our share because we don't want to be a part of a small group claiming a lottery payout as historic as this one. Way too much attention and way too much money for us. So the idea of four million dollars in the bank and not being a part of this bizarre story suits us fine."

George nodded his satisfaction with Mike's explanation as he looked at his copy of the numbers. "I know these are approximations. So it could be less or more but probably not by much. You're estimating the cash option is about fifty percent of the $188,000,000 or $94,000,000, and you figure the feds will take twenty-five percent of that amount. I'll bet there's more taxes down the road. Anyway, you have us looking at a net of approximately $70,500,000 which divided four ways gives us each about eighteen million."

Walt had his smartphone out and using the calculator app divided that net amount by three. "See the trouble starts when we divide it into thirds. Unless, like Caitlin suggested, we each buy a portion of the Gearon's share or bring a forth along." Walt paused, and felt compelled to add, "As long as it isn't my wife." Then in a scolding tone, he said to Mike, "You know your bailing really complicates matters."

Mike understood the reprimand. "Walt, we are flying blind here. There are no tax experts, money managers or lawyers who probably know a dozen different ways to handle this. I was just trying to..."

Walt didn't let him finish. "I got a great idea," he interjected. Folding his hands and placing his chin on them, his eyes darted back and forth from George Crowder to Duffy and Caitlin Hart. Then in a surprisingly calm and controlled voice, he said, "Look, I know you guys aren't so hot on wanting to be part of this either. Do you want to sell your shares, too?"

It would come to pass that even though he was sworn to secrecy about what happened on Wednesday, April 25th, 2012 at Bar OSA, Walt would occasionally feel a strong urge to tell all. To his credit, though, he realized this itch was based on his desire to brag about how he truly got things rolling that afternoon. It would remain a constant source of frustration to him that the real story couldn't be told.

Noticing Ambrose stiffen at hearing his question to the Harts and George Crowder, the plumber held up his hand and said, "Ah ah ah, you're not supposed to speak, professor."

Dowling folded his arms and pretended to pout. "Just fooling with you," Walt laughed. Then to the surprise of everyone at the table, he added, "I vote to have Ambrose's ban on speaking lifted."

"You?" George exclaimed with a throaty laugh. "I thought you'd be the last person to want him jabbering on."

"Yeah, well..." Walt rubbed the churlishness off his face and grinned. "I've taken a liking to the professor, and it's not just because of the extra money we're getting thanks to his bowing out of the lottery. I just think he should be a part of whatever happens here this afternoon."

Still standing, George put his meaty hand on the professor's shoulder and said, "I couldn't agree more. What about it everybody? Let Ambrose speak?" A mix of affirming gestures carried the motion.

What did I do, Walt asked himself. Putting forth a proposal to allow Ambrose to rejoin the conversation, his question about selling shares seemed to go by the wayside. But it hadn't, he soon found out, all thanks to the man whose voice was restored by his impulsive action.

"Thank you, Walter," Ambrose sang, cheery that he could be a vocal part of this unusual gathering again. "I must say, Mr. Gearon, you surprised me with your imaginative proposal to sell your shares. I'm sure there are all kinds of creative ways to transfer money with less tax consequence. However, given the truly obscene amount of money you all have to work with, why not let the government have a few extra dollars if it means accommodating everyone's wishes today. And that brings us to Walter's last question where he wisely,

I might add, asked the Harts and Crowders if they wished to sell theirs?"

Walt could have kissed him. Particularly because both the Harts and George Crowder were not quick to dismiss the idea. Rather, George signaled he was going to make a phone call and then walked in his uncomfortable way toward the entrance of the restaurant. The Harts asked to be excused and retreated to their office off the kitchen. While they were gone, the others sat silently for a moment.

"It's your idea then, Walt, that all of us sell you our shares and you claim the lottery prize?" Mike asked, breaking their self-imposed silence.

"I honestly can't see any other way," he replied. "It's fairly obvious that Duffy and his wife went off to talk about it and I'm sure George is on the phone with his wife discussing what they want to do."

Ambrose took a satisfying sip of his Cuban Manhattan and looked around at the site of his eighty-second birthday celebration. Now the post-party meeting had transformed Bar OSA into a unusual sort of boardroom where soon-to-be, very wealthy men and women, he among them, talk money. He'd already celebrated by putting a deposit down on a luxury cruise to Alaska in July; booking himself an expensive penthouse. Even though his new found fortune was just shy of a million dollars, he knew the cruise fare would hardly put a dent in his budget. My heavens, he thought to himself, do I even have to think in terms of a budget. The actuarial tables suggest otherwise. How are the others going to come to terms with their substantial fortunes, he wondered. His mental meandering came to end when the Harts, holding hands and looking fondly at each other, returned from the kitchen and George, putting his phone away, returned to take his seat next to him. The retired football player looked at Ambrose and grinned broadly.

# CHAPTER 15
# TRUST ME

What is it about that blunt two word phrase that intuitively sends a signal that you should do just the opposite? Perhaps it is because we are too used to hearing it come from the fictional mouths of villains, ogres, big, bad wolves, vixens and ne'er-do-wells in movies or books. Or worse, from friends who have disappointed. There is also an aggressiveness to it that can't be denied. If the message a person wants to convey is well-intentioned, they could certainly strengthen it's positive impact by saying instead, "You can trust me." or "I am someone you can trust." To give it even more gravitas, that individual might also include what it is that requires your trust, i.e., "You can trust me to deliver that porcupine in two days time."

Interestingly, we put our trust in all sorts of people, places and things without giving it much thought. We trust a cabdriver to get us to the airport on time, hopefully without airing his oftentimes strident political opinions. We trust a pilot to fly us to our destination and that the fight attendants will serve us a decent Bloody Mary that will help further bolster that trust. Even though we can't spell it, we trust anasthesiologists who put us under to also bring us back from wherever it is they sent us. We trusted Walter Cronkite.

In God we trust. And while there are times that call for a certain wariness, we trust our instincts. I mention this last because instinctual trust plays a vital role in this story. Trust me.

At this point in our tale, though, trust of any design was the last thing on George Crowder's mind as he returned from his short phone call to his wife, Debbie, who had assured him that whatever he chose to do that afternoon at Bar OSA, she would be happy, deliriously so. They were both of one mind that less money and no publicity had a lot going for it. Duffy and Caitlin Hart had also come to that conclusion and upon their return from their kitchen meeting seemed happier for it.

Taking his seat, his battered back mercifully behaving for him, George wore a warm smile that for years intimidated, some say terrorized NFL linemen who dared set up residence opposite him on the line of scrimmage. While the ones he faced went to great lengths to display fierce, menacing mugs all the while spewing fire-hot trash talk, George merely smiled at his opponent, never uttering a peep. It was very, very effective. Since his playing days, that same smile now produced the opposite effect as people found the big, intimidating man most engaging whenever he flashed it.

"Absolutely amazing," he said to no one in particular, pronouncing amazing as if it had five A's in it. His daughter-in-law had brought that particular approach to the word back with her from a recent buying trip in New York and, like a fast-spreading germ, soon all the Crowders were giving the word more emphasis than it needed.

"What's amazing?" Mike Gearon asked without adding the extra A's.

"The weirdness of all this," he replied.

"I couldn't agree more," Mike said.

"Making it even weirder, Debbie and I also realized money doesn't hold the same charm for us as it did when we were younger."

"It still charms the hell out of me," Walt said with his familiar greedy grin.

Ambrose, too, was anxious to weigh in on George's comment. He put his fork down on the now empty desert plate, his stomach rumbling as it tried to come to terms with the arrival of a large slice of heavily frosted cake and a sip of a Cuban Manhattan. "I believe what Mr. Crowder said about the flirty charms of money has considerable merit. Those of us fortunate to have lived with suitable wages during our working years and now have some form of retirement income that allows us to live contentedly in our golden years have a unique relationship with the almighty dollar. Because we are able to comfortably cover the basic necessities with enough left over to enjoy our myriad but measured pleasures, we are mostly satisfied with our lot and don't cotton to change, which, I'm afraid, reared its ugly head by our winning this lottery."

Walt, who was leaning back in his chair, sat upright and pointed a finger at the professor. "You know, I kind of understand what you're talking about," he admitted. "But like it or not, we did win and the money is there for the taking. You know if we were all younger, we wouldn't be having this conversation. We'd have been at the lottery office last Thursday at dawn camped out, waiting for it to open.

George laughed loudly. "Walter, my man, you are so right. If I won this kind of money, say, thirty-five years ago, I would have bought a share of the Oakland Raiders instead of having to borrow from Al Davis to get our property management company up and running. Of course, I loved him for doing that," he said respectfully of the Raider owner who had passed away just seven months previous.

Walt raised his hand and shamelessly declared, "If I won back then, I'd either be broke or dead by now. Probably both. I'd be into fast cars, especially Corvettes. I'd spend a lot on fishing gear and then I'd buy one of those big RV buses like John Madden's where I'd hit the road and fish and drink in all 50 states. I'm still a spending fool, but I think I have a better control of it now." Which, of course, he didn't as he was seriously thinking about putting a deposit down on a bright red, 638hp, 6.2 liter V-8 Chevrolet Corvette.

Mike Gearon's reminiscence was foggy. "I know I fantasized about doing or having all sorts of things, but I can't remember anything specific except for one."

Katherine nudged him and said, "I'll bet it had to do with buying me a large diamond ring."

"Kat, I didn't know you thirty-five years ago."

"I know. But you know me now and it's never to late for a large diamond," she teased. "So what's the one thing that stays in your memory?"

"I don't think I ever told you. It sounds silly, but I would have hired someone to drive me everywhere. Any time of day or night. Imagine, never having to drive or look for parking," he said wistfully. "That was my dream. It still is."

Katherine poked him. "Well, it's your dream come true. Don't I do all the driving and parking?"

"In 1977, I was waiting tables in Santa Monica," Duffy recalled. "I always thought that if I won a ton of money, I would do something that was spur-of-the-moment, totally outrageous and really expensive,"

"Like what?" The Redhead asked.

"Well, you know… I, uh… Like I had all sorts of what I thought at the time were creative ideas," he stammered.

The Redhead was not to be put off by his hemming and hawing. "Duffy Hart, I can read you like a financial statement. You had something in mind. Spill it."

"Okay," he acquiesced. "Without packing a thing, not even a toothbrush, I would have flown me and my girlfriend to Paris first class where we would check in at the Ritz. We'd leave our clothes' sizes with the concierge who would then have the best shops in Paris come to our suite and outfit us for a week's stay."

"Who was this girlfriend?" she demanded to know.

"Angie Dickinson."

Walt was undone. Wide-eyed and clearly impressed, he asked, "You dated Angie Dickinson?"

"No, but I used to wait on her pretty regularly. She liked the restaurant I worked in." He looked at Caitlin and explained with an awkward smile, "She was part of the fantasy. You know, like the plane, Paris and the Ritz."

"Well, she's old enough to be your mother," his wife said dismissively while at the same time giving him an affectionate peck on the cheek.

George saw Duffy glance at his watch and decided their short but fascinating visit to 1977 had gone on long enough. If they continued traipsing down memory lane, someone was bound to go off topic and bring up Star Wars and Roots, Elvis dying and certainly the Raiders' Super Bowl win. To that, he said, "Hey, people, I think it's time we return to 2012. Otherwise, we'll be here until midnight." Everyone at the table checked the time.

"Walt," he continued, "you asked if we wanted to sell our share. Debbie and I talked it over and decided we do. It's going to cost more than the Gearon's, though."

"So how much do you want from your winnings?"

"Eight million and you pay our share of Ambrose's cut."

Walt leaned back in his chair, folded his arms and looked at his table mates. "I am going to pretend that there's nothing crazy about what is going on here, even though I know there is. So, Duffy, are you and Caitlin headed to the lottery office with me or are you selling your share, too?"

Duffy and his wife spoke at once. Duffy hushed up, pointing to The Redhead who became their spokesperson. "We want six million and, of course, you pay Ambrose's share."

"At least you guys are willing to take a bigger chunk of the money than the Gearons. I still don't get it, though."

"Walt, are you okay claiming the prize on your own?" The Redhead asked with genuine concern.

"Why wouldn't I be?"

Duffy laughed. "Because, we'd have a real problem if you didn't."

"No problem there," he assured them. "I can handle my fifteen minutes of fame. So what does all this wheeling and dealing add up… Wait. Shouldn't somebody be writing all this down?"

Caitlin raised a hand that held a pen. "Katherine, there's a calculator app on your iPhone, isn't there?"

"There is."

"Okay, we ladies will handle the bookkeeping."

Planning to help, Ambrose suggested, "Now that you are down to the numbers phase of this meeting, why don't I switch places with Mrs. Gearon so you two ladies can deal with this gold-plated crunching."

After the shuffle of chairs, Caitlin asked Mike, "What determines the amount of the cash option?"

"It's the estimated cost of funding the annuity that would pay the winner or winners annually. The lottery people say it's usually somewhere between forty-five and fifty-five percent. I picked fifty."

Caitlin looked down at the array of numbers and said, "Based on that, each share after taxes is $17,625,000. Seeing as we're guesstimating what the true cash option will be, we might as well just round the numbers out to a million. So for discussion's sake, each share is eighteen million."

Upon hearing that, Katherine suddenly began to giggle; a high-pitched, girlish chuckle that had always charmed her husband and now caught everyone's attention. Blushing, she put a hand to her face and said, "I am sorry. The craziness of all this… It just got to me. The last time I worked with numbers, Mike and I were trying to figure the what it would cost us to build a small flagstone terrace. I rounded out numbers then, but this gives new meaning to the practice. It's totally surreal."

"Hey, I got a great stone guy for you," Walt said with enthusiasm. "He's a little weird, though. The company name is The Flagstone Family. They're in RIchmond. He refers to himself as Fred Flagstone and his accountant wife as Wilma. It's silly, I know, but they do know their stuff."

George interrupted, "Let me guess, Barney Rubble and Bam Bam are part of the crew and they all wear caveman coveralls."

"Gentlemen, time's a-wasting," Ambrose warned, draining the last of his Cuban Manhattan. It appeared Duffy was in no hurry to replace it.

The Redhead took over. "All right, here is what I have for you. The Gearons are selling their share for four million, we're selling ours for six and the Crowders are selling theirs for eight. The buyer, who we hope to dear God is Walt, will also pay whatever gift taxes are due as a result of giving us our monies and the full amount of $820,000 owed to Ambrose.

Mike added, "I checked and the maximum gift tax for this year is thirty-five percent with the first five point one million of lifetime gifts exempt from taxes. This could all change in 2013, of course. Best to check with a tax expert on how to handle it."

The Redhead picked it up from there. "So that means if you buy the Gearon's share for four million, you're out about five point two million. For us, the total is eight point one million and for the Crowders a hefty ten point eight. With Ambrose's so-called commission, the grand total is about twenty-five million, more or less."

"So what does that leave me?" Walt asked.

"Are we still rounding off?" Katherine asked as her fingers worked the calculator app on her smartphone. The amount she came up with was $46,880,000.

Caitlin peeked over, read the amount and said to Walt, "Not a bad business day for you, Mr. Gillespie. For a measly twenty-five million, you get your share of eighteen million and what's left of ours. That totals forty-seven million dollars." Leaning back in her chair, she said with a wink, "You should buy the house a round."

Walt's response was a distracted smile. The Gillespie mind was now a disorganized mess of questions and thoughts. Somehow, though, he managed to give voice to one puzzling notion: "I really don't understand you guys. Does claiming the lottery money scare you so much that you're willing to give away millions just so you don't have to show up at the lottery office?"

George was the first to answer. "I can't speak for everyone, Walt, but there are many reasons Debbie and I are doing what we are doing, but this isn't the time to go into all of that. And I might add that the less you know about our views as regards this lottery, the less inclined you'll be to think of us whenever the topic comes up. And once you claim the prize, my friend, it's going to come up a lot."

Mike chimed in, his tone also serious, "One of the conditions of the sale of our shares is an absolute assurance from you that we are never connected in any way with this lottery. Simply put, we can't be part of the story. George is right, Walt. When we leave this restaurant today all any of us have to remember about the luncheon is that we were here to celebrate Ambrose's birthday. Nothing more."

"So who's the biggest fool, I wonder," Walt mused aloud as if he had heard nothing the two men just said. "Is it Ambrose for taking what amounts to be pennies from a multi-million dollar jackpot? You guys for taking just a fraction of what your entitled to? Or me for going it alone as the lottery winner?" Then, as if the money were a burdensome load, he added, "Even if I do come away with forty-seven million."

"Let there be not a fool among us," Mike intoned, thinking something that sounded comically like Shakespeare might lift Walt's reflective and seemingly somber mood. Feeling a scolding nudge from his wife, he left it there.

"Walt, we are all getting what we want," she said emphatically. "There is no one here who feels they're being short-changed. There is certainly no one here who feels dissatisfied with the decision they've made regarding the money. We are all fine." She reached over and put her hand on his arm and added. "I hope you are, too."

"Oh, I am," he assured her. "I'm just trying to make some sense of all this."

"Don't try," advised George.

"Actually, I could use some help," he said in a humbling manner. "In order to keep all of you out of it, I'm going to need a story, and maybe we can also talk about how we manage to..." The plumber suddenly stopped mid-sentence as another thought, a ticklish one this time, bullied its way forward, demanding attention. "You guys know I could stiff you all and there's really nothing you could do about it," he blurted out. "What if I just kept all the money?" He'd asked it in such a friendly, engaging way all manner of evil intent was absent.

"Katherine and I would be out the buck we put into buying the lottery ticket. Other than that, no great shakes," Mike Gearon replied just as congenially. His response was so matter-of-fact, so casual, Walt was convinced the retired broadcaster thought he was just kidding around.

George was just as cool in his response. "I agree with Mike. Life goes on." Then inching closer to the plumber, his eyes fixed on him, George's tone deepened and he said in a playfully threatening manner, "Now, let's suppose that instead of this lottery funny money, you took my NFL pension check. It isn't much but it's mine and I earned it. How would I feel about that? You really don't want know."

"Seeing as I have already put a healthy deposit down on a luxury cruise, I certainly would not take kindly to a greedy grab like that," Ambrose commented, glancing at Duffy to see if one more Cuban Manhattan might come his way.

Walt held his hands up in mock surrender. "Okay, okay. You obviously didn't take me seriously, and that's for the good. Maybe what I should have asked was how do you know you can trust me?"

The table was silent for a moment. Eyes darted back and forth, evidence each of them was trying to fashion some kind of rational response. But what's a rational response when everything about this unusual situation was, to put it bluntly, irrational?

George shifted in his seat. His back was beginning to act up again. He knew the plumber required some kind of answer. Accepting that he had nothing profound to say, he said with a shrug, "That's a good question. To be honest, Walt, I never gave trusting you any thought. I can't speak for the others, but I just assumed from the way everything has been going that trust wasn't even an issue."

Walt shook his head vigorously. "No, no, it's not. I was just... Oh, I don't know, the thought came to me and I had to say something about it."

"Can we trust you, Walt?" The Redhead asked directly.

The plumber's blushed and stammered, "Yes, you can. You certainly can. As I said, it was just one of those crazy thoughts that popped into my head. I mean, think about it. I could really do that. I wouldn't, of course."

Ambrose put his hands up and called for silence. "Walter, you probably now regret bringing the subject up, but you shouldn't. At some point, any one of us was sure to. Now that it's on the table, I would like to offer my thoughts."

"Whether we want to hear them or not." George muttered, giving the professor a gentle poke. "Go ahead. We're all ears as you never fail to entertain."

Ambrose was in no mood to deliver this speech sitting down. Pulling his chair back, he slowly made it to his full height where he took a moment to study his audience. He thought it was a fine group of casual acquaintances who had come to celebrate his eighty-second birthday. It mattered not that the party was just a front. Clearing his throat, he began, "Trust, my friends, is at the core of what we're all about here. I want you to think about its importance. Soon, millions of dollars will change hands and not one of us will have, as they say, signed on any dotted line to insure that it happens as planned or happens at all. That is because there are no lawyers here to draw up long, tedious-to-read contracts that we wouldn't bother to read anyway. Nor have we sought the advice or counsel of those with sound financial instincts and knowledge. I daresay, If they ever learned of this, they probably would scoff at the insane and amateurish way we went about handling such a large amount of money. But the good news is they will never hear of it. So far, the only evidence of this meeting are these sheets of speculative numbers that will be collected from all of you and shredded or torn into tiny little pieces. As it must be, there can be no recorded evidence of this meeting today. That is why trust is so very important. Everything we do or say here depends on trusting each other implicitly. Perhaps it is a naive notion but this blind trust is the only thing that will make this work. Let me finish by saying that I, for one, have complete faith in Walter, as I do the rest of you."

"Hear, hear," George cheered. "The professor is right. Duffy, the man deserves another Cuban Manhattan."

"God bless you, Mr. Crowder." Turning to Duffy, Ambrose whispered, "Maybe one that is a tad smaller than usual?"

"I'll make a real one and you drink what you want."

The Redhead was anxious to get into the nuts and bolts of getting the money and then its eventual distribution. To that, she asked Walt about his need for a story.

"It's been a week since a winner has come forward. I'll probably need to explain that. Not to the lottery officials, but I'm sure I will be interviewed."

Duffy answered while he made Ambrose's drink. "I'm sure you will be. Why not stick pretty close to what happened last Wednesday. That will make it so much easier. You were here drinking with... Oh, don't forget to mention the name Bar OSA on Shattuck Avenue in the heart of the Gourmet Ghetto..."

"I'm sure you'll get a good plug," Mike said, jumping into the discussion. "Duffy's right, though. Tell them you enjoyed a beer and some conversation and then left. On the way home, you heard them talk about the Super Lotto drawing on the radio and decided to play some of your favorite numbers. It's important to remember it wasn't a quick pick. You then put it in your shirt pocket and promptly forgot about it. Tell them you didn't remember it until you went to launder the shirt and found it."

"Should I tell them who I was drinking with?" he asked.

George and Mike looked at one another and shrugged their shoulders.

"I doubt you're going to get asked, but if you are, I don't have a problem with you mentioning us," Mike replied.

"I don't either," George added.

"And what about Dick Clark?"

"What about him? He wasn't there."

"I know he wasn't there. He's dead. You were the one who told us, Gearon," a flustered Walt replied. "What I wanted to know was whether I should mention the Dick Clark Memorial?"

"Sorry, I couldn't resist," Mike said. "Honestly, I don't see the media asking about the specifics of what we talked about, but if they do, remember it's a good story. Just don't tie it into buying the lottery ticket."

George shook his head and spoke up. "Don't listen to him, Walt. With all due respect, Mike, you're a professional cute guy. It's in your nature to be as entertaining as possible whenever there's a camera or microphone around. Hell, even when there isn't," he said, chuckling.

"Guilty as charged, George. What do you suggest he do?"

"Walt, here's how you can reduce your fifteen minutes of fame by a good ten minutes. Be as boring as possible. The media folk who get the assignment to cover a big lottery winner are going to want someone whose enthusiasm borders on hysteria. All the better if he's got a fun story. What they don't want is someone who has the emotions and vocabulary of a crash test dummy."

"I believe I had several of them as students over the years," Ambrose joked.

"George here knows whereof he speaks, Walt," Gearon said. "In his playing days he hated post-game locker room interviews so much that he just dumbed down whenever the reporters came around. It eventually earned him the nickname Clam."

"No one ever called me that to my face, though," George growled. "I'm sure it's in the Guiness Book of Records as having the briefest run as a nickname."

"Clam Crowder," Walt said aloud. "Yeah, I can see why you didn't like it. Anyway, I think I'm going to take your advice. I'm better at being boring than being a chirpy, in-your-face kind of guy."

"Remember now, this will only shorten the time the press or the public will be interested in you," George counseled. "The real challenge will be dealing with your family, friends and acquaintances who will come out of the woodwork to make contact with you. That won't be easy."

"I'm up for that," Walt said with a confident bravado. "Speaking of that, I want you to know I can't tell my wife about any of this."

The Redhead looked confused. "How can you not tell her."

"No, what I I mean is she can't know about any of this," he replied. "She can't ever know about how this all came to be. Look, I love her to death but the reality is Jeannie cannot keep a secret."

Ambrose accepted his second Cuban Manhattan whispering a sincere thank you to Duffy. Before he took his first sip, he asked the plumber, "How will your spouse react when she learns you're only going to see a small portion of what she will consider an historic payout?"

"That won't be a problem. I handle all our finances. Jeannie's never shown any interest in it. Money, taxes, investments... It's all a foreign language to her. Plus, it bores her. All except the spending of it, of course. What money she makes from her job, she keeps in a separate account. If it ever did come up, I would just blame Uncle Sam and taxes."

Duffy put his palms on the table and said, "Okay, I think we've pretty much wrapped this up. What else do we need to know today?"

The Redhead took charge of answering that broad question. "Before we all leave, let's make double sure we all have phone numbers for each other. It's going to take some six to eight weeks before Walt will see any money, so we have plenty of time to get whatever information he will need to wire us our money. Figure out which account you want it deposited in and then make sure Walt has all the proper routing and account numbers."

Ambrose felt it was his duty to officially close their meeting: "It is ten to three. We are done here with room to spare. I want to thank you all for sharing some of these moments with this insufferable fool. I do so appreciate it." Lifting his Cuban Manhattan, he toasted, "Here's to trust."

## CHAPTER 16

# THE UPS AND DOWNS OF SUDDEN WEALTH

Don Meyers shifted in his seat, straightened his back, rolled his neck to lessen the tension, licked his lips and shouted, "Hooowaaa." With made-for-television looks, he was just thirty seconds from the red light on the remote camera cueing him to open Friday's edition of Channel 8's News at Noontime. The early morning and noon news anchor knew that the woman he met the previous night in the St. Regis hotel bar had promised to watch and he wanted to impress. That meant veering off-script on the day's lead story; giving it what he called the Meyers Spin, even though he knew it would have the station's news director tearing his hair out. If he had any.

In their kitchen, Mike and Katherine Gearon had a small flat screen TV that sat eye level on a bookshelf surrounded by cookbooks. While they prepared lunch, they would usually catch ten or so minutes of a hanging-on-for-dear-life soap opera. They enjoyed speculating and sometimes reimagining the preposterous plot lines the show dished out daily. Today, though, they were tuned to Channel 8 for a far more important reason. There had been a news tease that said a lottery winner had finally come forward and their crack news team would have the breaking story. Breaking being the hot adjective on newscasts.

"Good afternoon and welcome to the Friday edition of the News at Noontime. I'm Emmy-winning Don Meyers." Mike wondered how the station engineers managed to squeeze his ego into their tiny TV. "The mystery is finally solved. After a little more than a week, Walter Gillespie, a plumber from El Cerrito has come forward to claim one of the largest jackpots in Super Lotto history. Before we check in with Tiffany Tomara who is at the lottery's Hayward office, let me be the first to welcome Mr. Gillespie into the nation's One Percent Club. As you know, Walter, it's pretty darned exclusive. I wonder if you'll get a congratulatory call from Mitt Romney." With that, Don emitted an ever so subtle chuckle signaling that even if the viewer didn't think it was funny, he thought it was frightfully witty.

On their way back from Sedona to Phoenix several years ago, the Gearons passed a huge billboard advertising a Phoenix TV news team. The larger than life man and woman reminded them of how eerily similar news anchors were, regardless of race, ethnicity, size or gender. They joked that they were all born and bred at a desert ranch just a few miles from the highway they were on. Don's looks and his rather lame ad-lib gave further credibility to that possibility.

"Standing just outside lottery headquarters is Channel 8's Tiffany Tomara. Tiffany, what can you tell us about California's newest rich guy. And remember, if he's single, tell him he can find you on Match.com."

"Thank you, Chuck. I'm here in Hayward outside the California Lottery Office where a plumber by the name of…" Here she looked down at her notes. "…Walter Gillespie of El Cerrito has just been presented with that oversized check the lottery officials like to give winners of large jackpots and this one certainly is that. I was there for the presentation which just wrapped up. I was hoping that..." Tiffany glanced behind her and couldn't believe her luck. There was Walter just feet away. She waved him closer with her microphone and introduced herself. Standing next to her, his girth and height only emphasized the petiteness of the attractive Channel 8 reporter. "First, congratulations, Mr. Gillespie. Tell us in your own words what it must have felt like when you were given that huge check?" Walt rubbed his face and remembered what George had said about being boring. The hell with it, he said to himself. This is too much fun. I'll do it my way. "Well, Tiffany, I think I'm going to have a hard time finding an ATM that will take the check they gave me."

On it went. Walt's responses to Tiffany's questions were funny and well-delivered. The Channel 8 reporter was thrilled as his bravura performance made her look good as well. In a matter of a minute and a half it was over. Tiffany thanked him for sparing the time and then she was off to cover a story in San Jose. What she really wanted to do was head back to the station and kick Don Meyers in the balls.

Turning off the television, Katherine and Mike headed into the dining room for lunch. Katherine was first with her assessment of Walt's performance. "If that's his idea of being boring, I'd love to see him when he's really on. His comment that he was sure his ex-wives were lawyering up was very funny."

"What about the crack he made about leaving it all when he dies to an animal shelter that takes in depressed tortoises? I have to give him credit. He was really amusing," Mike said. "It's a good thing it's Friday. The weekend is a month in the news business. He'll be forgotten by Monday.

"What about social media?" his wife asked.

"I don't know how involved he is on... What do you say? Are you in social media or on social media?" Mike asked.

"Either works for me," his wife replied, not really caring about social media at all.

"I think right now Walt's biggest challenge will be his dealings with family and close friends." Holding up his glass of Newcastle Brown Ale, he added, "Here's to everything working out for everyone, particularly Walt."

Katherine reached across and put her hand on her husband's arm. "I want you to know I am very comfortable with not having to deal with the complications of suddenly having eighteen million dollars. Although, Kevin and Jansis and Caroline and Raf might think otherwise."

Mike put his hand on hers. "We both know the money would always be the elephant in the room. No, Kat, we did the right thing. Look at us as a family. We're happy and our kids are doing just fine. Kevin and Raf with Jansis are making a success out of the brewery and Caroline has a great future in public relations and marketing and she's working with them as well. We know they want children…"

"And I really want grandchildren," Katherine exclaimed. While she now felt comfortable with her children's decision to wait and marry in their mid to late thirties, she realized she'd be left with less time to be the doting grandmother she dreamed of being.

As do I," Mike emphasized, feeling much the same way, perhaps even more so as he was nine years older than Katherine. "And maybe before I'm eighty when I can't knee them."

She gave him a startled look. "Knee them?"

"I don't know what you officially call it. It's where you put a kid on your knee and play bouncy bouncy."

"It's obvious I'm going to have to give you grandparenting lessons."

"I was thinking about how best to deal with this four million we're about to receive," Mike said. "Our investment picture is sound because of Paul's great advice."

"We're going to have to tell him where we got this money."

Paul Farana had been the Gearon's financial manager for almost three decades. He was not only the senior vice-president of a Walnut Creek wealth management firm but he was also one of their closest friends.

"I don't think we have to worry about that. When it comes to client confidentiality, Paul takes his cue from a priest hearing confession. Paul will take our story to his grave," he assured her.

"So what do you suggest we ought to do with it?

"When we get our check, I think we should buy more shares of whatever stocks we currently own and then put some money into CD's. I was thinking that at some point, rather than just leaving a big chunk of cash for the kids when we die, we can borrow a page from what Walt's going to do when he gifts us our money. We can help the kids now with some of it. We'll just explain we are doing well in the market."

"All that sounds fine to me. Now, Mr. Gearon, I also want to do something extravagant and utterly financially wasteful," Katherine said, plopping a large radish from her salad into her mouth.

"Lets wait until until we see the money," Mike cautioned.

The Tiffany Tomara interview was also seen by George and Debbie Crowder whose reaction to Walt's remarks pretty much echoed the Gearon's. George had almost spit his coffee out when the reporter asked Walt why his wife wasn't with him and he answered, "She's at work, Tiffany. We're both going to stay on the job until the lottery's real check clears."

"Debbie, you know I went for eight million with the idea of not only propping up our businesses but also doing something for some of my old NFL colleagues who haven't fared as well as we have."

"How are you going handle that?" she asked.

"I haven't the slightest idea, except that whatever I do will be anonymous," he answered. "Maybe I'll pick Tom Flores' brain.

Anyway, we've got some time to think about it as it's going to be between six and eight weeks before Walt gets a check from the lottery. I assume he won't waste any time sending us ours."

"I just can't believe we're going to have that kind of money" she sighed. "Please, let's go on some kind of fun trip."

"Well, Charley's in Manhattan and Carly's in Santa Monica. So we have free places to stay in those two fun cities," he said with a straight face.

"George, we'll have enough money to stay in a luxury hotel's presidential suite if we want to. We don't have to bunk in with our children," she laughed. She knew, though, that she'd married a closet ascetic.

"Just kidding. How about Hawaii? Let's have a family Thanksgiving on Maui. The kids will love it."

"Won't they think we're being a little too extravagant?" she asked. "We're not going public with the fact that we're multi-millionaires, you know."

"I'll tell them I earned the money at a card show."

"They know you better than that," she laughed. "George 'Clam' Crowder at a card show! That's like John Madden going on Dancing With The Stars."

"Ooh, that paints a really bad picture," George remarked. "Listen, as to the kids thinking we're extravagant, don't worry about it. Not that much is going to change as to our lifestyle. We're not moving to a really pricey house or buying two expensive cars. You won't see us purchasing new jewelry or updating our wardrobes... All that's noticeable stuff. But a once in a lifetime Thanksgiving getaway? No, I don't think the kids will see that as anything more than Mom and Dad being generous."

Debbie gave her husband a sideways look. "As to that list of noticeable things, my dear; houses and cars I get, but you're headed into dangerous territory putting jewelry and clothes in that category"

Ambrose Dowling remained blissfully unaware that Walt had staked his claim on that Friday, April 27th, 2012. Instead, after a morning devoted to one of Anthony Trollope's heftier fictions, he took himself downtown to Nordstrom department store where he treated himself to a double-breasted tuxedo and accompanying accessories. Inspired by the formal dinners of Trollope's more well-off families, the professor had decided that while on his luxury cruise, he was going to dress for dinner every night even though there were only two designated formal evenings. He was proud of the fact that not only could he tie his own bow tie, but he was a master at making the it look appropriately imperfect. At the time he had no idea his formal attire would cause single, elderly ladies on board to think he was a ship's dance host.

Duffy and The Redhead heard the news of the lottery winner while en route to Bar OSA from their home high up in the north Berkeley hills. When they had time they would do an on-line search for more news. For now, though, thanks to the privacy their van afforded them, they were free to talk openly about it as once in the restaurant conversations involving personal matters would be impossible.

"You really think we can buy the building?" The Redhead asked while applying what little makeup she required.

"Oh yeah," he shot back. "We'll have more than enough. In fact, we'll have enough so that if we have to get into a bidding war with whoever it is that also wants the building, we'll be ready. It's a dream come true, Caitlin. Do you know how many restaurant owners own their own premises? Probably a handful. We're very lucky."

"Everything happened so fast. I mean we made that decision to take six million just like that," she said, snapping her fingers. "You know why we did it?"

Duffy glanced at his attractive passenger and cracked, "Because we're a pair of loony tunes."

"Well, one of us is," she teased.

"So why did we do it?"

"Because that's what Ambrose, the Gearons and George did. We had no choice as I'm the one responsible for them accepting a lesser amount of money."

"Caitlin, what on earth are you talking about?" he asked while parking in the yellow zone in front of Bar OSA.

"Remember when we all started talking about that big lottery and I said something about you guys taking two and a half million and throwing the rest into a charity pot of sorts?"

"I remember. We had a good laugh and decided we'd call ourselves the Dicks. But that was just innocent bar chatter."

"And then in my typically oafish way, I told the guys they were old and didn't have that much time left to spend all that money and that there were better things to do with it," she said. Her chagrin was evident. "You see, I may have indirectly influenced them into taking what they perceived to be a more reasonable amount of money given their age."

Duffy turned in his seat to face her. "Caitlin, I think we learned there were far more reasons than just age that went into their decision making. Look at it this way, perhaps, in some strange way, you inspired them."

The Redhead's eyes widened and she exclaimed, "Inspired them. Criminy sakes, who inspires people to lose millions of dollars?"

"Uh, how about someone who sells money-losing wineries to very rich people."

As she always did before heading into the restaurant, Caitlin flipped the visor down for one last look in the mirror. She passed her always tough inspection and gave herself permission to get on with her day. Then it was time to inspect her partner and she was just as unsparing. "You need a haircut, darling. And that shirt has seen better days."

"Maybe I'll get one of those four hundred dollar cuts you talked about yesterday and get fitted for a bespoke suit."

"They won't let you back in Berkeley," she laughed.

"Before we go in, Caitlin, let me say one more thing about this crazy but wonderful situation we find ourselves in."

"Sure."

"I read somewhere that sudden wealth is no real solution for unhappiness."

"But we're not unhappy."

He held up a hand. "I know we're not. Let me finish my thought, please. It seems to me that when you start thinking about sudden wealth, you realize there's no limitation as to what it can and cannot do. The way I see it is sudden wealth is a powerful intoxicant and we, by that I mean Ambrose, the Gearons and the Crowders, have somehow managed to curb its seductive powers and deal with it in an insanely sane way. From the very beginning with Ambrose's decision to take only what he wanted, we took charge and decided we would manage sudden wealth rather than having it manage us. And in a very large way, that conversation you started nine days ago influenced all of us. So there's no need to feel anything but good about what you did."

The Redhead leaned across and gave her husband a peck on the cheek. "You're sweet, especially when you make sense. I even understood that insanely insane bit. I noticed, though, that you didn't include Walt."

"Ah, there's the mystery element. Depending on what Mr. Gillespie decides to do once the lottery has showered him with millions, we'll find out if sudden wealth is really in our future or if you and I have to deal with our rent going up here."

"If it's the latter, I'll kill him," she growled as only a redhead can.

Duffy leaned across, kissed Caitlin's reddening cheek and then leaned further to open her door. "And just how to you plan to take him out?"

Exiting the van, she turned around and winked at her husband. "I'd hire Ambrose to talk him to death."

## CHAPTER 17

# THE SNEAKER WAVES OF INSTANT WEALTH

The change in Walter and Jeannie Gillespie's life was not subtle or evolving. It resembled more a sneaker wave; catching each one unaware and challenging them to find some way to contain their panic and figure a way out. Jeannie was the first to be swept up; the wave engulfing her at work in the middle of that fateful Friday afternoon. On an average day, in the heavily scented cosmetic's section, her co-workers and she would gab on and on about such scintillating topics as hair-coloring, filler versus surgery, yoga versus spinning, reality TV, shoes and men, particularly those who sported designer stubble faces and waxed chests. Soon after her husband's noontime appearance on television, though, the topic and tone of their conversations changed drastically. Almost to a number, those who engaged her first congratulated her on winning so much money. Then, after asking if she was going to continue working, they would proceed to describe in detail some nasty crisis that, as they carefully explained, only a ready influx of cash would remedy. These predicaments were varied; exorbitant daycare costs, medical bills, a relative's expensive rehab, credit card debt, a car that conked out. The list seemed endless. A caring person, Jeannie expressed sincere sympathy when she could and, because she always had a ready reserve of it, empathy when needed. Neither comforted nor assuaged the person to whom she was listening. Inevitably, they would express disappointment or in some cases outright anger that Jeannie did not offer to open her soon-to-be fattened purse to help out. After two hours of this, she decided that spraying people's wrists with a floral scented sample was not in her future. She would have done the right thing and given formal notice had her manager not been the one with the biggest financial need and the angriest reaction. Instead, she left an hour early with no intention of ever returning.

Walt's sneaker wave waited for him in his hilltop house in El Cerrito. It came in the form of his sister's husband, Salvatore Romagna. Soon to see the last of his fifties; the swarthy, wavy-haired man was shaped by too much pasta, fettuccine con vongole to be exact. The longtime manager of a big box sporting goods store in Hayward was slouched on the brown leather sofa in Walt's media room with a can of Pabst Blue Ribbon that he'd helped himself to. When he heard the front door open, he yelled, "Hey, Wally, get your ass in here."

His brother-in-law's loutish summons infuriated him. He hated that nickname and he knew Sal knew that. Plus, he didn't like being ordered around in his own home. What he needed now was time to collect himself. "Yeah, I'll be right there. Have to hit the john," he barked.

He found Jeannie in their bedroom. He knew she'd be there hiding from their guest who'd made himself at home in their den. Fully clothed, she was stretched out on the bed. Walt stared at her and realized she could have been swaddled in an army drab Snuggie and she'd still look incredibly sexy.

"When did he get here?" he asked, bending down and kissing her on the forehead.

"About ten minutes ago," she said. "God, he's such a sleaze. With his Mafia-wannabe act and his touchy-feely ways, I just can't... Look, I know he's family but I can't be in the same room with him." Frustrated and feeling imprisoned in her own home, she folded her arms and sighed. "Anyway, I told him I had a headache which is partly true. I had an awful afternoon at work. As it turns out, it was my last day there."

"I'll get rid of him and then you can tell me all about your afternoon. After that maybe we can get touchy-feely."

"Oh, by the way, I did as you instructed and let all calls go to voicemail. There were so many, I finally turned the ringer volume down on all the phones."

Walt knew from experience there was a way of shortening Sal's visits and that was to remain tight-lipped. His brother-in-law loved talking to or at someone but he abhorred listening. Thus, once he had had his say which was always gruffly delivered, he usually left without so much as a push or a prod simply because he had no interest in what you had to say back to him. The key was to let him talk. By tossing in a few nods and grunts; making sure they were all non-committal gestures so he couldn't get a firm yes or no about anything, his sister's husband usually went on his way. Even so, there was a part of Walt who wanted to storm into his den, rip the beer can from his pudgy hand, pull the short, jowly-faced man off the sofa and frogmarch him out to his car. However, he dearly loved his sister and would do anything to keep the peace in the family. This time, though, what awaited him in his den would put that commitment to the test.

Sal had draped one leg over the arm of Walt's prized leather sofa. Holding the can of beer out to welcome him, he said with a well-practiced wise guy accent, "Hey, Wally boy, you did well by the family today. I mean really fucking well. Looked good on TV, too." Putting the beer on the table, he rubbed his hands together. "So, what are we going to do with all this money? And how soon are we going to get it."

Sal's use of first person plural didn't shock or surprise him. He fully expected this kind of performance from him. With his back to his brother-in-law, Walt fished around in the small fridge which housed a wide variety of craft beers for something suitable. Picking a bottle of Big Daddy IPA, he debated drinking it or hitting Sal over the head with it. Remembering he didn't want to confront him, he just shrugged his shoulders, took a sip and muttered something unintelligible.

Walt didn't have to worry about an extended visit this time as Sal surprised him by announcing he had to leave soon as he was wanted back at the store and according to him they couldn't function without him. Taking a last sip from his can of beer, he put it down and ran his hand through his thick mop of hair. "I only dropped by to offer my help in dealing with this new world of high finance you now have find yourself in. I know you got a couple of years on me, Wally, but I see myself as the true patriarch of the family and in that capacity, I can help you out when it comes to seeing everybody in the family is taken care of and they don't run roughshod over you." Wasn't that exactly what Sal was doing, Walt thought. "Anyway, I know a great young CPA in Pinole, a fucking whiz. Oh man, what he can do with taxes and shit. You just gotta forget his age."

Walt put his beer down and made for the door. "Thanks for dropping by, Sal. Tell Margaret I'll give her a call. You know, I don't think I've seen or heard from you since you had trouble with your dishwasher connection. When was that? Early January?

The less than subtle slight went right over his head. With a struggle, he lifted himself off the sofa and approached Walt. Putting his hands on Walt's shoulders, he looked up at the much taller man and smiled widely. Oh jeez, he's going to kiss me, Walt thought. Instead, Sal took an opened hand and gave him an affectionate slap. "Some good times ahead, Wally boy," he gushed, heading out to the driveway to get his car. "Hey, by the way, how's my son doing? I hardly see him."

"Fino's a good plumber."

Sal's laugh was derisive. "I hope so. You'd have to be a real dumb ass to be a bad one." These were his parting words.

Angry and confused, Walt stood stock still in his driveway, looking out at the tall buildings of San Francisco and the green hills of Marin in the distance. It was a view he never took for granted but now it was a distraction. Even so, he decided to stay locked in place for a few minutes to ruminate on what had just happened and what it portended. The thought that his extended family might feel entitled to a share of his winnings as Sal had suggested prompted him to take a quick inventory of relatives. On the Gillespie side, locally there was only his sister, Margaret. He had an aging aunt in Minneapolis and two cousins back east somewhere but he wasn't sure where exactly as they were not close and didn't stay in touch. What there was of Jeannie's family lived in Chico. They consisted of her mother and her mother's sister and husband. That's all to the good, he thought. The downside was he was thick with in-laws past and present thanks to his two previous marriages and Margaret choosing Salvatore Romagna for better or worse.

Interestingly, Walt's preoccupation with a sudden influx of money and potentially problematic kin had put his hypochondria on hold. Since winning the lottery, he'd only entertained one thought regarding his health. On the drive back from the lottery office, experiencing an unexplained tingling in his left foot, he considered how his newfound wealth might help tame his on-going anxiety about his state of well-being. He decided he'd make appointments to get an MRI, PET Scan and a CAT Scan just as soon as he could. He might even throw in a blood, stool and urine test and while he's at it get his eyes checked and his teeth cleaned and X-rayed. Then it dawned on him that there was the inevitable three day wait for test results, and no matter what they revealed, they would not take into account any possible deteriorating changes to his health that might pop up in that seventy-two hour period. As a result, he'd be to out thousands of dollars, yet still wondering if some awful disease had suddenly taken seed somewhere in his body. Now, standing there in his driveway, he was weighted down with other burdensome thoughts and unable to appreciate the lightness of being free of his hypochondria. This was his state of mind when he saw Fino driving up his street.

They sat in the same room where Fino's father tried to take over the handling of Walt's finances. Unlike Salvatore, Fino sat straight with his hands on his lap. He was obviously uncomfortable. When Walt looked at him, the young man gave him a self-conscious grin. Walt was rightly suspicious as he knew his nephew was a dedicated petulant scowler. He'd never seen even the slightest glimmer of a grin.

"So what brings you around?" Walt asked with a wariness that it was probably for the same reason his father dropped by unannounced.

"You said I could." Checking the time on his smartphone, Fino chuckled, "And I'm right on time for a change."

His nephew's civil demeanor had him stymied. Besides never smiling, a chuckle would be out of the question. Further, he sensed no hint of hubris in his nephew's voice, mood or movement. To top it all off, there wasn't one fuck in those two sentences. Something was wrong and Walt needed to know: "Okay, Fino, what's going on? You aren't your usual surly self."

"I'm in love, Uncle Walt," he said softly.

"You want a drink?" he asked. "I definitely need one."

"Sure," he said with enthusiasm. His uncle had never offered him a drink before. "A beer, please. Doesn't matter what kind."

For the second time, Walt found himself digging into his small fridge. He'd only taken one sip of the beer he had opened when Fino's father was there. This one he'd drink.

Jeannie, aware Sal was gone, had come downstairs. She walked in just as her husband was handing his nephew a Drake's 1500.

He had an Anchor Steam which he took over to a matching leather armchair. Seeing Jeannie, he bounced up and returned to the fridge and pulled out a bottle of French rose that was a favorite of hers. "Will you have a glass?"

"I'd love it," she said, noticing that Fino had risen when she came in the room. Like Walt, she was immediately suspicious of this gentlemanly action. "Hi, Fino. Are you all right?"

"He's in love," Walt explained.

Jeannie took a seat on the sofa a distance from Fino. She was still in ill-fitting, baggy jeans with frayed cuffs, scuffed running shoes and an extra large sweatshirt that had seen better days.

Glancing over at Fino, she said, "So, what do you think?"

"What do I think about what?" he asked.

"You don't know what happened to Walter?"

"No, I don't. Is everything all right?" He turned and looked at Walt. "Are you okay?" he asked with genuine concern.

"Yeah, I'm fine. More than fine." Still doubting Fino's transformation, he said, "We'll get to me soon enough. Right now, I want to know more about this great change that's come over you."

Fino was delighted to be first up because that's the way it is when you're in love and Serafino Romagna was just that; deeply, madly, insanely in love.

"So how long have you..."

Fino put a hand up and stopped his uncle in mid-sentence. "Let me start from the beginning. Last Friday I went to this rave with my roommate, RIco, at the Craneway Pavilion in Richmond. It was pretty typical. Most of the crowd was high on Ecstasy, dancing with themselves, drinking Red Bull and Grey Goose and generally being lovey-dovey and brainless. I was getting a drink when I bumped into this girl who had just gotten a bottled water. I checked her wrist to see if she was under twenty-one what with her buying something non-alcoholic. Turns out she was twenty-five, stone-cold sober, bored to tears with the whole scene and the most beautiful woman in the place, if not the world. At least to me."

Walt laughed.

"So what happened?" Jeannie asked eagerly, loving stories of budding romance.

Fino leaned forward and continued. "We went outside and talked for awhile. I don't know. We just hit it off. I drove there with Rico and he knows if I'm not around to leave at a designated time, it means I got lucky. I never have. Gotten lucky, that is, so I wondered if he'd end up looking for me. Anyway, I found him and told him I was getting a ride from a somebody I just met. I thought he was going to go up on the stage and holler, "Hey, Fino's finally getting laid.' So anyway, she has this new little Fiat and we left and went to Daimo in Berkeley and had bowls of their Wow wonton soup and just kept talking and..." Fino leaned back and sighed, obviously reliving moments from that special evening. "Anyway, she drove me back to my apartment and we agreed to meet later that day and go to the A's game. I've seen her almost every night this week."

"Does this love of your life have a name?" Walt asked.

"Kaya Hamada," he answered. "Born and raised in Berkeley. She went to Cal and now teaches third grade at Marin Elementary in Albany. She's got a nice flat she rents just a few blocks from the school. You know something, I never thought I would be jealous of a bunch of third graders," he commented.

"I don't understand."

"They get to spend more time with Kaya than I do."

"Oh, you do have it bad."

"She has such an exotic name," Jeannie said.

"She's Japanese, Irish, English and a splash of French," he explained. Fino looked at them both and judging from their expressions, sensed what they were thinking. "I, uh, get the feeling you're wondering how I seem to have done a one-eighty."

"That's a good way of putting it," Jeannie responded. "The Serafino Romagna we know is rude, loves the F-word and is extremely arrogant. Now here you are all sweetness and light."

"This is not an act," he insisted, pointing at himself. "The other Fino was the act. It started with me playing the part of a loud-mouthed jerk because it pleased my father. He was my first and my last bully. It sorta toughened me up."

This did not sit well with Walt and Fino could tell from his angry expression that he was concerned about his sister. "Hey, Uncle Walt, the only part of my father's body that gets a workout is his mouth. Physically, he's a pushover. I doubt he ever got in a fight in his life. He gets by with a lot of swagger and bluster. The truth of it is he'd never raise a hand to anybody, especially my stepmom. He worships the ground she walks on."

"So it was verbal bullying?"

"Yeah, but when you're a kid that's still pretty impacting. That's why I became a kind of feisty, in-your-face guy in school. It was a protection. By the time you hired me, it was pretty well ingrained. Right after junior college, I got an apartment with Rico and we started hanging out together. Both of us found this louche behavior still worked as a good way to disguise our insecurities."

"Louche?" Walt exclaimed. "Where'd you pick up a word like that?"

"I read a lot," he answered. "Anyway, I am not, as Aunt Jeannie said, all sweetness and light. I'm really an insecure, nice guy who has found a terrific lady" Fino took a sip of his beer and asked mischievously, "So, are you two a little homesick for the old Fino?"

They both laughed, appreciating the positive change in their nephew. Walt pointed to his wife to give Fino an answer and sat back to enjoy his beer.

"Fino, even the old you can't come close to livening things up the way Walter did this morning," she replied, feeling more relaxed about the young man who before this meeting would just stand around ogling her.

"That sounds X-rated," he joked. "So what happened?"

"I can't believe you don't know. Don't you ever listen to the news or watch TV?"

"Not when my boss has me on a job that takes up most of the day. Don't tell me Uncle Walt did something that went viral?"

"I don't know how viral, but I was a big news story today," Walt boasted. "I'm sure the press conference will be on all the local TV evening news."

"Jeez, what did you to?"

He was glad for the opportunity to rehearse again what would become the story. It was pretty much word for word what he had told Jeannie before going to the lottery office. Missing in the tale were names like Dowling, Hart, Crowder and Gearon. There were known only as some guys at the bar. He did, though, lay it on a little thick with the Dick Clark story.

Through out the telling, Fino sat there with his eyes wide and his mouth opened. When Walt wrapped it up, his nephew just sat there quietly as if in shock. After a time, he said, "I don't know much about lotteries. How much will you get?"

"I won't know until I get a check and taxes are paid. They say it will take at least six to eight weeks. Whatever it is, it is a hell of a lot of money," Walt explained cooly.

"God, you must be hearing from everybody and his brother," he remarked.

"The lottery people recommended we let everything go direct to voicemail for awhile. We're doing that. We also turned the ringer volume down on our cells. They suggested we change phones and I'm doing that tomorrow. They give you all kinds of good advice including how to interview lawyers and CPA's. They said the press conference I did was a good thing to do because it gets the press interest taken care of in one shot.

"I'm sure lost in those voicemails are several from my father. I'm surprised he hasn't shown up here."

"He just left," Jeannie replied, her disgust evident.

Fino shook his head. "I should have known he was here by what you have on. No doubt he rushed over to tell you about the big plans he has for spending your money."

"You're pretty much right on," Walt remarked, checking his watch. "Anyway, you said you came by to ask me something. What's on your mind"

Fino cleared his throat. "Actually, it's about money."

"So I'm now about to get hit up by another Romagna," Walt said, angry with himself that he'd fallen for Fino's nice guy act.

"What? No! I don't want your money," he insisted, his face reddening. "You won the lottery and you can do whatever you want with it. That's not what I came here for."

"Then what did you come here for?"

"A raise," he muttered. "I came to ask for a raise."

"A raise," Walt mumbled as he rose from his easy chair and began pacing.

"Hey, Uncle Walt, a lot has happened to you today," Fino said abruptly. "Maybe this isn't a good time. Why don't we put this off until you can deal with it with a clear head."

Walt returned to his leather easy chair. Settling in, he stared at his nephew and realized they may well have an ally in Fino; someone who could be invaluable in dealing with his extended family. Walt knew, though, that like Jeannie, the young man must forever remain in the dark about how his lottery win actually came to be. Scheming was not one of the plumber's strong suits. In fact, he had a profound distaste for it. But this all started with a dodgy plan and it now seemed like scheming and maneuvering just goes hand in hand with the acquisition of instant wealth. He was beginning to wonder if the other partners in this subterfuge got the better deal even though he earned many more millions of dollars.

"Yeah, that's a good idea, Fino," he said. "But I promise we'll talk about that raise soon."

Fino stood and addressed both of them: "I'm really happy for both of you. I mean that. Hey, you know what you two ought to do? Take a trip. Go somewhere and don't tell anyone where you are. Uncle Walt, I can look after the business. Let things cool down. Of course, my father might issue an all points bulletin for you, but fu..."

Walt smiled. "I agree. Fuck him."

Perhaps it was a combination of his distaste of scheming and being tired that lead Walter to believe his reformed nephew had an excellent idea.

## CHAPTER 18

# THE PARTNERS ARE SUMMONED

Anyone out and about in Berkeley on the first day of May faced an unseasonably chilly fifty-three degrees. With cloudy skies and pesky winds, scarves of every material, design and color were wrapped around necks of varying sizes and conditions. Because scarves were also a local fashion statement, these necks would have been swaddled in them even if it had been sunny and seventy-five. Minnesotans would have had a good laugh.

It was chilly enough that Duffy Hart left the front windows of Bar OSA closed. As a result of that and having had a roomful of luncheon diners, the restaurant was warm and inviting. It was also empty which was fortunate as Walt in a moment of mild panic over the weekend called everyone requesting they meet up on Tuesday at three. By the time he arrived, Mike Gearon, George Crowder and Ambrose Dowling were already huddled together at the Inbetweener's end of the bar chatting about Obama's chances at a second term; something they all wanted to see happen. They had yet to be served as Duffy was busy toasting his kitchen and wait staff with small shots of Patron Silver tequila. It had been a busy lunch and this was his customary way of telling his crew they did a good job. Returning to the bar, he spotted Walt taking the furthest barstool.

"Hey, everybody, the big lottery winner has deigned to enter our humble establishment," Duffy announced cheerily. "I'd say the least he can do is buy the house a drink. Hell, he can buy the house if he wants. Or maybe this block of Shattuck Avenue."

Like a loggerhead sea turtle, Walt's head grew smaller, retreating further into his thick wool scarf. An Oakland A's knit cap was pulled down over most of his forehead. "Shit, Duffy, that isn't funny."

"If you haven't noticed, except for those three not so big spenders you're sitting next to, Bar OSA is empty," he said with a sweep of his arm to emphasize its absence of paying diners and drinkers.

"Yeah, whatever," he mumbled as he unwrapped his scarf and removed his A's cap. Running his hand over his bristly crewcut, he greeted the others, "So, how's everybody doing?"

Always ready with a response, Ambrose, who sat next to him, patted Walt's arm and said, "I see you are in mufti."

"I don't know what the hell you're talking about, but that's par for the course," he huffed. Picking up his scarf, he asked, "Are you talking about this?"

"No, Mr. Gillespie, that is a scarf. In your case, though, it does play a part," Ambrose replied. "Mufti describes the plain clothes one dons when their job or profession requires them to normally wear a uniform. You are obviously minus your Gillespie Plumbing getup. Thus, you are in mufti. Weren't you on the job today?"

"No, and not because I didn't want to be," he pouted.

George leaned forward. "For someone who just won countless millions of dollars, you look like you just came from putting your dog down."

Walt was more grizzled than usual. While he had paid no attention to what he was wearing, one couldn't solely judge him by that as the thrown together look, like year-round scarves, was Berkeley-chic. It was his general pallor and tired, red eyes that gave him away.

After everyone had chimed in on his wayward appearance and expressed concern over it, George spoke up again: "I'm guessing it has been pretty crazy since you made your television debut which, by the way, was very entertaining. Obviously, you decided my advice of being disappointingly boring wasn't worth heeding."

Walt looked over at him and grinned. "You're beginning sound like Ambrose."

Before Walt could explain the spiraling madness of his existence, Duffy approached the group holding a bottle of Agrapart & Fils champagne in one hand while somehow managing five champagne flutes in the other. "Walt, that was a very nice plug you gave us on TV. Our business picked up over the weekend all thanks to you. But I have to say many of the new diners and drinkers were only here in the hopes of running into you and your money."

Remembering the bar owner's suggestion that he buy the house a round, Walt pointed at the champagne bottle and said, "You aren't sticking me with the bill for that?"

"What? This bottle of seventy dollar bubbly? I wouldn't think of it. I just thought we all ought to celebrate your good fortune." Then he mouthed silently, "And ours, too."

The champagne poured and distributed, they all toasted the now obscenely wealthy plumber from El Cerrito. Anyone witnessing this celebration would never know that all of them were multi-millionaires thanks to Ambrose's mistaken purchase of a Super Lotto ticket. They hid their jubilation well. Make no mistake, though, they were all neck deep in euphoria.

"Thanks for the champagne, Duffy," Walt mumbled, but not unappreciatively.

Mike Gearon got them back on track. "Like the others, I'm curious to know why you called us here today, but I'm also curious about how it's been going for you these last four days."

Walt ran a hand over this mouth, took a deep breath, exhaled slowly and then emitted a soft "Oh, man. It's been like totally crazy. Our home phone voicemail is full and it's mostly relatives and close friends. We haven't called anybody back yet except my sister. My company phones are useless. They're crammed with messages from charities, financial services companies, investment firms, inventors… Shit, I can't name them all. There was even a so-called seer who said I wouldn't live to see the next sunrise unless I wired her five thousand dollars. One guy wanted me to fix a second floor leak in his house for free because now that I won the lottery, I don't need money. At least he called with a plumbing problem. E-mail is another issue."

"Are you on Facebook?" Mike Gearon asked.

"No, but Jeannie is. She uses her maiden name, though."

"Don't even think about going anywhere near it," Mike urged while the others agreed with a nod of their heads.

"No fear of that," he replied. "Right now, Jeannie and I are living like a couple of hermits. This is my first time out since Friday. Do you know in that short space of time I have only had face-to-face dealings with three people and they were all lights out weird. First my sister's husband wasted no time in chasing me down. In my own home, in so many words, he congratulates me for winning the money for the family. He likes to use the word family the way the mafia does. Then he goes on to say he will take charge of seeing how it's spent and distributed. No sooner does that asshole leave than his son, Fino, turns up."

"Isn't that the nephew you warned us to keep an eye on if anything odd should happen to you?" George asked.

His question prompted a warm smile from Walt. "Yeah, but it turns out Fino is okay. In fact, he's more than okay. It's a long story for another time, but trust me, he's someone I can depend on. Maybe the only one, excepting you guys, of course."

"You haven't told him about…" Duffy began to ask.

"Jeez, no, not even Jeannie," he exclaimed, slightly offended the bar owner might not trust him to keep his mouth shut.

"What about your third encounter?" a curious Ambrose asked.

"You know the homeless guy selling the Street Sheet out in front of Peet's?"

"There's a bunch of them," Ambrose said. "I know them all."

"This is the thin, white guy with a grey beard and a red bandanna."

"That's Eager Eddie. He works the neighborhood. A talkative guy."

"I walked by him on the way here and gave him a dollar. I've given him money before and he knows me. Anyway, he takes the dollar and then reads me the riot act for not giving him more. As I walked away, he's waving the dollar at me and shouting, 'This is chicken shit, man.'"

"All in all, Walt, it sounds par for the course," Mike said. "Katherine and I have a financial advisor who has a client who won a big lottery. While he won't go into detail about him, he did tell me he'd been really harassed early on but eventually things settled down."

"That's why I wanted to talk to you all today." Before he continued, he first glanced behind him at a bustling Shattuck Avenue. "Look, this place isn't going to stay this quiet much longer."

Duffy laughed. "I certainly hope not."

Confident they were out of earshot from Elena and the kitchen crew, he began to explain in a hushed tone why he called them all together. "First off, I want to let you guys know that Jeannie and I are disappearing for awhile. We're leaving as soon possible. We don't know how long we'll be gone, but we are definitely getting the hell out of here. What I need is a recommendation for someone who knows their way around a lot of money. Somebody who can handle everything; wills, trusts, taxes, investments and, of course, seeing that you guys get your share of the money. I don't know anyone like that. I have a bookkeeper who's been with me for more than twenty years but she'd have a stroke if she had to deal with the kind of money we're talking about. If one of you has somebody you totally trust and you think they could take me on as a client, I'd like to talk to them before we go. Oh, one more thing: I want somebody who plays by the book. No tricks or dodgy stuff. None of that kind of bullshit. You know anybody like that?"

Mike wasn't shy about recommending his financial advisor. "I think I have just the guy. He's a former lawyer. His name is Paul Farana and he's a senior vice-president with PHE Financial in Walnut Creek. I can't say enough good things about him."

George Crowder looked at Mike with disbelief. "You're a client of the Beacon Deacon? So are Debbie and I."

"I never heard him called that before."

George took an almost ladylike sip of the champagne. "Its kinda silly. Farana is Italian for... Actually it's Sicilian and it means torch or beacon. As you probably know, Paul is really active with his parish church and he's a strong supporter of De La Salle where his son, Robbie, played football. I sometimes lend a hand with the team during the season, so I got to know them both. Anyway, a couple of years ago, I dubbed him the Beacon Deacon. I don't think he likes it so that's why you probably haven't heard it."

"Would you agree Paul is the go-to guy for Walt?" Mike asked.

"Absolutely. I can't think of anyone better," he replied. "He's as straight arrow as they come. And he's used to working with wealth. I'll bet you and I are his two poorest clients."

"Not in a few weeks," Mike responded. Just saying that made him feel good.

Duffy had been listening with keen interest. While The Redhead handled the restaurant with an acumen that would make any business owner envious, she lacked investment know-how as did he. Before Walt could reply, he spoke up. "If he's all you say he is, The Redhead and I would like to meet with him. We could certainly use him."

That was all the convincing Walt needed. He asked how soon they could set up a meeting. George waved his smartphone in the air to signal he'd get right on it. Deciding he'd take the call outside, he slowly and a little painfully lifted himself off the barstool and shuffled toward the door. While he was walking out, he asked Ambrose if he was interested in talking to Paul.

"Thank you, Mr. Crowder, but at this point in my life, investing long term and buying green bananas are two things I pass on."

"Hey, none of us are into long term either, but I understand," George shot back. "Oh hi, Jan, is Paul in?" he shouted into the phone when the PHE receptionist answered. "Sure, I can hold."

George's news that Paul would meet with them in his Walnut Creek office the following morning at ten lightened Walt's spirits considerably. He thought he might now be able to celebrate his good fortune rather than constantly fret over it. Rubbing his hands together, he exclaimed, "Enough of this bubbly stuff. Duffy, I'm buying whatever these guys want to drink or eat."

Whatever needed to be said in confidence had been said and now the men, armed with cocktails of their choice, slipped easily into what they referred to as bar banter. Duffy Hart was a fan of this kind of chatter; feeling there was always a chance something of value could come out of it. For that reason he was not shy about taking the lead. "Can I tell you guys about something that's been bugging me lately?"

Mike pointed to him standing there and quipped, "It's your bar and you do have the floor."

"I will skip a witty reply to your sarcasm, Mike, and get right to it," he said, swatting his friend's arm with his ever-present bar towel. "For some reason, whenever I don't see a regular for awhile, my first thought is they may have died. Why do I entertain such a morbid thought? They could just be traveling or entertaining friends or family. Heck, they might just be taking a break from eating tapas. The point is..."

Suddenly, he felt a warm breathe in his left ear as two familiar arms wrapped around him. The Redhead and Katherine Gearon had been enjoying tea in her office while the rest had dealt with Walt. Deciding to join them, the attractive pair had quietly approached while Duffy was expounding on guests and their possible demise.

"So my husband has found yet another way of bringing up his current favorite topic," Caitlin said, having cut him off mid-sentence with an affectionate hug from behind.

"And what topic is that, my dear Mrs. Hart?" Ambrose asked.

"He thinks Bar OSA has too many older customers. He's convinced that by 2015 or so anyone who is still dining with us will not have enough teeth in their mouths to chew their way through a paella."

"I could always buy some blenders so we can make paella smoothies," Duffy suggested.

"That is a thoroughly disgusting thought."

"You could be the first restaurant to offer valet parking for wheeled walkers," George kidded.

Katherine had joined Mike at the bar and they laughed at their friends' exchange. "Duffy, you have a ton of young people coming into Bar OSA," Katherine said.

"I know, but it's the older gang that are regulars. The young ones are flighty and will skip off to the next tapas bar that opens," he replied, knowing this wasn't going in the direction he wanted it to.

So it was no surprise to him that Ambrose would come to his rescue. "Ahem, gentlemen and ladies," he began. "As one of those senior regulars, allow me to submit that Mr. Hart's concerns are legitimate. However, they have nothing to do with an imminent business problem. He is simply thinking the way most people do when dealing with an older person who suddenly vanishes from their lives for a period of time. They automatically suspect the worst. Their first thought is that person must have shuffled off this mortal coil when, in fact, they might just be taking a cruise to an exotic Polynesian island with a shipload of vegan nudists."

"I think I'd prefer to be dead," George said.

Looking over her husband's shoulder, The Redhead watched as a brand new Mercedes Benz convertible pulled into the yellow zone in front of the restaurant. "Oh, now that is a good looking car," she blurted out.

"I like white cars. Of course, knowing car people, the color is probably known as Arctic Snow or Holy Communion White," Mike Gearon joked. "Anyway, you're right. It is a very handsome car."

Duffy spun around to look. "That, my friends, is a pricey Mercedes Benz E350 Cabriolet. You have good taste in cars, darling, just like you do in husbands."

Walt, whose back was to the window, shifted around in time to see his brother-in-law's head rise above the car roof on the driver's side. Now fully out of the Mercedes, Sal Romagna brushed back his dark, wavy hair, straightened the front of his Tommy Bahama silk shirt and then, looking around to see if anyone were paying him any attention, walked around the front of the fancy car. I had earlier described him as swarthy. In this instance, now aware he was being observed, he put his swarthiness on full display like a peacock spreading his feathers during a courtship ritual. Once on the sidewalk, continuing to make a show of his good looks, he extended an arm, took aim at the new Benz with his key and locked it.

Watching his primping and strutting from his barstool, Walt's response was predictable. "Oh, shit!"

## CHAPTER 19

# WALT, WEALTH AND WRONGDOERS

As if he had just been cued and the camera was rolling, Sal Romagna entered Bar OSA in a puffed up manner that he'd refined over the years. Straight ahead was his brother-in-law who was slumped on his barstool. "Fino told me I'd find you here," he barked from across the room as he removed his stylish Maui Jim sunglasses.

"Yeah, I'm here," Walt groused, continuing to stare into his beer glass; hoping if he didn't look up, his obnoxious relative might disappear.

"So who are your friends?" he asked as he approached the Inbetweener's end of the bar. He surveyed the group in much the same way a drill sergeant looks over a lineup of raw recruits.

Walt grimaced. The last thing he needed was his sister's husband bringing his smarmy wise guy act to Bar OSA. In almost a whisper, he said with some reluctance, "On the far end there, that's George..."

"Hell, I know who that is." Sal beamed as he walked over to the former football player. Extending his hand, he introduced himself,

"Sal Romagna. I'm Wally's brother-in-law. You know you are one of my all-time favorite Oakland Raiders. Kenny Stable first, Dave Casper second and then you. It's a real pleasure to meet you." Looking back at Walt, in a derisory tone, he asked, "So what are doing hanging around with my brother-in-law?"

The clumsily presented, left-handed compliment didn't bother the former Raider, but Sal's use of the term brother-in-law as a pejorative really rankled him. Might as well have a little fun, George thought. "I'm surprised you don't know. Back in my playing days, Walt was the official Raider team plumber."

They all made some attempt at stifling their laughter but to no avail. Duffy tried wiping his mouth with his ever-present bar rag while The Redhead threw in a cough. The others tried turning laughter into throat-clearing. Sal just looked confused.

"Hey, I'm only kidding, Sal... I can call you Sal, can't I?" George asked with a friendly smile. "The truth is we enjoy each other's company and this little corner of the world is the perfect place to meet up."

Mike stuck out a hand and introduced himself. "And this is my wife, Katherine."

Duffy Hart followed. "And this is my wife, The Redhead."

"So what am I supposed to call her?" he asked her husband.

"I can speak, you know," Caitlin snapped, her voice cold. She was angry at the boorish and lecherous way Sal had sized up Katherine and her during their husbands' cordial introductions.

""Like I said, what do I call you?" he asked again, unaware of his own loutish behavior.

"I'll say it slowly. I am called The Redhead."

"Hey, Wally, this is a tough crowd you hang out with."

"Oh, you couldn't be further from the truth, sir," Ambrose remarked. "I assure you the teat that produces the milk of human kindness suckled all of us as babies."

Duffy groaned. "That's a stretch even for you, professor. You make it sound like we all came from the same litter."

"You guys always talk like this?" an addled Sal asked, his eyes darting from one to the other at the bar.

Before anyone could answer him, Ambrose grabbed his hand and pumped it vigorously. "I am Ambrose Dowling, known around here as the village elder. Now you have met us all. By the way, I'm sure you've heard this before, Mr. Romagna, but you sound exactly like Joe Pesci."

Walt's brother-in-law loved hearing that and he heard it often. With much pride, he gave his usual reply, "I'm sure people tell Joe Pesci he sounds a lot like Sal Romagna."

"Is it a practiced thing or did you just come out of the womb sounding like a wise guy?" Ambrose's asked in a tone that was both innocent and disarming.

If Walt's brother-in-law were offended, he didn't show it. Instead, he just shook his head, gave the professor a pat on the cheek and walked toward Walt's corner stool.

"What do you think?" Sal asked, nudging his wife's brother.

"What do I think about what?" Walt shot back.

"The car, for chrissakes. What do you think I'm talking about? It belongs to a friend of mine at the Mercedes dealership in Oakland. Ernie let me borrow it for a test drive. I like it but the color isn't me. White's a chick's thing."

"Can you afford it?"

Sal smiled at the question. Poking him in the chest, he said, "Wally, we are rich. I know the money's not going to be here for a few weeks, but that shouldn't stop us from making some plans."

Hearing this exchange, Duffy decided to be a bit mischievous. First, though, he would be a good host. "Hey, Sal, can I get you something to drink?"

"Yeah, gimme a Bud."

"We don't have it."

"What kind of bar doesn't serve Bud?"

"A discerning one," Ambrose muttered.

"I'll find you something, Duffy said. "So did you go in on the lottery ticket with Walt? Kinda sounds that way."

When asked a challenging question, part of Sal's theatrics included looking down and brushing nothing off the front of his Tommy Bahama silk shirt. Then he would raise his head slowly, wearing a tough-guy look designed to intimidate.

"Look, uh... What's your name again?" he said as if he had rehearsed it.

"Duffy Hart. I own this fine establishment."

"Good for you, Duffy" he said, pointing an accusing finger at him. "So let me explain something to you. A family, a real family always shares good fortune. That's the way it is meant to be. Now on top of that, this kind of money requires expert management. My brother-in-law here..." Sal paused to pat Walt's back. Seeing he had everyone's attention, he said, "Let's be honest. What does he know about money? He's a plumber."

Walt's reaction to Sal's insensitive and insulting comment came in two stages. Firstly, he asked Duffy for a shot of Patron Silver tequila which he downed in a single gulp. Then, sliding off his barstool, he stood beside his brother-in-law with his back to the others. Leaning down, fresh with tequila-breath, he whispered in the shorter man's ear, "Outside." When Sal, still wearing his cocky smile, continued to stand there, Walt said in another fierce whisper, "If you don't, I am going to carry your sorry ass outside."

This much can be said for Salvatore Romagna. The man could keep his cool. Acting as if he were in charge of his forced departure, he told the others in his best Joe Pesci voice, "Hey, as much as I'd like to stay here with you nice people, I'm in a yellow zone. I just need to have a private word with Wally here and then I'll send him right back to you. And no hitting the guy up for money." If only he was joking.

All six watched as the two men stood on the sidewalk in front of the new Mercedes Benz. Facing each other, they were perfectly framed in the Bar OSA windows. Now all their audience at the bar needed were closed captions to hear what was going on. It was apparent Walt did most of the talking and seemed to be in charge. On three occasions, he punctuated whatever it was he was saying by poking Sal in the chest, the poke strong enough to send Sal back on his heels. His brother-in-law poked back but was careful to make only the slightest physical contact with Walt's good-sized torso. The chest-pokes were much discussed in the bar. Then it was over. Sal walked to the driver's side of the car gesticulating the whole way. Now that he was a safe distance from his adversary, he began shouting at Walt. Passersby looked uncomfortable as they walked by. A homeless guy seemed to appear out of nowhere. He stood next to Walt, pantomiming Sal and Walt's movements until angry stares from both of them sent him on his way.

George spoke for the group when he asked Walt upon his return, "Anything you care to talk about?"

The plumber did indeed want to talk. Addressing them all, he explained, "What you saw out there was a long time coming. I hate being called Wally. It goes back to when I was a kid. The other thing that set me off was his getting on my case because I'm a plumber." The shot of tequila and the confrontation with Sal had left him exultant and suddenly the air seemed clearer and the future more promising.

"So your epiphany to confront the Joe Pesci-soundalike was caused by his incessant use of a despised nickname and his insulting your profession. To that, I say bravo," Ambrose exclaimed, lifting his glass.

"No, it wasn't religious or anything like that," he replied with a straight face. "It was just one of those spur of the moment things."

The professor passed on telling him there was also a secular meaning to epiphany. Instead, he remarked, "Isn't it amazing how quickly the brain can process so many thoughts when it doesn't require putting everything into words. Instantaneously, you can make a wise but risky decision on the spot just like that. And that's what you apparently did."

"I suppose so," Walt mumbled, taking a sip of his Stella Artois. "All I know is I'd had it with that clown. My sister, Margaret, is all about keeping the peace when it comes to the family. That's why I have always let him act like a jerk around me."

"I think that came to an end this afternoon," Mike Gearon said.

"You did get a little worked up out there," Duffy commented.

Walt shrugged and started to smile. "Yeah, I guess I did."

"You're brother-in-law didn't seem so tough when you were talking to him. We decided you won the chest-poking competition."

Walt remembered Fino's description of his father. It was a revelation as he always thought Sal could be a handful. "No, it turns out he's all talk."

"Big hat, no horse. huh?" Duffy threw out.

"You could say that."

"Is he like that with your sister?" The Redhead and Katherine wondered whether Margaret was safe around someone who might be ill-tempered.

Walt glanced over at her and shook his head. "No, absolutely not. That's what's so strange. He's a totally different guy around her. He worships the ground she walks on."

"You just can't let him out in public, huh?" Ambrose quipped.

"Something like that."

"We gather that you must have put him straight as to the money and who it belongs to?" Mike asked.

"Oh yeah," he said with a victorious smile. "That said, though, my plan is to spread some of the money around my family. I mean you almost have to if for no other reason than you want them off your back. I warned Sal to watch his manners around me because I'm going to see that Margaret gets a substantial amount. I told him that between now and then, I'm going to subtract ten thousand dollars every time he calls me Wally or takes a cheap shot at me being a plumber."

"So what's next, Mr. Gillespie, man of action?" Ambrose asked, hoping the plumber wouldn't mind hosting him to a second Cuban Manhattan.

"There's the meeting with the finance guy tomorrow and then Jeannie and I hit the road for awhile." After another sip of the Stella Artois, he added, "Settling matters with Sal has really put me in a good mood. I think I can handle anything now." He lifted his almost empty glass and toasted his silent partners.

The meeting adjourned, they began to make their departures. "I'm out of here," George announced. "Debbie and I are meeting Tom and Barbara Flores in San Francisco. We missed his induction into the Bay Area Sports Hall of Fame in March, so this a chance to congratulate him."

"Maybe you can borrow John Madden's bus and just stay overnight in front of the restaurant," Mike Gearon kidded.

"Maybe I can get Walt to buy it for me," George responded.

While Walt was outside outlining to his brother-in-law the new rules of their relationship, Bar OSA began to fill up much to Duffy Hart's delight. Among the new arrivals were two Inbetweeners. Dyson Ward was a handsome black man in his mid-seventies. A retired Berkeley city engineer, he was one of the more popular regulars; known and liked by all who were gathered there that afternoon. Dyson, who was an extra large in height, weight and voice, was a double XL in personality. Everyone was delighted to see him and welcomed him cordially.

When the hellos and how-are-you's subsided, Dyson looked over Ambrose's shoulder at Walt and congratulated him on winning the lottery. "They say money brings out the worst in people, Walt. Don't you go changing on us," he warned while flashing a toothy grin. "Of course, there's always the chance your money may bring out the worst in others. I've heard that happens, too."

"It's already happening." Pointing to the gang gathered around him, he continued, "They've just seen an example of it," Walt said.

"Dyson, didn't you win a bunch of money on Jeopardy?" Mike Gearon asked before Walt had a chance to retell his encounter with his brother-in-law.

"You should know, Gearon. You and your partner Smith interviewed me on your radio show right after I won. I was a three day champion," he boasted.

Ambrose turned and looked up at Dyson with his short, wiry-grey hair and trimmed matching beard. "When was this, Mr. Ward? My Emily and I were big fans of Jeopardy."

"Ten years ago. I won close to sixty thousand dollars."

"Did it bring out the worst in you or the people close to you?" the professor asked with a wink.

Dyson laughed heartily. "Not really. My relatives were more Family Feud types than Jeopardy types. It took them awhile to learn about it. By that time, I had already paid taxes on it, covered some of my daughter's college bills and had enough left over to take my wife here for a paella dinner. Duffy, I remember you bought us a bottle of Rioja to celebrate."

While they were talking about Dyson's 2002 Jeopardy experience, the second Inbetweener had managed to find a space near Mike and Katherine Gearon at the Bar. His name was Nathan Gross. Unlike the engaging Dyson Ward, he was barely tolerated by the Inbetweeners. A slender, well-dressed man with thinning hair and pinched features, the former salesman now into his tenth year of retirement felt he still possessed the persuasive powers that allowed him to have a successful career selling a variety of goods and services no matter the product, it's quality and, in one case, it's legality. Thus he was always peddling one idea or another every time he visited Bar OSA. It did not go unnoticed. This particular late afternoon, his eyes were hungrily fixed on the plumber who was nursing both his beer and his euphoric mood. Nathan nodded to those close to him and then worked his way to the crowded corner, squeezing himself between two women at a table behind him and the large body of Walt who sat at the bar.

"Congratulations, Walt," the retired salesman said, tapping him on the shoulder and placing a business card on the bar in front of him. "This is what I call perfect timing. Your winning that money could not have come at a better time."

"How's that?" he asked warily, knowing full well the Nathan Gross was ready to deliver a pitch which Walt was most assuredly not going to swing at.

"Read the card," he ordered. "It's my latest venture."

Walt read aloud from his card. "Nathan Gross, INVESTAPRENEUR. What the hell is an investapreneur?"

Hearing Walt and knowing Nathan, Duffy came over to that end of the bar to run interference should he need it.

"As an investaprenuer, I bring money and innovation together. The kind of relationships where doubling if not tripling your return isn't unheard of." Nathan paused and leaned in to catch Walt's eye. "How's your back and prostate?" he asked out of the blue.

"Both are just fine."

"No, they aren't. No back that belongs to a man your age is fine. And as for your prostate… Anyway, I am helping a brilliant Vietnamese scientist get his business up and running in the states. He manufactures a highly praised pain-management belt for sore backs and an herbal medicine for enlarged prostates. Plus, you get a piece of his downtown Saigon bike rental company. All for a mere five hundred thousand dollars…"

He got no further. Duffy had taken his card from Walt and handed it back to the pitchman. "This is a no-hustle zone, Nathan. Walt is hands off as long as he's at this bar."

"You're joking."

"No, I am not," Duffy shot back. Having never officially eighty-sixed anyone from Bar OSA, he was sorely tempted to make Nathan his first as the salesman never ate there and usually bought just one glass of wine, the least expensive on the menu when he did come in. And, to Duffy's knowledge, he'd never left a tip, vacuuming up his change after paying his bill.

"I'm not interested anyway, Nathan," Walt said, sliding off his barstool. Standing next to the perpetual pitchman, he said, "You want to know why? My back is terrific, I pee like a sixteen year old and I hate bikes."

Nathan continued to stand there as Walt took his leave. Duffy caught his eye and signaled him to come closer. In a low voice, he said. "Nathan, why don't you just stay retired. These sales' pitches of yours are getting further and further out there on the believability scale. Nobody's falling for them."

Within minutes, the Gearons and Ambrose had taken their leave. Ambrose told them he saw no reason to come to Walnut Creek and wished them well with their meeting. Nathan now sat alone at the end of the bar thinking Duffy was right. It was time to let go of these far-fetched schemes. Just then he felt a tug on his coat. He turned to see the two older women at the window table smiling at him.

The one who had done the tugging said, "Excuse me, we couldn't help overhearing you talk about bad backs and stuff. Uh, would you like to join us and explain more about it?"

## CHAPTER 20

# A SORTING OUT OF MATTERS

It bothered him. Enough so that Walter Gillespie was now convinced he was not acting in his own best interest when he chose to keep his wife in the dark about the real story of their lottery win. So the night before the group's appointment with Paul Farana at PHE Financial, he decided to remedy that even though he was well aware of his spouse's propensity for gossiping. His reasoning was sound. Theirs was a marriage of honesty and trust in all matters and he didn't want to lose the joy and satisfaction that came from being one half of such a blissful union. That evening at a dinner of Chinese takeout, he took his wife's left hand; allowing her to still handle her chopsticks with the right. While she hungrily worked her way through the shrimp chow mein, Jeannie listened intently as he told her the true tale of their unlikely win. When she asked him why he'd taken so long to tell her, he spoke of his legitimate concern that she might not be able to resist spreading the fantastic tale far and wide and that worried him. He also let her know that he'd warned the others about her passion for storytelling. Hearing that, she leaned toward him, kissed his cheek and whispered, "Call it what it is, darling. It's gossip, pure and simple." When she asked why he had decided to tell her now, he explained about the next day's meeting and how he wanted her there. Then he stumbled through a clumsy but romantic explanation of not wanting to live with, in his words, "the heavy burden of that kind of deceit for the rest of my life." The best part came when he blurted out there should never be secrets between them. It earned him her assurance that he could trust her completely. Then putting her chopsticks down, she rose from her chair and cooed in a soy-scented voice, "Let's go use our lips for something other than talking and slurping Chinese noodles."

Now they were in the left turn lane of a Walnut Creek intersection. On the far corner was the modern, seven-story office building that housed PHE Financial. Walt checked the rearview mirror and saw the Harts and Ambrose Dowling were behind him. Duffy was driving and, like Walt, waited patiently for the green arrow; a Jackson Browne piece playing in the background.

From the backseat, Ambrose stared out at the car-filled multi-lane intersection and began to complain of the long wait. Striking a tone of exaggerated desperation, he shouted over the music, "I just know it. I am going to die in a left turn lane of the intersection of Ignacio Valley Road and Could-Be-Anywhere Avenue. What did I do to deserve such an ignominious passing? I know I should have never asked to come today. Just look at where we are. Suburbia is a mortal's purgatory, Mr. and Mrs. Hart. It's a damnable place. I daresay even Dante couldn't imagine another ring of hell quite like this."

The Redhead turned to look into the cavernous back of the van where the professor was belted into the corner behind Duffy. "Ambrose, you will survive this. That's the bad news. The good news is I now know how far I can travel in the same car with you. Eastbound, I'm good until Orinda. Northbound, maybe Pinole. Southbound, definitely San Leandro. I want you to consider that before sponging another ride off us," she said, her smiling eyes contradicting the scolding tone in her voice.

Just then they got the green arrow. "Look, we are moving again, Mrs. Hart. As regards your hastily constructed rules of transit; yes, I will remember them. However, I'm certain Uber has no such restrictions."

With outstretched arms. Mike Gearon welcomed the others as they poured out of the garage elevator. "Ah, the gang's all here. Welcome to the ever expanding metropolis of Walnut Creek," he said in his rich, broadcast baritone. His wife, Katherine, and the Crowders were standing next to him. It had been agreed they would go up to PHE en masse.

Walt had caught them off guard by bringing his wife, Jeannie. Initially, they were uneasy as they knew of his concern about her being a hopeless chatterbox. Knowing of their trepidation, she assured them right off they were meeting the new, improved and much quieter Jeannie Gillespie. With her forthright and pleasant manner, the attractive, well-figured woman easily won them over.

"I'm so glad Walt decided to tell me how you won all this money. I promise never, never to share it with anyone. Even if the CIA were to give me some of its notorious truth serum, my lips will prove resistant." She glanced lovingly at her husband. "I forgot to tell you, honey, I quit Facebook this morning. Do you guys have any idea how difficult it is to permanently delete your account."

While she was talking, Walt looked around at the spacious lobby and wondered who did their plumbing maintenance and repair. Then he realized he was about to receive enough money to buy the building. On the heels of that bizarre notion came another realization. He was far more comfortable thinking about the former.

The tastefully but not extravagantly furnished offices and board rooms on the fifth floor were designed to let a visitor know straight away that PHE Financial was careful with their clients' money. Stepping out of the elevator, the gang of nine were greeted warmly by Paul Farana's personable assistant who ushered them into the company's comfortable conference room where she began to take coffee orders. They had just a moment to enjoy the views of nearby Mount Diablo before Paul Farana entered the room carrying only a legal size note pad. After placing it at the head of the long table, he circled the table, warmly greeting those he knew and introducing himself to those he didn't. The greetings completed, he took a seat at the end of the long table. Of medium height and build, Paul Farana was dark-haired with a handsome, square face that wore a constant smile. Coco Chanel said at fifty you deserve the face you have. If that's the case, at fifty-five, his was a visage that spoke of a life well-lived in all the best possible ways. He was also in a suit and that immediately endeared him to Ambrose Dowling who decided on the spot to move his accounts to PHE Financial.

Taking a seat, Paul pulled a pen from his inside jacket pocket. Pulling the tablet toward him, he said, "George gave me just a sentence or two about why you are all here today. To say it was irresistible is an understatement. So how can I be of help?"

They had earlier decided to let Mike Gearon tell their story which he did in an impressive adjective-free, facts-only rendering of how they ended up winning the second largest lottery in Super Lotto Plus history and the rather unorthodox way they were dealing with it.

He concluded by saying, "Yesterday, we all agreed that having our accounts at one source and handled by the same person was a good idea. Quite simply, George and I couldn't think of a better person to handle it than you."

While Mike had explained all, Paul's brown eyes had darted back and forth, settling for a moment on whichever person Mike was taking about. When he had wrapped it up, Paul took a moment to digest it all. He'd taken a few notes which he quickly scanned before responding, "First off, thank you for thinking of PHE and, more specifically, me. I think you are doing the wise thing here. By that, I mean keeping it all in one house with just one person handling the accounts. It will certainly help maintain the confidentiality you all desire. That said, let's get started. First we need to set up accounts for the Gillespies and Harts. Then we need to..."

"You can add a third client to that list, Mr. Farana," Ambrose interjected. "I, too, am interested in having an account here. By the way, do you always wear a suit to work?"

Puzzled, Paul responded, "Yes, I do. Most of the time away."

"You sir, are a rarity; a coat and tie man in a tee-shirt, jeans and hoodie business world. I for one greatly admire that."

The Redhead poked the professor. Is this what it's like to have a precocious child, she wondered. "Ambrose, let Mr. Farana get on with..."

"Paul. Please, call me Paul," he said to all of them. Glancing at Ambrose, he added, "I''ll be very happy to open an account for you and I'll be sure to wear a coat and tie when I know you're coming in."

"Thank you, sir, and I will have the pleasure of being the poorest one among those you sign up today."

"He will also be the most difficult one to deal with, Paul," The Redhead warned the financial advisor.

Paul laughed at their interplay. He liked all of them and saw no problem in dealing with them. Ambrose might well prove to be a nuisance, albeit an entertaining one, but it was Walt who would require his close attention for awhile. He'd not spoken directly to him about what awaits the plumber as the public face of the group. Paul, though, was well aware of the pitfalls of instant wealth; parents demanding houses and allowances, wives suddenly wanting to be ex-wives leaving with half of everything, siblings wanting money and lots of it simply because they were siblings and friends and extended relatives expecting money on a regular basis some even resorting to threats and robbery if they don't get what they think is their fair share

Looking at Walt, Paul said, "Mike Gearon mentioned you and Mrs. Gillespie are going away for awhile. I understand why you want to put some distance between you, your family and friends for awhile. I currently have a client who was a big lottery winner and I also represent several highly paid professional athletes. We've been through some difficult times together all thanks to sudden wealth. I just want to alert you to the fact that you are now going to see another side of your family and friends and it won't be a pretty one. They will all come down with pleonexia which means exhibiting extreme greed for wealth and material possessions. One pro athlete client told me it got so bad he didn't even trust his house plants."

Walt chuckled at his last line. "Thanks for the heads up, Paul, but it's already started. Nothing I can't handle yet but I do think getting away is the best thing for now."

"Just know I am always ready to help even to the extent of being your spokesperson," Paul said. Rubbing his hands together, he continued, "Now let's get going on opening these accounts. By the way, you don't have to fund them right now but I want to get them open and ready to go. Kara, who is a senior registered client associate and assistant vice-president..."

George held up his hand. "Forget that fancy title. Her most important title is being Paul's right arm."

"She is that and more," Paul said. "I just wanted to say that she'll be right in to get us going on the paperwork. Now, Walt, as regards the California Lottery, they will have you sign a form authorizing the wiring of funds. I'll give you the correct wire instructions which you'll then provide them. During that time, you'll be able to monitor your account to confirm receipt of the funds. Later, when things have cooled down a bit and you're finally comfortable with the idea of seeing an account that has eight figures in it, we'll discuss what to do with it. How does that sound so far?"

"It sounds... I was going to say crazy, but it sounds great. Really great," he replied enthusiastically, squeezing his wife's hand.

"There's something else we need to do right away and that's set up a temporary trust."

"Why is that?" he asked.

"The trust spells out who gets what amount should you predecease the division of funds."

"Why would I do that?" the almost retired plumber asked, his voice wavering.

"I think what concerns Paul is should you die before we get our share of the money, the trust will see that we, in fact, get it," George Crowder explained.

"I know that," Walt snapped. He knew what predecease meant. It was just not a topic he was comfortable dealing with. They're all so much into trust, he wondered why they couldn't just trust him to stay alive for the next six to eight weeks.

"The benefit is that it keeps everything private and out of court, unlike having a will and having it go to probate," Paul explained. "It's good short term protection."

"I don't plan on dying," Walt insisted.

Ambrose decided to respond to Walt's shaky but confident statement that he had full control over his mortality. "Nobody does, but it happens, Walter. My lord, you could walk out of here today and all of sudden get hit by a giant SUV driven by a woman in bright spandex anxious to get to her yoga class. No doubt, they'd find your body in neighboring Concord."

Finally accustomed to Dowling's sometimes rascally manner, Walt began to laugh. He realized he'd overreacted when Paul talked about the trust. It did make perfect sense, he decided. Looking across the table at the professor, he responded, "Ain't going to happen, Ambrose. And if it does, I hope she ends up tossing me into Pleasant Hill instead. I've got some good customers there."

Ambrose was not to be put off. "Joke if you must, Mr. Gillespie, we must always be aware that our undoing is out of our hands and always awkwardly timed. In 1911, Bobby Leach successfully went over Niagara Falls in a barrel. Then fourteen years later, in New Zealand, he slipped on a banana peel and died."

Walt's forehead wrinkled as he squinted at the professor and asked with a laugh, "What the hell does that have to do with anything."

Ambrose shrugged. "You know, I thought it might have some relevance to the matter at hand, but now having heard it out loud, I may have been mistaken. However, I always wanted to slip it into a conversation, so mission accomplished."

This time The Redhead gave the professor a harder than usual nudge. "Ambrose, if you want a ride home, cool it," she snapped. "Otherwise, we are dropping you off at the nearest assisted living residence and leaving you there in a basket with only your first name attached to your shirt."

The Crowders and the Gearons realized they'd just be in the way if they continued to stay as Paul and Kara would have their hands full getting the others set up with their new PHE accounts. As they rose from their chairs, Mike spoke for the foursome when he suggested to Paul that they best get on their way.

"Before you go, I want to say something to all of you," Paul said, waving to them back to their seats. Leaning forward in his chair, he scanned the room to see that he had everyone's attention. "When I drop my wife at BART every morning, she tells me to have an unusual day. Sounds crazy but that's what I usually have. As a CPA, she does, too. That's because we take care of people's money. We don't watch their dogs, clean their houses, do their gardening, wash their cars, prescribe their medicine... No, we keep an eye on their money. Even scarier, I put their money to work for them. People are funny, odd, eccentric and downright weird about money and that's why we have unusual days. As you can see, I can't wait to tell her about this morning's meeting." Paul noticed their surprised expressions. "You should know that I will tell her," he emphasized. "The deal here is trust me, trust my wife. Besides as an accountant and tax expert, she will be invaluable when it comes to dealing with Uncle Sam. Oh, and by the way, I'm certain he's the one relative who will love you as he will be getting more than his fair share thanks to the unorthodox way you're dealing with this. Speaking of that, I understand your reason for taking the direction you took. There are viable, practical and potentially money-saving alternatives to handling a lottery jackpot, but they would involve a battery of financial people and an accountability on all your parts which is clearly what you want to avoid. This is just an observation... Well, more of a left-handed compliment, but I have found that with sudden wealth, it's usually the money that takes control of things. Perhaps it's your ages, your experiences... I'm not exactly sure what the reasons are but you all seem to have taken control of it. That's to your credit."

"As a way of explaining, it's time to roll out a way overused, tired old chestnut, Paul," Mike sighed, running a hand over what few remaining hairs he kept cut short were left on the top of his head.

"Let me guess. Money changes everything."

"And he reads minds as well," Mike laughed.

"It can change things for the good, you know," Paul offered. "Change is that way. Sometimes for the good, sometimes for the bad and that includes everything; the weather, our mood, money... Even our health." Walt thought he could have left that last one out of his litany of changes.

Katherine decided to jump into the conversation. "Of course it does, Paul. But we are dealing with a specific situation here. It's not the money but the ridiculous amount of it that has Mike and me so concerned. We both feel strongly that it would complicate everything. And they are complications we would prefer to keep out of our satisfied life."

Kara, an attractive and according to Ambrose a suitably well-dressed woman in her late twenties, walked in to the room with an armful of forms and a cheery smile. "Hi again, everybody. Time to get started," she said. Taking a seat nearest Walt and Jeannie, she began to distribute PHE Financial-inscribed pens around the table.

Once again, the Gearons and Crowders rose as one. This time George spoke for them. "Debbie has to get back to the shop and I have business in Montclair. We'd better get going."

Mike looked at the people whom he'd gotten to know well over the last few weeks. People he'd grown very fond of. I suppose this is it, he thought. No more fake birthday parties, clandestine meetings or end-of-the-bar gatherings to plan or strategize. What lies ahead, he wondered. For Katherine and him, it meant four million dollars appearing in their PHE account sometime in the next few weeks without their having to do a thing. They had talked about how they could help their kids and their spouses with some of it, but for now that was the extent of their ambitions for it. But what of the others? He knew Walt and Jeannie Gillespie, who were off to parts unknown with no return date, had made it quite clear early on that they would go on a spending spree. Ambrose Dowling was talking about going on back to back cruises where he plans to wear a tuxedo every evening. The Harts were hoping to buy the building that houses their beloved Bar OSA and George Crowder was planning to help former NFL teammates who had fallen on hard times. While only George mentioned something charitable, Mike knew the rest of them would not ignore the basic urge to do something good with some of it. What they all were, he knew, was grateful. Perhaps, it wasn't always expressed but it was clear that their lives were guided by thankfulness. Maybe that's why they all got along so well.

While Mike Gearon was wondering whether this gathering at PHE Financial was a final act of sorts, George Crowder gave voice to it. Walking over to Walt, he extended his hand and said, "I guess we'll see you when we see you. Good luck and if you ever need our help... That's right, I'm volunteering everybody. What I mean to say is you have our contact numbers. Just holler."

Walt took his hand and then let it go to give the big man a hug. That started it. Everyone was on their feet and moving from one to the other giving affectionate hugs all around. All except for Ambrose, that is, who was a resolute handshaker.

# CHAPTER 21
# WALT LEARNS YOU CAN GO HOME AGAIN

While lunch was respectable enough on that Wednesday, December fifth, the diners had made a quick exit and now Bar OSA was playing host to only two. Alone at the corner of the bar nearest the window, armed with his thinking rag and a leave-me-along expression, an angry Duffy Hart was busy rubbing the spotlessly clean countertop. At the same time his wife, Caitlin, stewed and fumed in the privacy of their back office. The reason behind their mutual ire was Saul Benares, their much despised landlord. They were just inches away from signing on the bottom line to purchase the building when he decided to toss in another condition of sale. They'd just learned that the crotchety gent wanted a dining allowance of five free dinners a month for five years with a maximum of five guests. Duffy had called him and told him nobody sold a house to a prospective buyer with the condition that the seller then be allowed to come over for dinner five times a month and bring five of his nearest and dearest with him. Saul's blunt response was, "This ain't a fucking house. This is a building. You want it, you feed me." The Redhead, who had been doing most of the leg work on the property purchase while Duffy ran the restaurant, was also contending with another interested buyer. Since June, each had raised their offer and The Redhead feared their competitors wouldn't stop outbidding them. Her first thought that afternoon was if giving him a meal ticket meant they could own the building, then they might have to agree to it. Her next thought was screw him. He was an odious man who was loud, rude and obnoxious. There wasn't a server at Bar OSA who could abide waiting on him.

Her husband was thinking along the same lines. Tossing his thinking rag in its special drawer, he instructed Elena to watch the place while he went back to the office. When he walked in, Caitlin swiveled around on her small office chair and asked, "So what do you think?"

Duffy kissed the top of her head. "You go first," he said.

"My original thought was we should do it and put up with him for another half decade."

"Whoa. A half decade. You put it like that and it sounds forever. What was your next thought?"

"Screw him. Tell him we've made him our last offer and live with the consequences. What are your thoughts?"

"Pretty much the same. Remember whenever our lease was up, Saul would throw in these ridiculous conditions. There was that time he wanted us to agree to sell him wine and booze wholesale? We refused and then we caved when he asked for comped meals instead. What a mistake that was."

The Redhead leaned back in her chair and smiled up at her husband. "I honestly thought one of the benefits of buying this property meant finally putting some distance between us and him. I don't think I can handle another five years."

"Five years or a half decade, either way I know I can't."

"So what do we do now?"

Duffy leaned against the small filing cabinet and folded his arms. "How about we tell him no deal on the meals and he has our last offer. Then we keep our fingers crossed. The good news is we can always relocate in Berkeley, probably close by. I'll miss being Alice's neighbor, though," Duffy said of the famous owner of Chez Panisse.

The Redhead placed her hand on his thigh and caressed it. "The real good news, husband of mine, is we have chips. Lots of them."

"Caitlin, please take your hand off my leg. I have to walk back out there and I won't be able to in the condition your stroking causes."

"Hey, look at this way; people will now know you dress on the left."

"Do you want me to call Saul?" he asked, trying to sound businesslike.

"I've been dealing with him. Let me have the pleasure."

Duffy returned to the bar, his mood now cheerier than usual. A seasoned restaurateur, he automatically scanned the room and noticed the head count had improved by one. At the far end of the bar in Inbetweener territory, a large man in work clothes with a scruffy crewcut occupied the last barstool. He sat patiently while Elena drew him a pint of Stella Artois. Duffy blinked twice, not believing his eyes. Had everything that had happened between April 18th and December 5th been some sort of bizarre dream, some perverse joke. he asked himself.

Approaching that end of the bar, he said tentatively, "Walt."

"Hey, Duffy, it's been awhile." Walt Gillespie threw out his hand and Duffy shook it vigorously. "Okay, okay. I need that for work," Walt said, laughing at the restaurant owner's shocked reaction.

The apparently still-on-the-job plumber was sitting exactly where he sat on that fateful April afternoon. He wore the same faded blue shirt with the Gillespie Plumbing logo half hanging off the pocket. Every indication was he had just finished some kind of nasty job. This would not have been so frightening except for the fact that after that peculiar Wednesday in April, Walt became the proud owner of many, many millions of dollars. What happened, Duffy wondered. So he asked him directly.

Walt ran a hand over his thick five o'clock shadow and thought a moment. With a dispirited look of resignation, he explained, "I spent it all, Duffy. Well, more to the point, I lost it all. First Jeannie took half in an ugly but quick divorce. She ran off with a Christian fundamentalist minister who was also a yoga instructor in Newport Beach. He named all his yoga positions after biblical characters. Evidently one morning she was doing the Delilah Dip and the Sampson came out in him. I naturally took it bad and dealt with her leaving by drowning myself in booze and gambling for awhile. Then I ignored Paul's advice and invested in two businesses that went belly up. One might have been porn. Then I fell victim to a Ponzi scheme and lost what little I had left. So here I am back fixing Berkeley's many faulty pipes and trying to get my life back together."

Duffy was visibly stunned. Distracted by imagining Jeannie doing the Delilah Dip, he stammered, "Walt, uh... Please, tell me you're joking around. Otherwise this beer's on me."

Walt let a smile slowly form. Shaking his head, he laughed and said, "Of course, I am. But you can still pay for the beer. You have a no idea how long I rehearsed that story. Jeannie helped me, or course. She came up with the yoga stuff."

"Everything's okay then?" Duffy asked, still puzzled by his outfit.

"More than okay."

"And that's the absolute truth?"

"Of course, it is. Life couldn't be better and I couldn't be richer," he said with an equanimity that confirmed his well-being.

"My god. I haven't see you since... Let me see. Yes, it was the meeting with Paul. Where the hell did you go? What have you and Jeannie been doing? And what are you doing here?" Duffy asked in rapid fire succession. Then before he could get an answer, he said, "Wait! Don't say a word. Let's get everyone here first. It's been about six months or so since we've seen each other. I mean we have seen each other... A lot, in fact, but you've been a giant mystery. Did you know that sometimes we played a conversation game called Where's Walt. We'd try to guess where you might have sought asylum for awhile."

"Did anybody guess Cabo or San Diego or a bunch of the Western States?

"I think Mike and Katherine Gearon mentioned Cabo."

"Give the lucky couple a third of the prize."

Phone calls were placed. The Gearons and Crowders said they could be there in half an hour. Ambrose, it turned out, was just a block away and said he could drop everything and be there forthwith; everything being a late afternoon coffee at Peet's with an Arnold Bennett novel.

They had no reason to worry about what to talk about while they waited for the others as Caitlin Duffy burst from the back office, ran down the length of the bar, put her arms around her husband and shouted, "We got it! I don't believe it, but Saul agreed to our offer. He'll take just the money, Duffy. No fucking free dinners." She was so excited her last sentence was loud enough that it bounded off the Bar OSA bare walls and into the ears of the half dozen gathered there. Horrified, The Redhead covered her blushing face, looked around the room and apologized for her outburst. It was only then that she noticed Walt.

Unwrapping herself from her husband, she moved around him and with trepidation approached Walt. Like Duffy, she couldn't believe what she clearly saw. She took a few seconds to take in his questionable appearance. "Walt, what on earth has happened to you?" she finally asked.

Walt looked at her husband and held up his hands. Laughing, he said, "Sorry, Duffy, I don't think I can tell that story again without screwing it up."

"At least tell her about the Delilah Dip."

Walt rose from his stool and gave The Redhead a clumsy hug. "Everything's fine, Cait… Oops, sorry. Forgot where I was. Anyway, everything's better than fine and we're waiting for everybody else to show up so I can catch you all up. Now what is it that has you so excited?"

"Do you remember us mentioning we were planning to buy the building with some of the…" Realizing where she was, she stopped to reword her explanation. "What I mean to say is our offer to buy this building was just accepted after a song and dance revue that went on for months with our crazy landlord."

Knowing most of them in Berkeley, Walt asked. "Who is it?"

"Saul Benares."

He repeated Saul's name, disgust apparent in his voice. "I did some plumbing repairs for him some time back. Took me forever to get my money. The guy's a bonafide jerk."

"Well, it turns out he's a Berkeley jerk and that worked for us." When Duffy asked for an explanation, she explained, "I phoned him as we discussed and told him that he had our last offer and there was no way we would agree to any comped meals. Without so much as pausing, he said, 'Fine, the place is yours.' I couldn't believe he'd accept our offer."

"Did he say why?"

"Yes, and it explains why he's a Berkeley jerk which is naturally a cut above your basic North American jerk. He said he recently learned the other buyers were planning to put a franchise business in here. He spit the word franchise out like it would poison his tongue and make his face break out. He told me as a member of the Hillside Club, he couldn't imagine facing his fellow members if he allowed that to happen in North Berkeley. I hope you don't mind, but I told him once the papers are signed, he's welcome to come by for a celebration meal." Seeing the concern in her husband's eyes, she added, "Duffy, considering what he's doing for us, one night is fine. It won't kill us. Hell, I'll wait on him myself."

"You may have to," he laughed.

As if it were a Hercule Poirot mystery where the natty detective brings everyone together to recreate the murder scene, all of our characters were now in the exact same place they were on April 18th during the unforgettable Dick Clark memorial. Ambrose was seated between the two big guys, Walt Gillespie and George Crowder. Duffy was behind the bar while Mike and Katherine Gearon stood beside The Redhead and behind the three men on the barstools. That's where the similarity to a whodunnit ends. As the monies had been distributed months ago, the only mystery that needed solving was what on earth had Walt and Jeannie Gillespie been up to all this time and why was he now sitting in Bar OSA wearing a shirt that obviously had seen grimy combat in the last few hours.

Understanding that his work outfit needed explaining, he addressed that first. "Before Jeannie and I took off for... Well, Cabo to start, I gave my nephew, Fino, a substantial raise and asked him to run the company for me while we were gone. I told him that if he did well, I'd turn Gillespie Plumbing over to him. He did better than well. The kid did great. Fino has so much work coming in, he had to hire on three more guys. He's even keeping the Gillespie name," he said with that special kind of pride a father has for his son's accomplishments.

Ambrose asked, "Walter, my friend, how does that explain you wearing that tattered old shirt that was really meant for last year's charity pickup. I don't mean to speak for the group but I will. We expected to see you in... Oh, I don't know, perhaps a Tommy Bahama resort outfit or maybe a Savile Row bespoke suit. Certainly, something that would have given us a hint of your new rich and famous lifestyle."

George placed a hand on Ambrose's shoulder. Leaning in, he said, "I have an idea. Let's just let Walt tell us in his own words and in his own way what they have been doing since that meeting at Paul's office."

"Let me answer the professor first, George," Walt said. "Starting this week, I am working three days a week for my nephew. I love it. Plumbing is what I know how to do and I get great satisfaction out of it and satisfaction is what I'm working for these days. Plus, it it keeps me busy while Jeannie's away. She's doing volunteer work in Richmond three days a week at a women's center. It's a charity we're thinking of supporting financially. I already do their plumbing repairs."

Sitting there, dressed as he was on the day of Dick Clark's death in April, Walt Gillespie looked to be the same affable but oafish man, but he had changed. He was now calmer, more reflective and wiser. And, of course, much richer. Without question the months between May and December were transformative for him.

They were not so life-changing for the others. Even though they all saw substantial gains in their net wealth, none of them felt richer as none of them ever measured personal wealth by the amount of money they had in the bank. If they felt anything, it was more blessed. Approximately four weeks after their meeting with Paul Farana at PHE Financial, a Tuesday to be exact, within the space of a few seconds millions of dollars were wired into their respective accounts. That morning when they all saw their new, eye-popping net worths, they immediately started texting and phoning. It was agreed by all they needed to find an evening to whoop it up. The date picked, now they had to decide on just how they'd go about their whooping. In a moment of giddiness from the visions of dollar signs followed by lots of zeros dancing in their heads, the Gearons suggested they charter a jet to New York for Martinis at The Monkey Bar in midtown Manhattan, then dinner at any Danny Meyer's restaurant and an overnight stay at the Peninsula Hotel on Fifth Avenue. Now that a high level of splurging had been introduced, George Crowder recommended they divert the plane to Chicago as it's closer. Once in the city of big shoulders, they could dine on extra large steaks at Benny's Chop House on the Near North Side and then check into the Four Seasons on the

Miracle Mile. Wary of the flying involved, the Harts suggested they take a luxury van to the Napa Valley for a multi-course French Laundry dinner and a stay at Meadowood Resort. The could even play croquet which made George Crowder wince. Being ever so sensible, Duffy explained, "The Redhead and I have to be back to open Bar OSA the next day. We're still working stiffs."

Certainly they could have afforded to do all three of those obscenely priced outings in three successive nights if they so desired, but once the giddiness had worn off, they opted for a potluck dinner at the Crowder's condo in Rockridge; the Harts bringing paellas, the Gearons the wine, bragging the Rioja came from Trader Joe's and the Crowders supplying dessert from the Market Hall Bakery. Over dinner, they laughed at their thrifty approach to celebrating but it spoke volumes about how the money initially impacted their lives. Quite simply, it didn't. Their daily routines continued to be what they were before the fortunate kick up in funds and no one brought up the idea of splurging other than to kid about it. They all agreed, though, that perhaps when they were more comfortably adjusted to their new wealth, they might be less frugal and more open to extravagance. They did, however, put some of their money to work right away. The Harts immediately pursued buying the Bar OSA building even though they knew dealing with Saul Benares would be a bumpy ride. For the Crowders, aside from putting more cash into Debbie's store in Rockridge, their big expenditure was taking their whole family to Maui for Thanksgiving. George's interest in helping retired NFL colleagues who had fallen on hard times was still in the figuring it all out stage. The Gearons, after informing their children that they had invested well, explained they were in good enough financial shape to help them each with substantial down payments towards houses. They nodded approvingly when their son and daughter swore to pay it back, but In reality, the children's sincere promises fell on loving but deaf ears.

And what of Ambrose? He would have joined the three couples for their celebration dinner had he not been at that moment having a glass of chilled rose' and steamed mussels at an outside table at a small waterfront cafe called Le Mere Germaine in Villefranche in the south of France. From his table, he could see at anchor the gleaming white Crystal Symphony, the cruise ship that got him there. After only four days at sea, he'd fallen head over heels in love with this indulgent form of travel. "This is, in my estimation, the most perfect type of assisted living," he said to anyone who would listen. He was so enthralled, he booked two more sailings while on board and now on this Wednesday, December 5th, all three were but special memories as he was back in his beloved Berkeley trying to figure out when and where to go on his fourth cruise.

Before finally sorting through Walt and Jeannie's fascinating May-to-December experiences, we can report without hesitation that as far as the Gearons, Crowders, Harts and Ambrose Dowling were concerned, that same period of time proved that the creative and efficient manner in which they handled their winning the second largest SuperLotto in California history was a success. Going in, their priority had been to protect their privacy and their richly satisfying personal lives. Like a well-funded IRA that showers its rewards upon you in retirement, each had invested time and energy over the years into strengthening their character, their family structure, their health and their well-being. This constancy resulted in lifestyles that were not to be tampered with. In summation, it was mission accomplished as they each received the amount of money that suited their purposes and no one was the wiser.

That leaves the Gillespies. It is, perhaps, best to let Walter tell the story in his own words. Wisely, he first asked the avuncular man in the old Harris Tweed coat sitting next to him if he could try and refrain from inserting himself into the commentary.

"Then lead us not into temptation, Walter, by saying something that begs for comment," Ambrose replied, hoisting his beloved Cuban Manhattan in a mock toast.

"I will keep that in mind."

## CHAPTER 22

# AND THEY LIVED HAPPILY...

Bar OSA began to fill earlier than usual. Fortunately, Duffy Hart's evening servers had shown up on time so Elena was not alone in handling tables full of hungry and thirsty patrons. That meant Duffy would not have to leave the other alumni of the Dick Clark Memorial of April 18th who had the corner of the bar to themselves. Walt was about to tell the story of the Gillespie travels of the last six months when the bar owner called timeout to refill drinks and order some montaditos for the group. Ambrose took advantage of the break to assure Walt he would in no way interfere. He promised to be a model of restraint.

"That's impossible," Mike Gearon laughed. "You can't help yourself, Ambrose."

"I agree," George added. "Rumors have it the Vatican's Swiss Guards have Ambrose's name on a short list of people who are not allowed to attend the Pope's Midnight Christmas Mass for fear of his interrupting the Pontiff at some inopportune time."

"I would imagine that would be anytime during a Catholic Mass," Mike said, remembering back to his altar boy days.

"I would respectfully wait till the prayer after Communion. I might add that whatever I propose to say, I would say it in Latin, perhaps Carthaginian Latin to impress," the retired professor said with his trademark twinkling eyes and impish grin.

Now that drinks were in hand, montaditos on the bar and eyes and ears trained on the plumber, Duffy commanded, "Okay, have at it, Walt."

"You're all nuts. You know that, don't you?" he charged, his voice contrarily jovial. "Now here I am about to tell you how Jeannie and I became just as nutty." After a heavy but satisfied sigh, he was off and running. "At first, we both felt like we were on the run, but that feeling didn't last long. A couple of days maybe. Then we were like a couple of excited kids who were just let loose in Disney World and told everything was free. In our case, it felt free because money was no object. Trust me, I never thought I would ever say that in my lifetime."

"Hey, we're all filthy rich but we would probably have a hard time saying it," Katherine remarked with a laugh. "Although, I'd like to give it a try." She glanced at her husband and quickly added, "Just once, darling, to see how it feels."

Walt assured her it felt exhilarating. "I have a customer who is a travel agent. I called him and said we wanted to go to Cabo and price wasn't a consideration. He booked us into an oceanfront suite at a luxury resort called Esperanza. I swear their nightly rate was just a few dollars shy of my monthly mortgage. The suite came with an infinity pool and a butler. My first thought was a fat lot of good that will do me as I don't swim and I know how to dress myself, but we found out that a butler is a very cool thing to have."

"I had one for my penthouse suite on the Crystal Symphony and I concur," Ambrose managed to sneak in while Walt took a breath. Then he pantomimed zipping his lips.

The plumber ignored him. "Before we left we got a new e-mail address and new cellphones that only Fino and Paul knew about." Recalling their departure, he laughed aloud. "We didn't pack much, figuring we'd buy what we needed when we got there. We lasted two weeks at the Esperanza then it got way too hot. While we were there, we met a couple from the San Diego area and the guy did a good job of selling us on his hometown. He was in real estate and said if hight rents didn't scare us off, he had a couple of places in a gated community called Mar Largo Estates which is close to Rancho Santa Fe. He mentioned Rancho Santa Fe like we were supposed to know all about it."

"I do," The Redhead said. "I have a friend who lives in the area. It's high end. Ridiculously so."

"It sure is. And this Mar Largo Estates turned out to be a gated community within a gated community. Then there was another gate to the house. The realtor we met in Cabo owns two houses there that he rents out fully furnished with country club privileges. He said he usually puts potential clients in them short term to let them see what life is like there. He jokingly called it Airbnb on steroids. This time, though, they were going to be traveling for two or more months, so he wanted someone to stay longer. We figured why not and headed off to San Diego."

"You always said you wanted to live in a gated community," Duffy reminded him. "Then you end up with a gated house within a gated community within a gated community. Wow! Trifectagate!"

Walt, as it turned out, wasn't all that enthusiastic. "Yeah," he muttered, "but it ended up being too confining and way too rich for our blood."

"We have an author friend, Mel McKinney, who calls these communities prisons of wealth," Mike Gearon said.

"Well, if you had to do hard time, this is a great place to do it," he said, chuckling. "The funny thing is most of the people who live in Mar Largo have homes all over the place. Sometimes they're around and sometimes not. When they are, you see them in Bentleys, Mercedes, Jags… Cars like that. Not a Prius in sight except for the rental we drove. I just love the car and so does Jeannie."

"Did you make any friends?"

Walt thought a moment. Shaking his head, he said, "No, not really. Pretty hard to get close to most of them. A lot of CEO types."

"Any SOB types?" George asked.

Walt laughed. "Yeah, a couple, but you find them anywhere, George, even here in Berkeley. Actually, most of the people we met were okay. Friendly enough, but as I said, you can't get close. The men are all about business and they are really bad at small talk. You know, like the way we're talking here. For them, it's all about money; making it, investing it, acquiring companies with it. Oh, and spending it. Jeannie said the wives were really good at that last one. She also thought the women were glamorous but also very competitive. Anyway, not really our crowd." Walt took a sip of his beer and wiped his mouth. "But look, I don't want to go bashing them. We met all types and most were pretty nice and treated us well. It's just that their world is way different that ours."

George raised his wine glass. "Well, we're glad to have you back in the fold of us small talkers."

"There are a lot of reasons why I couldn't live there. One is that I found it tough to buddy up with the guys who are all about the business of acquiring things. See, I'm all about fixing things. I suppose that's why I'm back in uniform," he stated proudly. "Jeannie was the same way. In her case, the women were all about getting worked on and my wife is all about working on them. We just didn't fit."

Duffy finished off a montadito called a matrimonio which featured sardines, anchovies and a dollop of aioli on a toasted baguette slice. "Where did you go when the two months were up?"

At first, he was embarrassed to admit it. "We, uh, stayed another month," he said, feeling silly about admitting it after his lengthy explanation as to why they felt they didn't fit in.

They were surprised. Mike Gearon was first to ask, "What kept you there for another month?"

"Golf," he replied. "We fell in love with the game. Played practically everyday."

"Frankly, I'm disappointed, Walter," Ambrose said. "I was expecting you to say something exotic and posh like falconry."

The news didn't disappoint Duffy and The Redhead who beamed when he mentioned golf. There were many passions in their lives but golf certainly ranked among the top three. Mike Gearon knew this and, catching the eye of his friend on the other side of the bar, suggested he let Walt finish his story. "Then you guys can talk golf until closing time," he said.

"Come on, just one question," Duffy begged.

"When it comes to golf, it's never just one," Mike remarked.

"Can you and Jeannie play tomorrow at Tilden? Say around nine?" he asked hurriedly.

"Sure, but just so you know, we don't bet. We're not that confident in our game."

"We don't bet either. Well, maybe for drinks," The Redhead said.

Mike feigned frustration. "See, this is how it starts."

Duffy held up his hands in mock surrender. "Okay. That's it. Sorry. Walt, the floor is yours again."

"Yeah, well like I said, Jeannie and I stayed for another month at Mar Largo. Besides playing golf we talked a lot about what else we'd like to do while we were, for lack of a better term, on the road. We decided we'd rent one of those large luxury motorhomes. You know the kind of bus that music stars drive from concert to concert, only ours was smaller. Our plan was to spend a few weeks traveling the Western States doing a little fishing, playing as much golf as we could and visiting National Parks. Six states and eight weeks later, we turned in the bus and headed home to El Cerrito. We had the time of our lives. Spent a ton of money but it was worth it." Walt picked up his beer and drank through a smile brought on by a fleeting memory of their time on the road.

"Are you entertaining questions now, Walter?" Ambrose asked.

"I suppose so."

"During your stay in Mar Largo, where, by the way, you passed up an excellent opportunity to learn falconry, were you ever found out?"

"What do you mean?"

"Did the tony residents of Mar Largo ever discover they had a big hotshot lottery winner in their midst?"

"That was one of the weirdest things about our stay. We didn't get found out until the last week we were there. Suddenly Mar Largo became Solicitation City. Everybody wanted a piece of us. Well, maybe not us, but you know what I mean."

George looked around Ambrose at the plumber and noted, "I read somewhere that there aren't that many people walking around with more than twenty-five million to their name. Jeez, Walt, you were probably king of the hill down there and didn't even know it."

"You know the odd thing," he said. "When we added up the cost of five months of living high off the hog and the amount of money we had Paul dish out to family members, it turns out we hardly put a dent in our net worth."

Now that they heard about the Gillespie's costly time away from home, they were curious to know more about how they handled their family members. George steered him in that direction when he said, "That must have been a fun list to make considering the run-in you had with your brother-in-law the last time we were all here."

"Oh yeah," he laughed, running a hand through his short hair that was still trying to qualify as a crewcut. "I gotta be honest with you. Right from the start, we thought of it as nothing more than a payoff. We figured if we gave them a generous amount of money, they'd leave us alone. Whatever evening we wrote up our list of people we must have been in a real charitable mood because we included my two ex-wives even though I'm not obligated to them in any way. Then we gave Paul all the names and addresses and had him issue the checks. What a wonder that guy is. He even wrote a letter in our name telling each person we wanted to share with them some of our good fortune. He included that with the check and a note saying if they had any questions, they should contact him as we were traveling.

"And what was their reaction?" Mike Gearon asked. "Or do we want to know?"

The plumber sat back in his chair and folded his arms. The others inched closer to him eager to hear every word. "You might not want to know. It won't restore your faith in humanity," he said with a grin. "Of course, we got all this secondhand as Paul was our first line of defense."

"I gather he wasn't overwhelmed with thank you notes and gleeful expressions of gratitude," The Redhead said.

"He said he got one thank you and that was from one of Jeannie's kin. Then one of my relatives who I don't even know very well called him and asked if that was just the first payment. We got a laugh out of that one. Then there was someone who called to find out if accepting the check meant she couldn't ask for more when she needs it. Another in-law called to complain that it was a pretty chintzy sum considering the millions I won. Paul also heard from one of my ex-wives who wrote back saying if I had added another zero to the amount, and I am quoting here, 'she might think about thanking the bastard.'"

"Maybe you ought to hit the road again for the Holidays," Duffy suggested.

"Oh, we're cool," he said. "Since I got back I was able to talk to my sister and she was really happy and thrilled with the money we gave her. That's all that matters. We both love her to death and we were more than generous. I couldn't believe it but even her husband thanked us, but I'm sure she pressured him into doing it."

"Walt," Duffy said, putting a hand on his arm, "you can at least feel comforted that you are among friends here and none of us will be hitting you up anytime soon or for that matter ever. However, the price of your drinks here at Bar OSA will go up."

"Gee, thanks, Duffy. That makes me feel much better." Walt looked at his watch and did some quick math to see how much time he had. "Hey, I have to pick up Jeannie in Richmond soon but there are a couple of things I want to say before I head out."

"I detect a certain sobriety or should I say seriousness in your manner, Walter," Ambrose said.

What the elder of the group actually heard was simply the settled tone of the new and improved Walter Samuel Gillespie. While he still looked it in his raggedy plumber's uniform, he was no longer rough-edged. During the couple's time away, he had successfully shed his sometimes clumsy social mannerisms. He was now more composed, more relaxed with others. Contributing to these changes was how he now dealt with health and aging. Once away, Walt soon realized his hypochondria had evidently stayed in El Cerrito. Wondering if most of his aches and ailments weren't psychosomatic, he decided to not give his state of health any thought; dealing only with hunger and tiredness. The result amazed him. He ate better, slept better and Jeannie swore he was more passionate. Walt had also come to realize that there was an enormous difference in getting older and being old. There seemed to be no sense in continuing to deny he was getting older. It is what one does. He did not, however, have to be old. Shaped by these uplifting notions, Walt's outlook on life changed enough that he and Jeannie decided that there was more they could do when it came to handling their new found wealth. Now it was time to share those thoughts with his lottery partners. In the early goings, Walt had always admired how casual and comfortable they were with each other and themselves. He, too, was beginning to feel the same way. This is going to be easier than I thought it would be, he told himself.

"You're right, professor, I do want to say something serious," he said to Ambrose. "While we were away, Jeannie and I, as I said earlier, talked a lot about money, particularly the huge amount of it. We also talked about our future, where we wanted to live and how we wanted to live. We both agreed that we wanted to live in a world we understood. A world we get. We don't get Mar Largo. What we do get is our home in El Cerrito, our friends and neighbors; people we've known for years. It doesn't take much to live comfortably in this world. But we had one small problem and it concerned money. See, it's okay to be well-to-do, but stinking rich ain't gonna cut it in our neighborhood." Then he looked directly at The Redhead. "I told Jeannie about that funny conversation we all had in April when we discussed what we'd do if we won the lottery. I know I was the odd man out shouting about how I'd spend every stinking dime. Do you remember what you wanted us to do?" he asked her.

Caitlin Hart thought back to that springtime Wednesday. Shaking her head, she answered, "Sorry, Walt, it was just bar conversation. In one Martini and out the other as they say. I don't know where you're going with this."

"I remember," exclaimed her husband. "You, my always tactful darling, suggested that if we were to win, each of us should only keep a paltry sum and then put the rest of the money to work doing beneficial things rather than leave it to money-grubbing family members who probably never liked us in the first place."

Her eyes widened and she pointed a finger at her husband. "Yes, now I remember. Actually, I thought it made a lot of sense."

"Do you remember why you wanted us to only take a token amount?" Mike asked teasingly.

George answered for her. "I believe she said one of us was already living on borrowed time and rest of us were nearing that mark. So seeing as we weren't going to be around that much longer, we didn't require all that excess money."

"Oh God! I wasn't that direct, was I?" she asked, her cheeks aflame.

"In so many words," Mike replied, mimicking the speech of an old man.

Walt jumped to her defense. "Hold on, guys. Jeannie and I think The Redhead is right."

"You do?" Caitlin exclaimed.

"We do."

"And I presume you have an idea?" Ambrose said, taking a last sip of his beloved Cuban Manhattan.

"I do," he stated. "I got to thinking about what The Redhead said about age. She's right, you know. Maybe one of us might live to see his nineties or maybe a hundred but the odds are..." He paused, trying to find the right words.

"It's going to be Ambrose, you know, who accomplishes that," George quipped.

"Anyway, Jeannie and I talked to Paul about our wishes to give most of the money away and keep just enough to make us financially secure. He talked about a charitable remainder trust but we don't like that as its focus is too narrow. Too much going to one source. We want to be more wide-ranging and a lot more personal in our giving."

Mike Gearon's eye's lit up and he snapped his fingers. "I know what Walt wants to do," he blurted out. "We talked about it in the spring. Actually, we kidded about it. You want to make the DICKS Foundation a reality."

Walt shrugged his shoulders and said, "Yeah, but, Mike, that's not exactly what we'd call it."

Duffy held up a hand. "Wait a minute, Walt. Are you seriously thinking about creating a foundation and giving most of what you won to charity?"

"More than than that, I am thinking about what The Redhead suggested. We all keep four million and put the rest in the foundation. Look, guys, most of the money I won was yours to begin with anyway. I like it that we'd all be a team."

George said, "So Debbie and I would contribute four million and the Harts here would toss in two. Mike, you and Katherine only took four, so you're already in."

Ambrose held up a hand. "Calling it the DICKS Foundation might work. It could be an anagram for Doing Interesting Charitable Kindnesses Serendipitously."

The Redhead shut him down. "Ambrose, please don't do anything to encourage these guys."

George had a couple of questions that Walt answered to his satisfaction. The Harts followed with another query that put even more of a complete form to the concept. While they chatted, George once again went to his smartphone. "This could work, guys. I'm sure Paul can steer us to the right people to set up a charitable non-profit. Walt, can I assume some of the money can go to helping some of my old teammates."

Walt nodded. "I want us to use the money in as direct a manner as possible. I'm not saying this well, but I think I'm looking at our charity working more on the street level than on the corporate level."

Katherine help up her hand. "I think I may have a name for your…"

Walt stopped her. "No, it's our foundation. Everybody's involved including Jeannie and Debbie who aren't here today."

"Gotcha," she said. "So why not call it The Banter Foundation. We could make this end of Bar OSA our office and meet here quarterly or monthly to discuss what charity work we all want to do."

Duffy raised his hand. "Katherine, you are a genius. I second the proposal. What say, people?"

It was a splendid idea and easily accepted. It was, after all, bar banter that started it all in April. It seemed only appropriate they stay with a bantering format to handle the demands of a charitable non-profit.

The Redhead nudged Ambrose Dowling. "You are being awfully quiet, professor."

He turned toward her. "I was just thinking of how marvelously all of you have dealt with your good fortune. I feel I may have underestimated my value in all of this, seeing as I am about three million and change short of being a giving member of The Banter Foundation. However, as I have fallen in love with a terribly expensive recreation, namely cruising the high seas in luxury, perhaps I might be your first charity case."

George reached over and kissed Ambrose's cheek.

Walt patted him on the back.

The Redhead ruffled his hair while Duffy threw a bar rag at him.

Mike and Katherine applauded him.

Duffy took back his rag and saluted Ambrose. "Professor Dowling, consider yourself a founding member of the Banter Foundation. In fact, I know everyone here would be proud to nominate you as Head Dick of the group."

The Gearons were flying out the next morning to Hawaii and had to head home to pack. They said their goodbyes, promising to be available for the first official meeting of The Banter Foundation. At the heavy door to Bar OSA, after Katherine had exited, Mike Gearon paused. He turned to look back at the Harts and the Inbetweeners. "By the way, I forgot to mention something I heard on the way over here."

Duffy shouted back, "What was that?"

"Dave Brubeck died today."

# ACKNOWLEDGEMENTS

I must first express my deep appreciation to my wife, Mary Ann, who produced the art work for the cover and when needed became another pair of editorial eyes.

My second thank you is to a place. If it weren't for a tapas bar named Cesar which just happens to be next door to Chez Panisse in Berkeley, there would be no tale to tell. I want to thank this bar for allowing me to borrow so heavily as regards its welcoming decor, its array of delicious tapas and its broad range of drinks.

It's only appropriate then that I thank Cesar's owner and host, the personality-charged Richard Mazzera and his equally charming wife, Terumi. They made fashioning Duffy Hart and The Redhead extremely easy. My heartfelt thanks also go out to the Cesar employees past and present and those colorful and always fascinating regulars who inspired me to create the Inbetweeners.

Many thanks to Dave Nyberg for his tax expertise and his patience in handling all my questions. A very special thanks to Paul Giacoletti who was the inspiration for my character, Paul Farana. His many wise contributions were invaluable. I also want to thank Paul's executive assistant, Sara Holland, for her helpful contributions. A special thanks to Dennis Sullivan. As an attorney, Dennis could have had many billable hours all due to my peppering him with legal questions. But as a friend, he settled for an occasional

Martini. Bill and Gerri Groody deserve a special thanks as they never winced when I called and said, “Is this tech support? Good. What’s a pixel?” Thanks, too, to Patti Edmonds who allowed me to use her initials for my fictional financial services company. I extend a big thank you to Mel McKinney, a renaissance man and a published author whose on-going encouragement means a lot to me.

Finally, thanks to my family which now includes two grandsons, Sebastian Michael Castaneda and Drexel Grey Chase who will no doubt get around to reading this by 2040.

# ABOUT THE AUTHOR

Mike Cleary is a longtime Bay Area radio personality. While some may remember him as a Top Forty DJ or as the host of a successful children's TV show, he is best known as being the Mike of Frank and Mike in the Morning. The Frank was his close friend, Frank Dill. The highly rated show ran for years on KNBR in San Francisco. In 2007, he was inducted into the Bay Area Radio Hall of Fame.

A proud neatnik, Mike has a fondness for colorful socks, pocket-squares, Martinis and memorizing Shakespeare. To date, no one has asked him to recite any of the Bard's stuff he's committed to memory. He and his wife, Mary Ann, have recently retired from long distance running and now enjoy long distance walking. Their longest to date, a clockwise stroll around the island of Manhattan.

Mr. Cleary is happily married with two grown daughters. He resides in Piedmont, California.

Made in the USA
Las Vegas, NV
19 March 2022